PENGUIN BOOKS

Fresh Hell

Rachel Johnson is a journalist and broadcaster. Her previous books include *The Mummy Diaries*, *Notting Hell*, *Shire Hell*, *A Diary of the Lady* and *Winter Games*.

Fresh Hell

RACHEL JOHNSON

PENGUIN BOOKS

PENGUIN BOOKS

UK | USA | Canada | Ireland | Australia
India | New Zealand | South Africa

Penguin Books is part of the Penguin Random House group of companies
whose addresses can be found at global.penguinrandomhouse.com.

Penguin
Random House
UK

First published 2015
001

Set in Dante 11/13 pt
Typeset by Palimpsest Book Production Limited, Falkirk, Stirlingshire
Printed in Great Britain by Clays Ltd, St Ives plc

A CIP catalogue record for this book is available from the British Library

ISBN: 978-0-241-00412-8

www.greenpenguin.co.uk

To my brothers Al, Leo, Jo and Max
but especially to my only sister, Julia

Select Glossary of Key Acronyms

CBA – Can't be Arsed
DM – Direct Message
DOA – Dead on Arrival
ES – Evening Standard
FOI – Freedom of Information
GBC – Giving Back Centre
GIB – Good in Bed
HLD – Hung Like Donkey
IRL – In Real Life
KPG – Kensington Park Gardens
KPR – Kensington Park Road
LRB – London Review of Books
MAD – Making a Difference
MBA – Married but Available
MTF – More to Follow
NBF – New Best Friend
NBH – New Broadcasting House
NDA – Non-disclosure Agreement
NEET – Not in Education, Employment or Training
NFI – Not Fucking Invited
NFNH – Normal for Notting Hill
NHD – Notting Hill Divorcee
NHKS – Notting Hill Kitchen Supper
NHM – Notting Hill Mummy
OSP – Off-street Parking
PAC – Planning Applications Committee
PJ – Private Jet

PS – Plastic Surgery
PT – Personal Trainer
RBK&C – Royal Borough of Kensington and Chelsea
ResPark – Residents' Parking
REVEL – Rich Enough to Vote Even Labour
RT – Retweet
STD – Stop the Digs
UHNW – Ultra-high Net Worth
VHNW – Very High Net Worth
VVPP – Very, Very Pushy Parent

News item in the London Evening Standard

16 February 2015

Notting Hill
Dig Death

There was a death on Valentine's Day at the site of a controversial 'iceberg house' and deep double-basement dig in Notting Hill.

One witness told the *Standard* that the victim had been crushed between a convoy of heavy vehicles, but another said the victim had been impaled on a piling rig left stuck in the ground.

Ambulances and the fire brigade were called to the scene, but the victim was declared DOA (dead on arrival) at St Mary's Hospital, Paddington. A spokesperson for the deceased has requested privacy and the identity of the victim – rumoured to be a well-known personality – and any further details will not be released until initial police inquiries have been completed.

The accident took place at the site of a planned eight-storey house on Ponsonby Terrace that adjoins the new £20 million Giving Back Centre and is only yards from the exclusive Ponsonby Prep, the private school attended by the children of the area's many celebrity residents, and also, it is rumoured, the school that has been selected for Prince George by the Duke and Duchess of Cambridge.

Residents and Ponsonby parents have formed a Stop the Digs (STD) action group, enlisting the support of local luminaries, including comedienne Ruby Wax, Emma Freud, girlfriend of Richard Curtis, and Swiss-born playboy Julien StClair.

Controversy has dogged this particular development, which was contested by neighbours because the 'iceberg' extends out in front underneath the public highway and, at the rear, beneath Ponsonby communal garden square.

This is the first death linked to the construction of 'iceberg' houses, in which owners expand their properties downwards, creating an additional floor, or floors, underneath an existing basement, to house a gym, a cinema, pool, garage, panic room, wine cellar, or even bowling alley, so that the owners may enjoy a personal and private leisure complex in their own home.

(cont. p. 5)

Notting Hill Dig Death

(cont. from p. 1)
In 2010, the council of the Royal Borough of Kensington and Chelsea granted permission for thirteen such developments. In 2012, it received applications for 450, and only 10 per cent were rejected. One dig will extend the area of a house in Lansdowne Gardens by an additional 9,000 square feet.

Local residents complain that the trend for digging down causes massive disruption and long-term structural problems. Construction of such a house can take two or more years, causing residents inconvenience, with the closure of roads and the blocking of pavements, as well as prolonged noise and drilling.

'What has happened is unbelievable and tragic,' said Trish Dodd Noble in a tweet from the @GivingBackCentre feed. 'We in the close-knit, compassionate Giving Back Centre family are profoundly shocked.'

The Stop the Digs action group tweeted, 'Let us hope and pray that sense will finally prevail and urban communities will be spared years of disruption #tragedy #silverlining #RIP.'

The fatality last Saturday morning (when the borough permits building work until 1 p.m.) also raises wider concerns about safety, given the scale and number of similar projects underway across the capital.

Planning laws were drafted long before subterranean suites became fashionable additions to the houses of London's high-rollers, so councils have often been powerless to stop the new trend of iceberg houses.

Sarah Vere, founder of the Kensington-based support group Justice for the Victims of Basement Digs, released a statement: 'Perhaps this tragedy will put an end to this mania of the super-rich to make lives hell for whole neighbourhoods for years at a time, holing the substratum of London clay into Swiss cheese simply to create all these monstrous buy-to-leave mansions underground. This is a sign that the iceberg has now hit the *Titanic*.'

Two Bulgarian construction workers have been offered counselling.

(Turn to pp. 22–3 for feature: 'Sultans of the Sub-soil: Can London's Super-rich Sink Any Deeper?')

PART ONE

SPRING 2014

Clare

Lonsdale Gardens,
Notting Hill,
London W11

7 a.m.

The sunrise bodyclock gently beams daylight from a lustrous dome by the bed. I open my eyes gently, slowly.

I start with Pranayama and chant some of my favourite mantras.

I love and support myself.

I welcome this day as a gift.

Then I do my breathing to the familiar sound of the Blackers grunting under my window, as Hunter, the personal trainer to many of the local haves and have-yachts, puts them through their paces on the stretch of lawn between the weeping willow and the spriggy, waving-grassed, wildflower meadow.

The Blackers have been here a while – getting on for what, five years? They bought Si's house, opposite.

Si didn't need to sell the house. I think he just enjoys doing the deal, and the Blackers were desperate to have a house on the communal garden. They were trying to have children, I think – still are – and, anyway, the more money the rich spend, the happier they are.

It was tactful of them, though, to pay for the new John Deere ride-on mowing tractor when the old one broke last autumn out of their own pocket as a 'goodwill gesture' to compensate the residents for the annoyance of the endless work they're having done on their house, and they also host an annual 'Champagne, Canapés and Carols' party at Christmas, which is very much turning into the gold-plated neighbourhood invite.

She's a beautiful TV presenter, thirty-eightish, quarter Burmese, trained as a ballet dancer; he's an industrialist, waste disposal, late fifties, on his second marriage – and they're a rare mixed-race couple politically, as I saw first hand when I went round the other day, hand delivering the Spring garden newsletter.

The tiny Filipina housekeeper – the one who does all their shopping in the market with a wicker trolley – let me in, and escorted me through the double-aspect drawing room as if she didn't trust me not to steal her employers' *objets d'art*, or their Aboriginal paintings from the walls. She led me across a slippery parquet floor to Meredith's calm, light-filled study, where I found the mistress of the house barefoot, cross-legged, on a red Eames chair. The study overlooks the garden and is luxuriously tiled with those oblong, chestnut leather floor tiles from Bill Amberg, which I happen to know cost many hundreds of pounds each. Her sleek head was bent over the computer, and she didn't look up.

'Sorry to intrude,' I said, and then she looked startled and said she was really busy, 'reading herself in,' as she put it, 'before doing a programme on the corruption of GDP data with rock-star economist Thomas Piketty,' and then I looked down – I'd been admiring a vitrine containing a selection of her ballet shoes, from soft, shiny, pink silk ones the size of a baby's wrist to ones with ribbons and blocks and pointes – and noticed a brochure from a company called AirJet near her keyboard.

'Ooh, what's this,' I asked, taking the brochure – as it was very much not Piketty's 600-page tome, *Capital in the Twenty-first Century* – and she then said, oh, she 'had to' kit out 'their plane', as if this was an everyday chore.

It was a brochure of interior trims for private jets.

I flipped through, and she said that even though the wood looked solid in the pictures it was actually veneer, only a quarter of an inch thick, as solid wood was too heavy and made the jet less fuel-efficient. She said this as if she were really helping to save the planet.

I said, 'You can't go wrong with English oak,' which met with no response, so I asked, 'Are you going to the party tonight?' and she said, 'Which one?' as if she had a choice of many, and I said, 'The one for Denys?'

I assumed she knew Denys Bradshaw, the Tory donor and patron of the arts, who's terribly nice – as is she – as Denys was being given a special award for philanthropy in the Denys and Terri Bradshaw Gallery at the V&A, which was very fitting. After all, for those who've got so much they can't give it away fast enough, it's all about legacy and purpose. Giving life *meaning*.

I naturally assumed she'd been invited, as the Bradshaws are local, social and loaded, and so are the Blackers.

But, at my innocent query, Meredith's plump upper lip curled and she snatched the brochure back.

As I told Gideon later that day, 'She reacted as if I'd asked her if she was a Tory donor, too, or brought up the forbidden topic of Malcolm's directorship of HSBC, or something, and just shot back, "No, Clare," in a low voice. "I am not going to the Bradshaws'."' I had to sort of lean in to hear her, so I got a whiff of vanilla. She's one of those people who doesn't get angry; she goes quiet. She also walks with her feet splayed out and stands in first position, in case anyone forgets she was a ballerina.

'Mal may be a very successful businessman in his own right' – she allowed her voice to rise a decibel or two, as if about to break into the Internationale – 'but I'm a Socialist!'

Then Meredith proceeded to confuse me by saying the super-rich were like toddlers who treated houses and cars and yachts and planes like new toys to be played with for five minutes and then discarded, and went on about some friend of Mal's who'd bought a giga-yacht and only been on board once. But the implication was that the Blackers weren't like that. The Blackers were different.

She said the jet would save time and air miles, and that their friends could use it – and the Blackers are super-generous, it's true – so, by the time I left, she'd convinced me that their new acquisition of a private jet was already performing a valuable public service; it was literally Big Society in action.

So I try but fail not to think about the Blackers as I do my Pranayama breathing, but I always end up keeping time with Hunter.

He's counting out squat thrusts – I know the routine backwards; they work out daily, rain or shine – and, after this, there will be two sets of lunges, so that Meredith can work on her incredible butt (it's so unfair that she's skinny and got her own boobs *and* a bum), and then, *scrunch, skritch, scrunch, skritch*, he'll send them off on a jog around the gravel perimeter path (he uses these minutes to study his iPhone), then there will be three bouts of kickboxing each, and when they start stretching I'll tune in properly to the birds twittering and cheeping in the tall trees in the communal garden, and the roll of the wheelbarrow as Jimmy the head gardener and Lionel the plantsman go about their work and tend to my allotment. Yes, we have our own allotment now on Lonsdale Gardens, where residents can pick redcurrants, raspberries, roses, sweet peas and tulips from the cutting garden. Depending on the season, of course.

It's lovely.

Although most residents have second homes less than two hours away, in Gloucestershire or Oxfordshire (though some have third estates in Scotland, too, and winter retreats in the Caribbean), with walled kitchen gardens, groundsmen, gardeners and gluts of everything, not everyone is so lucky.

The people who live on our own very garden, for example, like poor Cathy, lurking in the lower-ground floor of one of those bleak 1950s council flats – Lonsdale Garden Court – on the corner of the square. Her son, Sid, seems nice, but I bet she's never picked her own anything in her life.

Even though the block does, in theory, have access to the garden via the gate on Lonsdale Rise, most of the tenants, it seems, just can't be bothered to go out and round to unlock it, which is probably a good thing as they don't have designer dogs who've been to puppy-training classes and had their shots done; some have Staffies on chains, Alsatians, and the like.

Yes, the allotment's so important, for children, and for the few without regular access to a country retreat, or to the organic-market-garden produce at Daylesford in Westbourne Grove, and who can't afford even the Portobello Market, where you can get plastic bowls of tomatoes and oranges literally for nothing at the end of the day.

It's so important – for everyone – to see things grow. To have a proper relationship with produce.

Since I put Nourish & Flourish, my garden-and-nutrition consultancy business, on ice to concentrate on Joe, I'm pleased to say I've had more time for – well, everything important, really. To think.

To breathe.

I breathe now, listening to the sound it makes in my still, empty, white room, where the only sign of Gideon is the arm of his oatmeal towelling robe extruding from the door to the wet room. I can't decide if I like the new arrangement – he's in Shoreditch two, sometimes three, nights a week. Part of me suspects that he's somehow, perversely, expiating his own guilt for not seeing more of Joe during his childhood by finding younger and younger interns. I'm sure that baby-blonde Eloise can't be the only one to –

I don't want to think about it. Breathe in. Breathe out.

I get off the bed that we ordered from Savoir Beds, bespoke to our own weight and preference – such a worthwhile investment, if you think about it, the £15,000.

I sit now on the chaise longue at the end of our bed, facing the sash window, through which the trees and mown lawns of the communal garden and the white stucco back elevations of the mansions opposite are framed.

I empty my head.

I don't need an app to do this. I know that busyness is essentially a hedge against emptiness, and I'm not frightened of not being busy – more of not achieving serenity.

I try not to switch on any media devices at all until 8 a.m. Some go to ranches in the Rockies for weeks at a time, simply in order to disconnect and unplug, but, luckily, I don't need to.

I do my facial yoga. I also do Bikram to cleanse my vital organs and stimulate my glands, but not in the bedroom.

I pad to the wet room and brush my teeth with Janina Ultra-white Toothpaste, and slather on enough Clarins beauty flash brightening balm to ice a Christmas cake.

I steel myself to look at my morning face in the mirror but, actually, what I see isn't bad: I don't look too ransacked this morning, thanks to my massage yesterday, when this amazing facialist I've found kneaded my face from inside my mouth.

I smile at myself. 'Be yourself, be sexy, be happy, and *smile!*' I say to my reflection.

It's all going to happen, I tell myself.

First, the school run, then getting ready for Donna's crucial visit, in less than three hours. Donna Linnet.

As the years pass, Donna has changed her offering. In a very real sense, Donna curated my current set-up: orchestrated the move into this house – what, eight years ago now? – and the successful conception of Joe, thanks to Ralph's . . . donation.

Now her USP is a holistic deep cleanse and detox of the whole self, body and soul, and of the living environment of both the client and their ancestors. She treats the family and the family house as a unit, as she believes it's possible to 'heal family shadows' by unlocking the power of the family tree. And now I need her again.

If anyone can, Donna will make it happen.

Before I prepare to dress, I suck in the air deeply through my nostrils, exhale and chant my final mantra: 'One mindful breath a day can lead to inner peace.'

Mimi

Home Farm,
Honeyborne,
Near Godminster, Dorset

I'm in the kitchen, with all the children, and the dog, leaning against the chunky wooden worktop between the blue-veined sink and the Aga, in the hazy, violet hour between tea and supper, wondering whether it's too early to have a drink.

Ralph's on his way home. I'm thinking, It's OK – you can hold it together. We've been here before. Those missed calls from Clare Sturgis on his phone . . . they don't mean anything.

They'll only be something about Joe, Ralph's biological son. Gideon turned out to be shooting blanks, so Ralph supplied Clare with 'the wherewithal' (phrase used by husband at first mention; ugh!) or 'the needful' (phrase used at second mention; marginally less awful). It was Ralph's moment of madness, I suppose, but he had his reasons.

And he had the financial incentive. Clare wanted our house, too, so she paid way over the odds for it, but the deal was clear: coming up with 'the goods' (not much better, why not just say 'sperm samples' from 'red-blooded English male'?, if that's indeed how they did it, which has always been a big 'if' in my mind), and that was the beginning, and end, of Ralph's involvement.

Plus, the children don't know about Joe. That's going to be awkward at some point.

14

So, those calls from Clare – can't think about them now, anyway.

There's an open bottle of white – emergency purchase from the all-night garage on the ring road – but I restrain myself from lunging towards the fridge. You don't need a bracer. Just have another cup of tea, perhaps, and keep going.

I'm trying to convince myself that last night doesn't count. A mere blip.

Like when the line drops on the *Today* programme and the nation gets a little thrum of adrenaline, pricks up its ears – the silence is suddenly more interesting than anything being said – and then some drone behind the scenes in some airless studio gets the line back up again, and the national conversation resumes, and the morning goes on.

So it's all going to be *fiiine*. I slide the kettle on to the hotplate. There's no way Clare's on manoeuvres, not again. She has Joe. She has our house. She has a private income. There is only one thing I have, in fact, that she could possibly want, but she knows she can't have it. Ralph's not on the table.

So let's look at the positives.

The car didn't run out of petrol on the way back from Godminster, even though the needle's below red.

Supper is under control, in the sense that it is sitting intact in the freezer.

In fact, today is – on one level – turning out to be something of a personal best on the domestic front, despite what happened last night during pudding, while everyone else was sipping Muscat and spooning their lavender-scented posset at Rose's 'modern Elizabethan feast' and didn't seem to notice when we slipped away from the long refectory table in the barn, which was piled with meringues and tuiles, brandy snaps and whipped cream, red grapes, wild strawberries, shortbread, right in the middle of Rose's sculptor husband Pierre's planned peroration over the syrupy Meursault about his new work, a piece of 'participatory art' comprising an eighteen-foot-high stone pillar with a slit in it.

Pierre's voice was carrying over the lawn. 'It represents whatever you wish,' he was saying. 'Water running down a mountain, and the human vagina . . . which people can enter if they want . . .'

We ducked into the gazebo, which was empty except for some fur throws on the stone floor and some tea lights glowing from the alcoves . . .

And now it's less than fifteen hours later – I grab Posy's phone from the table to check, rather than the mahogany clock mounted on the wall, as it is always wrong – and I barely know who I am any more.

I turn away from the familiar sight of children, home and hearth and crack open the kitchen window, and the smell, the sweet smell of the country, gusts through, warm air laden with pollen, grass, dung, diesel, teenage despair. I wish I'd bottled it, yesterday.

Freeze-framed it. But it's too late.

Life's like Snapchat. You take a picture, then ten seconds later, whoosh! it's gone. What you had you never get back.

I can't stare out of the window for much longer, or the children will suspect I'm going all Sylvia Plath on them, so with a decisive movement I twist the antique silver hot tap on and start swirling steaming-hot water round the coffee-ground-spackled plughole with my special brush made of broom root and twine made by the visually impaired of Sweden.

I know the scene behind me so well I could paint it.

Lucian, my baby (now aged six), is nestled in the dog basket, curled like a Dachshund puppy. Mirabel, eighteen, is roosting on the windowseat, wearing an old, grey cashmere White Company onesie of Rose's, discarded (by Rose) as soon as she found one moth hole. The iPad casts a green glow on her face. Posy, fifteen, is sitting at the table doing her homework, which means watching clips of *Lord of the Flies* on YouTube rather than reading it, while simultaneously watching a swotty video of how to crochet your own celebrity tea-cosy or egg-warmer (even though Posy's are already so accomplished that she's selling them for pocket money in the Post Office and Stores: so far, the Mary Berry is way out in front of her Nigella) and monitoring her Twitter feed and Vine. She is also reading out tweets.

'"What do we want from nails right now?" asks @vogue,' she says. 'Editor of *Glamour* Jo Elvin tweets, "Is it possible for one bum cheek to be fatter than the other?"' Then she says, 'Here's another bum one: "I'll have bum implants to get my dream guy," says Lauren off *TOWIE*.'

Everyone groans, including Cas, who is also doing homework, which is glancing through a potted summary of his A-level English book, *The God of Small Things*, online.

'No one reads the actual *book* any more, Mum,' he had said when I asked him why he didn't have a copy of the actual book. 'CBA' – i.e. can't be arsed – so then I bought him a Kindle and loaded the book, and when I asked him how he was doing with it he just said, 'Really well, about 3 per cent.' Aargh. Cas is seventeen, and he's never read a book, apart from sporting biographies and collections of Jeremy Clarkson's columns.

My older son sits opposite Posy, his tufty head garlanded by the blue-and-white striped mugs that dangle from cup-hooks on the Welsh dresser, so he looks like a young Roman emperor crowned by Cornishware.

Calypso is on the sofa under the window, snoring. Getting old now. She's on Special Needs Eukanuba for the sterilized senior dog. Every time I dig out her kibble from the plastic sack and tip it into her dish, I think, That's me soon. Sterilized. Senior.

I am wondering whether, as it's May, I should turn the ancient, cream, four-oven Aga off to save money, but I know I won't – it makes the whole room cosy – when the telephone rings, loudly.

None of the children twitches. They know it has nothing to do with them. Nobody ever makes contact with a young person on a telephone, let alone a landline. They have mobiles, of course, but they are maintained on silent, as 1. there's no signal at Home Farm, and 2. the only people who are ever going to ring them – as opposed to Facebooking them – are their parents.

As the telephone peals through the silent kitchen, at 5.30 p.m., it makes my gut twist again, and I feel like having a drink. I need something . . .

I should never have answered that call when it came yesterday, mid-morning. I should have left it, as the only people who ring during the day are cold callers, from somewhere deep on the subcontinent, asking me if a loved one has been in an automobile accident, or if I've been mis-sold pensions payment protection insurance, whatever that is.

Answering the telephone. That was my first mistake. If I'd left it then, I wouldn't now be feeling like a stranger in my own home.

'Hey, it's me. What are you doing tonight?' Rose had asked, a slight pant in her voice, as if I'd caught her in the middle of something, rather than her calling me.

It was eleven or so. Peak coffee-morning time. I was wondering whether to take Calypso for a walk, or whether to locate, if not tackle – too much of a commitment – the seat of the biblical moth infestation in the larder.

I could hear clattering sounds in the background.

'Um,' I said, playing for time. 'Well . . .' I don't know what to say. I live in West Dorset. I never do anything in the evenings except watch the *News at Ten*, then make a comment about how *Newsnight* isn't quite the same any more now Paxo doesn't present it.

More panting on the line. 'Sorry. Oops. Are you still there?'

Rose is my only real friend here. I've inevitably lost touch with many of my London friends, having left Notting Hill – what, six years ago: so easy to lose track – and there not being a proper motorway between the Jurassic Coast and West London; and I'm not one half of a socially dynamic power couple; plus the fact that they all have their own houses in the country, and abroad, so can't be arsed to come here.

'Yes, I'm here. Where do you think I am? You rang on the landline. What's that noise?'

'The brandy snaps. So easy, but you have to get the timing right, which is partly why I'm calling. I've got all these Art World People coming, didn't I say? You know, Pierre's Prae-mium Imperiale Award, and we're sort of christening the Biennale Barn.'

She spoke it as if anyone in the loop would know what the latest prize Pierre had won is.

'So, thought I'd do a modern take on an Elizabethan feast – and, of course, I'd love you – and Ralph – haha – to come.'

She sort of swallowed that last bit, and we both knew she was saying it only for politesse. Ralph never accepts a dinner invitation unless it's for something important, like his old housemaster Mr Squarey from Sunningdale retiring, and then he'll drive hundreds of miles without complaint; when con-fronted by other social challenges such as the 'country supper', he says he has a perfectly good home of his own, but what he really means is he can't face sitting next to two women and talking about children, ponies and schools.

'When?'

'Tonight. Late notice, I know,' she continued, a seductive note creeping into her voice, 'but someone dropped out.'

'Wow, dunno, um,' I said, perking up at the thought of an evening out on my own, and immediately worrying what to wear.

Rose has become palpably more into Pierre now he is a celebrated sculptor and collected in museums like the Guggenheim in Bilbao, and probably the one in New York, too, for all I know. After he won a huge cash prize at the Biennale, the Musgroves converted the old hay barn into the Biennale Barn, a fabulous entertaining space with a minstrels gallery-type thing, a table designed by John Pawson cleaving down the middle, light fittings by Tom Dixon – the whole shebang – and it's already been in the *Architectural Digest* twice.

Indeed, since Pierre's surprise late-onset success ('ENGLAND'S ANSWER TO ANISH KAPOOR', one sycophantic interview was headlined), Rose has even stopped cougaring men half her age – though she does convey the interesting possibility that, if Pierre went off grid again and devoted himself to wandering the hills collecting flints instead of making serious money from his art (now highly collectable, despite being based on huge representations of male and female genitalia), she could always do so again.

Rose leads a charmed life, in other words, which is bloody unfair. People say you only regret the things you don't do in life. But that's not true in my case. I regret the things I do do.

While Rose has money, a trophy husband and a faithful cleaner called Joan with a splendid collection of floral tabards, she also manages to rock and roll. In other words, Rose does what she likes, gets away with it, and even proceeds to enjoy it.

'Sorry,' Rose panted, going off line again. 'The brandy snaps are a triumph, but the herb dumplings are more fiddly than I feared. Using proper suet is always a bit iffy, but it makes all the difference.'

Instead of making a pointed remark about her Martha Stewarting, as I would have done had I been NFI – not fucking invited – I was right behind her forthcoming dinner and felt proprietorial, as if hosting it myself.

'So what's for mains? Roast swan? I won't ask if there's anything I can do . . .'

Rose always has a million things on the go: Rose's cheeses are now sold in Harvey Nichols and Selfridges food halls, and Court Place is so often featured in *House & Garden* that regular readers could find their way from the pantry to the parterre blindfold.

I didn't want to ask – it's rude – but I couldn't help it. After all, I was making up numbers.

'Will I know anyone? Come on, who's coming? Charles Saatchi? Grayson and Philippa Perry?'

'Among others,' Rose admitted.

'And who's the tethered mare?'

'Tethered mare' is our phrase for a mostly single white female at a dinner party who is supplied as juicy bait for an alpha male.

'*You* are,' said Rose.

'*Me!*' I squealed. I was buzzing at the prospect, which was sad, at the notion that I could be the tempting tethered mare, when it seemed like years since anyone had noticed me. Let alone found me attractive. Or showed it, at any rate.

'But who's my date? Who's the man?'

'Woman.'

Pause. This time the line went dead at my end.

'Woman?' I opened the freezer and removed the fish pie from Rose's farm shop as I spoke, to cook from frozen, and then one-handedly went to the fridge, opened the screw top on the garage bottle of Oyster Bay and gave myself a generous pour.

I didn't want to go to Rose's dinner to talk to a woman about schools. I sometimes saw Ralph's point about that, though I'd never admit it to him. The whole point of dinner parties was to talk to attractive men, surely.

'Yes. Woman,' repeated Rose, with slight impatience, as if I were slow.

'I think you'll enjoy – you can borrow that little dark-green leather biker jacket from ME&EM if you like. In fact, I think I might give it to you. I never wear it. The woman is Farouche, by the way,' Rose said, tossing this in. Casual.

'Get the fuck out of here,' I said, as none of the children was present to pick me up on my language. I'd just read a *Sunday Times Magazine* interview with her that ran over eight pages, and then Googled her . . . again.

'Well, I'd love to come,' I said, filing away the offer, now understanding why Rose wanted me to look biker chic rather than country casual.

I had been thinking about wearing my Boat Race crinkle wrap dress from Boden, as Ralph sometimes gives me The Look when I wear it, as a silent thank you for not wearing Uggs, sweatpants and fleece, I suppose.

But – this changed everything. I'd tried to get an interview with Farouche once, when I was a journalist, back on the *Telegraph*, for my column, when I got celebrities to tell me their fantasy funerals.

She'd turned me down. 'My funeral is going to surprise everyone,' she said, 'so I'm keeping it secret,' which I thought was an odd thing to say, but even odder was that she then proceeded to send me images – unsettling images – for months. A naked dancer straddling a chair, back view, her neat head bent towards her chest. A woman lying in bed, her right hand down her pink pants, as a man tucked her in under a sheet. And then that one of a medley of squares, with the naked Ingres lady crosshatched with other images – taken by Farouche – of women lying naked on beds and in baths . . . my face felt a bit hot as I remembered them.

I hadn't deleted them. Every time I'd seen something about her since, I'd had this funny feeling – a fluttering little kick inside, and wondered what she was like, in the flesh, and then I'd met her in Liberty, on the third floor, in Luggage. I was buying one of those Globetrotter-style suitcases with Liberty print, for Mirabel, for her eighteenth, and Farouche was buying a whole set in different sizes, and I introduced myself. Instead of brushing me off, we chatted for a while. She ignored a call on her mobile. And then she kissed me goodbye, and I remember: there was something delicious about her.

'I'd love to come, Rose, how sweet, but Ralph, he probably won't – if that's all right.' As I said this, I knew I wouldn't even give Ralph the option of coming. I'd seen those missed calls – OK, missed call – from Clare. Which made me officially fed up with Ralph.

'Good, come at eight, then. And don't bring anything!' she commanded.

Rose said this as if there were nothing I could bring that she could possibly want.

Clare

Lonsdale Gardens

It's all very well telling people not to mind growing old, that ageing is a privilege not accorded to all, but hello? I don't think that many of these people have to do the Ponsonby Prep school run.

I speed up, give my hair a quick onceover with the Babyliss Big Hair, and dress.

I have my clothes for the week already worked out in sections in the closet, and today it's elegant-casual: silk shirt, grey gossamer-weight cobwebby jersey, leather knee-length skirt, chunky ankle-boots from Fiorentini & Baker.

Joe doesn't have to be at school till 8.30 a.m., I know, but very few people can have any idea quite how long it takes to get one small boy who does two instruments, three languages and five sports a week ready for school, complete with a packed lunch that is sustainable, organic, healthy, and also one that a boy of eight might actually eat.

Nor how incredibly long it takes to look as if you – i.e. a woman over forty – haven't made any effort at all. The hours it takes, the money it costs, not to look 'done'.

Most of the other mummies are not merely much younger, it just so happens that they are also international super-models. They don't just wear Stella McCartney for Adidas, they really are Stella McCartney, and Claudia Schiffer, Laura Bailey, and so on, and then there are the reams of glowing thirty-somethings who flash side-boob at drop-off and still manage to look studiedly cool, cellulite free and have Instagram-perfect lives at all times.

I slide downstairs in my socks, gripping the side rail, as the dread age when I won't 'fall' but will 'have a fall' is on the horizon.

At the ground floor I pause, as the signal's stronger up here than in the basement.

I shoot Donna a text, reminding her of our imminent appointment, and make sure it's sent before going down, again gripping the banister with care.

Joe's already down, with Aida, our nanny. She's Californian, and it didn't take me at all long to induct her in the basics of engaged eating.

Aida came after I had to sack Mimi's old nanny, Fatima. I'd discovered she was sneaking Joe Dairylea triangles. This, despite the fact that she knew that all processed foods, especially those beginning with K, are banned from the house: Kraft. Krave. Krispies and Krispie Kremes. And Ketchup.

She didn't even know that you had to clean inside the tumble-dryer, but that wasn't such a sackable offence. Fatima was fifty-eight, so I like to think it came as a relief to her.

So Aida, Joe and I are all in the kitchen, for breakfast together. Gideon's not here; even Joe's stopped asking, he's not here so often.

I make us meditate for a moment before we start. 'Feed the soul, before the body,' I say, as Joe tries not to roll his eyes.

I have chia-seed porridge with a dollop of the magic gloop I keep in the fridge.

Joe and Aida have a short stack each of gluten-free, buckwheat-flax pancakes.

'Yum,' I say, as I watch him plough through it. 'What a treat, darling, pancakes and maple syrup!' I make a mental note to substitute agave nectar for maple next time.

Joe is playing with his iPad, smearing the screen as he eats. I decide not to let this bother me – I can blitz it with iKlear later. 'Any news on the puppy?' I ask.

Ponsonby Prep's latest parent-pleaser is to acquire a school dog, and each class in turn is getting to look after it, and all the kids to fall in love with it, and then at Christmas there's going to be an auction for the puppy, which I'm sure breaks every Kennel Club advisory but sounds NFNH – Normal for Notting Hill – to me, on the grounds that the whole operation is fuelled by money and emotional manipulation.

'What's Joe got today?' I ask with a sigh, as Joe explains there's going to be a 'competition' to see who gets the puppy – a currently nine-week-old Sprollie – to keep for Christmas, and I don't have the heart to correct him.

Joe's so excited he even raises his gaze from his iPad and looks at me with shiny eyes and says, 'In two weeks, it's our class's turn for Tracker. He's sooo cute, Mum!'

Aida rises and brings me his lunch box, where there's a grilled tuna wrap in greaseproof paper nestling next to a carton of Vita Coco, slotted next to a home-made granola bar and some kale crisps.

'You prefer the Cheesie Purple Corn ones, don't you, darling?' I say, as Joe stabs his iPad while pushing pancakes into his mouth. 'You say they're more –'

'Like real crisps,' Joe says. I see he's not doing his home-work, which was to find and illustrate an anagram of 'listen', on his iPad.

(Silent. I love how the school underlines its core messaging in assignments.)

I ruffle his tufty blond hair and then give it a tug and feel his scalp shift under my hands. He knows I love doing this, so lets me.

Then Aida shows me a small Braeburn. 'And a market-garden apple,' she says. I'm pretty sure it's from Tesco, but I don't comment. I have to pick my battles.

We finish quickly, antique linen napkins the soft, faded blue of Peter Rabbit's jacket in our laps, Radio Four playing in the background, listening to what is going on in the real world, outside the Notting Hill bubble, where people are being bombed in their beds in Syria, or swallowed by mudslides in South America, with a bland sense of detachment.

Joe knocks over the maple syrup and it spills a sticky brown tuppenny puddle on the table. I wait for Aida to rise from the table and deal with it. I've banned kitchen roll and disposable wipes of any sort, even flushables, from the house. We only use tea towels from Summerill & Bishop in Clarendon Cross for kitchen spills.

Aida does so, then sits back down. We both continue to watch Joe, and every mouthful he takes, as if his dear round face is a small TV screen, mounted on the table, and I don't have to look at my watch when, at 8 a.m. precisely, it begins.

The thudding, the metallic, ear-splitting noise as lorries converge on the Molton house next door, where a piling rig has been squatting on the pavement behind an ugly hoarding claiming that the builders are 'compassionate contractors' for many long weeks now.

The sound of beeps means they are reversing, and a growling, clanking sound means the conveyor belt carrying thousands of cubic feet of spoil from the depths to the surface has started cranking, bearing the first of many payloads of thick, brown London clay, as dense and as chock-full of little stones and pebbles as a well-fruited Christmas cake is with raisins and nuts.

And then there's the drilling and the digging.

It's as if a helicopter is taking off, and landing, and taking off – and landing, and it goes on all day, every weekday, and until lunchtime on Saturdays.

So, yes, I'd say this is irritation number one in my life. The double-basement dig bang next door. As Gideon says, 'But the Old Forsters were bound to sell sometime.' And, indeed, their orange units and black-and-white tiled kitchen, the grotty lino bathrooms, all were becoming a health hazard, destined only for the skip. Even their son, Alexander – now Chairman of the Tory Party – wanted them to cash in, downsize. So they sold up . . . to Patrick Molton. Who already lived on the garden.

'You see, Clare, the thing is, I need two houses now,' Patrick Molton told me when I found out, dumbstruck, that it was *he* who'd bought the house next door. As if on autopilot I went into the script for when a man hits you over the head with a brick, which is this.

Stop whatever you're thinking.

Stop whatever you're doing.

Take a breath and get quickly into the Lori Kaye Dance Position.

All you have to do is to open your palms out to the world, lean your body back, unzip your heart, let your heart out to breathe, let your shoulders drop, check in with your body to find out where you're holding tension, and focus in deeply on how your body and your heart are feeling. Simple. It makes it so much easier to speak your truth.

I don't even think Patrick noticed I'd assumed the Lori Kaye Dance Position so eager was he to explain that he 'had to' buy the house next door, in addition to the house on the garden he already had, and therefore his current and his ex would be sharing the same green space, living on the same garden, in a Mormon-style arrangement which he went on to rationalize.

'Tiggy's son doesn't get on with the boys, so they can't all watch the rugby in the same room, so the current . . . emotional geography doesn't work for us.'

Rugby and cricket have always been big things for Patrick, but phrases like 'emotional geography' are relatively recent, post-dating his divorce from Marguerite, the intervening period of mindless, presumably soulless (I sincerely hope soulless, anyway) shagging which followed it, and Marguerite's insistence that they both saw a therapist together.

Patrick was thrilled when he discovered that the therapist wasn't just any old therapist. She counted Gwyneth and Chris, and Matthew and Liz, amongst her clients. So she was the go-to therapist, after which he went-to with less reluctance.

So Patrick Molton's lashed out several million on another family house on the same garden so that his boys and Tiggy's son don't have to watch the Six Nations on the same fifty-inch flatscreen TV, and all he has to do to consciously co-parent with Marguerite is walk across the garden.

It's all worked out for Patrick, in other words, as it tends to, for husbands, after divorce.

'And all I have to do is some *minor remodelling*,' Patrick continued, as if doing us all a favour.

'What do you mean, "minor"?' I asked.

'Well, I am *going down*,' he admitted. 'But just the one extra floor,' he said, giving me his boyish, direct look, which Marguerite has warned me is the one to mistrust most.

'And it won't be too disruptive,' he continued, his blue Irish eyes boring into mine. 'Michael Alexis says we won't need to move out.'

But as soon as he names Michael Alexis I'm on red alert.

The threat level of a major, local, unwelcome disruptive

event from a close neighbour leapt with the mention of his name from 'ever-present' to 'severe'.

Though very handsome, Michael Alexis is, of course, the architect around here for anything really mega-antisocial.

'Michael *Alexis*?'

'Yes, Alexis. The Blackers right opposite, across the garden, are being very reasonable,' he went on, as if I should take my cue from them.

'Well, they would be, Patrick,' I snapped. 'One, they're not right next door to the works, they're on the other side of the garden; and two, the Blackers have put us through two years of hell already.'

The Blackers did the usual total renovation and major works when they bought, but are now in the midst of a major lateral knock-through. When the house next door to theirs came on to the market they bought that, too, as they were worried, of course, that if they didn't someone else would, and make their lives a misery with *their* redevelopment. That's how it goes round here.

As Patrick Molton's news meant that not one but two houses within seventy yards of mine would be undergoing major, major multimillion-pound works, simultaneously, I simply couldn't help it. I crumpled. There's only so much horror I can take.

He took my arm. I've never understood why women fall for him, but they do.

'Look, Clare . . . um, Tiggy and I' – I still can't get used to that pairing; it used to be Patrick and Marguerite – 'we'll be in the house *all the time* during the works, so I promise: it won't be awful at all.' That stare again.

Then, of course, it turned out Patrick was carving out a cavernous subterranean chill-out space, not even to park the Filipinas in some airless dungeon, which is what most of these double basements end up being for – who in their right mind wants to live underground, like a troll – but so the teens can watch sport in different rooms; and Tiggy and Patrick have been – needless to say – renting a whole separate house round the corner since before the work started and keeping a very low profile, as you might expect.

Intolerable.

Anyway. Breathe.

The neighbourhood disruption has, somehow, elided into irritation number two, which is Gideon. The Gideon Situation. Finding those texts between him and Eloise – I didn't even bother to ask this time. I think he must want me to find them. So I don't mind that he's been pretty AWOL, too, during the works next door, claiming that the noise is 'distracting' – pretty rich that, coming from an architect, pot and kettle, and also given that the real reason he's AWOL is because his hot new project isn't a skyscraper so much as his young blonde intern in Shoreditch. (They send each other pictures, or she does, anyway; I don't think even Gids is so idiotic as to think that anyone would relish receiving a detailed naked picture of *him*.)

Anyway, I've decided it's much easier, not judging. It is what it is. We are where we are. And at least there's no way Gideon can get her pregnant.

The HeadSpace app helps. And it is nice having the bed, and most of the house, to myself. Of course, I know why he's really away: he's emotionally detached, not just from me, but from Joe. The latest intern is a symptom, not a cause. I have to face it: he's never, really, embraced Joe as his son. Blood really is thicker than water; for him, anyway.

I've told him that there are many ways of being a father, just as there are many ways of being a man, but I know and he knows that he's only ever pretended playing Daddy with Joe.

So, yes, he's taken to overnighting in Shoreditch – he says he has early meetings every morning this week and it's easier to be nearer 'the site' (his latest skyscraper, which 'Londoner's Diary' has taken to calling The Phallus, and which I think is also a not-so-coded allusion to Gideon's penis).

My official response to this is that it's fine by me. Everything he does is fine. I don't really care now I'm writing him out of the script.

And problem three: I want another child. It's got to the point when not only can I not bear it when my friends – decreasingly, it has to be said, now we are in our forties – have babies. When a woman on TV, or even on the radio, gets pregnant, it's a dagger to the heart, too. I called Ralph a couple of times, to try to talk. After all, Ralph is Joe's sperm donor, so he is my first port of call on this. Plus, Ralph's usually quite patient – he wants to do the right thing by Joe, but he's never quite sure what the right thing is – but he didn't pick up. Nor did he call back.

But I can't dwell on the negatives, and I still have so much to do before we leave the house.

I start marshalling Joe.

As I shoo him up the stairs towards the front door I call back to Aida, 'I've got a meeting, so maybe you can do a shop?' I am, to be honest, struggling to find her chores to do: the house is immaculate, spotless, orderly. 'Make sure there's pods for the Nespresso. Ooh, yes' – I reach the top of the stairs, and call down – 'and can you run up to Clarke's for some basics: eggs, fresh herbs, milk, prosciutto, figs, pesto, bread . . .' I know I don't have to spell it out. 'And then do the fruit and veg and meat – put it on the account at Michanicou, Lidgate, yeah? See you later.'

Joe and I trip down the steps, laden with the day's bags, and when we turn on to Ladbroke Grove to cross the busy road, I take his hand. He shrugs it off.

Most of the other kids have scooters, and the parents have them, too, but I've put my foot down about one for me. It's not so much that I don't want Joe to skin his knee, I just can't bear to be one of those mothers – those try-hard MILFs who don't seem to want to realize that women age in dog years and our next stop is fifty, so zooming round on a micro-scooter in hot pants: not such a great look.

Eight minutes later, we have done his seven times table and we are nearing the Strip.

Children in a smart, laundered uniform of grey flannel shorts or pinafores with scarlet piping are skipping towards the imposing façade of Ponsonby Prep. Every few seconds, a blonde of no fixed age sporting a trout pout and shaggy rope-like hair will glide along slowly in a brand-new hybrid in search of a rare parking space on the Strip. Then she will dip into the recesses of the car to remove children, bags, lunch boxes, as if extracting random items from a bran-tub.

As Joe and I approach, there's a scene already, as is inevitable: Belle MacDonald, the supermodel, is on drop-off duty.

Usually, Belle wears tight white jeans that look as if they've been surgically stitched on by her gynaecologist, and something furry about the throat – the neck is a problem area even for supermodels – and close to her flawless, poreless, plumped face. But today she's in a school high-vis fluorescent yellow vest, shapeless over her grey Marc Jacobs sweater, Joseph chestnut leather trousers and high heels. But she's managing to stop traffic anyway.

Several daddies are loitering until the gates open so they can enjoy the sight of Belle's famous bum in tight brown cowhide, bulging like a shiny and cheeky conker, and hoping she might turn around to give them an uninterrupted vista of her cloven, leather-girt crotch.

Even though it's only May, everyone has an expensive,

burnished glow, especially Belle. I nod to her, and greet a few other mothers, and I know we're checking out each other's level of grooming and fitness just as men look at young girls: automatically.

I'm scoping skin and hair and outfits and boots and bags, and then I spot Julien, who's a new dad here who most mummies won't have seen before. He's accessorized by Fox, who's two years or so younger than Joe.

I don't rush up to greet Julien, as I'm keen to see what will happen next, which is generally that another, younger, thinner, and even hotter mummy than Belle stages a distraction. The photographers, who stake out the pavement opposite Ponsonby every schoolday, rain or shine, to give the celebrity mummies a good papping, are having a field day, as it's Belle's turn to do her civic duty and direct cars and escort their charges from Range Rover Evoque or Prius or Volvo XC60 to the pavement. And today that someone is Oksana. New, current, younger wife of Keith Dunbar, the founder and CEO of Dunbar Asset Management, who has so many billions under his management, and who is making so much more money than the whole of Mayfair put together that his City nickname is the Hammer of the Sassenachs.

Oksana's Porsche Cayenne purrs to a halt next to Belle MacDonald on the zig-zags, where there is a bossy sign saying 'SCHOOL. DO NOT PARK HERE'.

Belle approaches and lightly raps on the driver's window.

'Joe, watch this,' I whisper, as he grabs his lunch box and violin case from my hands and drums them against my legs – I never knew, until I had one, how percussive boys are – as we stand, as ever, unremarked and unphotographed, on the Strip.

'It's the owl babies' mummy, and you know what happened last time.' Joe calls the Dunbar twins 'the owl babies', as their eyes are very far apart and they are silent, watchful little girls.

Last time, Oksana accused the drop-off-duty mummy in high-vis of 'pulling her hair on purpose' when the poor woman reached into the car to help a child with one of her four bags and one of the two silver clasps on the trumpet case became irretrievably snagged up in Oksana's thousand-pound hair extensions, which then tumbled all over the back of her seat. The trumpet case opened, the trumpet fell into the gutter and, as the poor child sobbed her way up the steps into school, Oksana's hair trailed from the trumpet case like a lost fright wig on the morning after Hallowe'en.

It was awful. So humiliating.

As we all agreed afterwards, over soya flat whites at Daylesford, who on earth still has hair extensions? They're so nineties. It's been all about the destroyed blow-dry, i.e. spending £300 to look as if you've been dragged through a hedge backwards, for over a year now. The coffee klatsch at Daylesford spoke of little else, for at least three minutes, anyway.

This term, Oksana's lost the extensions – she's working a more natural, youthful look – but is now obstructing 'the safe flow of traffic' at drop-off.

'Oksana, you know you can't park here,' says Belle, rapping again.

Oksana chooses this moment to take a call on her mobile and buzzes up her window. She sits at the wheel, ignoring Belle, impervious to the chatter of the crowd.

I'm monitoring the gossip with one ear, as the skinniest, youngest and trendiest mothers with the most children and the highest-status husbands have gelled into a clump and are talking about the various trips they have planned *en famille*. In my experience, the only detail they will omit from this litany of activity-packed jaunts is whether any or all of the various super-tutors are accompanying.

Tutoring, like plastic surgery, and adultery, is ubiquitous – I think 70 per cent of all women are up to all three – but must be carried out in conditions of absolute secrecy, in order that the mask of inhuman perfection never slips at any point.

. . . 'We're going to a ranch in Montana, Mountain Sky? Yeah, with Eric and Eleanor and all the kids, then to Tuscany, and then the kids are doing a *sailing course* in Salcombe . . . and Tinkerbell's going to be a *qualified instructor*' . . .

. . . 'No, we much prefer Nepal to Bhutan . . . and even Burma's already *so over*!' . . .

. . . 'Oh, we'll be in LA, as I'll be filming – the kids *love* being on *set*; they have their own *trailer* – and Jed and Noah might be in the new Josh Rogen' . . .

. . . 'We're off to the *beach house* in St Lucia – you know, the house Peter got me as a surprise for my *fortieth* . . .'

. . . 'We went to this amazing, *amazing* place in the Maldives, it's the perfect post-safari-recovery retreat' . . .

Belle marches back up to the Porsche, having just tenderly detached a child from the booster seat of an armoured Hummer with darkened windows driven by the chauffeur of a very private movie star (a very famous one, over here filming, but not for long enough for everyone to try to be NBFs with her) and safely delivered him on to the pavement.

Belle pushes Memphis – for that is the name of the movie star's child – in the direction of the school steps. Then raps the window of Oksana's Porsche Cayenne again. For the third time. Speaks louder.

'Oksana! You can't –'

Oksana flings open her driver's door, so that it strikes Belle and she tumbles like a baby giraffe. There's no question about

36

it. In many ways – her height, her youth, her rudeness – Oksana is magnificent.

Several of us yelp in alarm as Belle goes flying.

Oksana's legs extrude from the vehicle, clad in charcoal, shiny-coated skinny jeans and ending in high-heeled gladiator ankle-boots covered with spikes and studs and, I think, actual diamonds. Then her torso, pitched forward in a battered but clinging grey James Perse T-shirt, and a tangle of gold chains jouncing on her breasts, which don't appear to be contained by a bra. Her hard nipples are the size and nubbly texture of unripe raspberries.

She unfurls and stands for a moment by the car, as if on the red carpet about to make an entrance to the Oscars. 'Oh, sorry, Bella,' she says, in a grating Russian accent. 'Total accident.'

The photographers opposite in parkas and biker boots start snapping, the dark Nile delta of Oksana's camel-toe in her spray-on Lycra jeans being an obvious target for their cross-hairs.

Oksana pauses so they get their shots, then pirouettes to the passenger door with a toss of her head. She opens the back door – shooing away her nanny, who must never appear in any pictures – and pulls out her five-year-old identical twins with white ringlets and identical expressions.

Bracing herself against the car door, she settles one on her hip, even though the child is perfectly capable of walking, aware that a child in arms makes for a far more appealing picture, and drags the other by the hand.

The nanny follows at an approved distance of two yards, out of shot, with assorted gym bags, instruments, lunch boxes and coats.

Oksana walks past her car and does a catwalk pivot for the photographers, who call out, 'Over here, Oksana!' 'Oksana, straight to camera!' And 'One for me, Oksana, babes, straight to me!' and 'Smile!'

As Oksana beams and twirls once more, and I walk up the steps with her, and agree with her when she says the parking and drop-off system is a joke, and that she's fed up with doing the school run by car.

We stand together on the pavement, and she scopes the street – but the paps have melted away. Something about Oksana's brazen, me-first attitude gives me hope – and, more importantly, confidence that I am entitled to execute the plan I have in mind.

I release Joe's hand, and at that moment the school gates open, heralding just another day at Ponsonby Prep, Notting Hill, London W11.

Mimi

Home Farm

'Mum! Shut the window,' says Mirabel. 'Freezing!'

I realize I have been staring out of the window, and the hot tap's still gushing and the telephone's ringing again.

'Mum!'

I lean across the sink and latch the window shut. Turn off the tap. Sigh.

All I can think about is what happened last night.

I went to the Musgroves'. In the end, Mirabel made me wear an old silk navy dress cast-off from Rose with exposed zips and frayed hems that she found in the dressing-up box, and flip-flops, and then she added a tiny Levi's denim jacket, stood back, and said, 'With your hair, the Lanvin works in a hot-mess kind of way.'

I parked the Subaru next to the Jags and the matt-black Range Rovers and Rose's silver Land Rover with the Court Farm logo, and flip-flopped over the gravel to the oak door open to the hall, and stood for a moment on the slate floor, on my own, wondering whether anyone would notice if I just slunk out.

Could I leave before I arrived?

But then I saw Joan in the kitchen, and she'd put on an extra-specially starchy white and crisp tabard for the occasion. She bustled out, beamed, and then she said 'everyone' was in the garden, and winked, as if there was a secret. How could I leave?

I walked through the house, admiring the pink masses of

blowsy peonies exploding like candyfloss bombs from round, silver-mirrored vases, passed the kitchen, where the white-aproned staff from the Court Place operation were slamming trays of canapés and decorating puddings in the kitchen, and went into the sitting room, filled with the scent of woodsmoke, with fires lit, and where French windows were flung wide.

I wandered out on to the lawn, which was bathed in buttery evening sunlight.

There was a woman in white sitting on a bench with her back to me, her dark hair almost knotting as it tumbled down her smooth, brown back. I knew it was Farouche. I wondered if she'd put two and two together, whether she'd remember me, either as Mimi Malone, or Mimi Fleming, or – far more likely – not at all.

I sat opposite her on the bench, put down my Kir, picked it up again and tried to say hi, but I couldn't. For some reason, no words came out of my mouth.

I knew she was tinier in the flesh – everyone always is – but I'd forgotten how ridiculously beautiful she was. And ten years younger than me.

I sat on the bench opposite, carried on staring – then, instead of saying anything, I couldn't help it. I laughed. I was going to start telling her who I was and remind her of our previous exchanges – it was our point of contact – but I held back. I felt, for a second, that I wasn't Ralph's wife, or the children's mother, or sister of the more famous Con. I could be whoever I chose to be.

She smiled back. There was a fringed suede bag on her lap, and she started delving inside it, then she looked up and fixed me with black eyes with eyelashes so long they tangled, underneath wild brows that flared a little towards the bridge of her nose, like the tips of eagle wings.

'Farouche,' she said.

Farouche. She spoke it as if she were a one-name brand, like Nigella, or Angelina, or Beyoncé.

I'd pretended I'd never heard of her, when on the phone with Rose.

'. . . She's quite well known, a sort of performance artist, she's called Farouche. Married to Julien StClair. You know, famously attractive. Was a modellizer for a time – such a horrid word, means he went out with a succession of models – then in mezzanine finance, now a wildlife photographer? But *he's* not coming. They're separated. She's a conceptual, avant-garde performance artist,' Rose continued. 'Quite well known.' She paused.

'When they split up, for the first time, before they had Fox, they marked the end of their affair by walking from two different points on the Great Wall of China separated by a thousand miles and meeting in the middle to say goodbye.

'And then, when they got together again, they had Fox, so he's very much MBA, only I don't think they actually married. Or maybe they're so avant-garde they did get married, can't remember . . .'

'Farouche,' I said, as I somehow managed to retrieve these details: modeliser . . . mezzanine . . . MBA – Married but Available . . .

I took such a clumsy pull of my Kir that it spilt down my front, staining the blue silk black.

'And I'm Mimi. I'm your date!' And then, for some reason, I gave her The Look.

I lowered my chin, pressed my lips together into a pout and held her gaze for a beat too long.

At this, Farouche cocked her head and looked at me as if she were a bird about to peck a juicy worm in her beak.

'Rose said I'd like you. But she said you didn't bother about clothes . . .'

We were staring at each other.

Then she lit a Gauloise Blonde. She was wearing a high-necked, creamy white broderie anglaise dress. I think it's called a baby-doll. It was very short, anyway. She lit her cigarette and the orange tip glowed, and she sat like a sprite against the emerald gleam of the grass, and the green hills of Dorset beyond her, and the clouds behind her were streaked with pink and gold, and even though she was backlit I was thinking how beautiful she was, with her untamed brows, her straight nose and high cheekbones, her full mouth, and how her glossy, clear skin was somehow both brown and rosy at the same time, so in her white dress she looked like a delicious, irresistible scoop of Neapolitan ice cream.

She looked at me, looked away, then she blew out a smoke ring with a 'poh' sound, then another, and gazed out over the heart-stopping vista of smudgy white clouds in the darkening navy sky, sunset spreading like Kerrygold over sheep-dotted, lumpy, green hills. Then she slowly uncrossed her legs.

Farouche wasn't wearing any pants. It wasn't even a question of slightly not wearing pants.

I could see straight up her white dress, to a dark but trimmed bush, bisected by a wavy pink line, like a fresh sea urchin, pink with close-cropped, black tendrils.

My whole body was buzzing, as if I'd run away from a charging bull and hurled myself over an electrified fence only to find myself at a cheese-rolling event and I was pelting down a hill and going faster and faster and out of control, and I knew I would fall over but I couldn't stop myself and I'd get hurt, and all because I was chasing a wheel of cheddar.

I had gone into shock.

And she knew it.

'Yes, Rose is a wonderful friend,' Farouche continued, as she drew on her Gauloise greedily. She offered me a cigarette, leaning forward so that we were close. I inhaled her scent – an astonishing amalgam of tobacco, tuberose, pepper and something almost rotten that instantly made me feel high. I wanted to come closer, to get a bigger hit.

I don't smoke. But I took one anyway and, as our hands touched, then – it was like hitting the third rail. The electricity snaked from our fingertips as if the hands of God and Adam were touching. She stayed leaning close, our heads almost touching, as she took a battered gold lighter from her bag.

She lit my slightly crumpled, fat fag for me; the oily shreds of yellow tobacco hissed and crackled as they flamed orange. As I inhaled, the smoke caught in my throat and I felt giddy, high.

'She has impeccable taste,' Farouche said, and I allowed myself to stare into her brown eyes, flecked with wildcat yellow, for far, far too long to allow any room for doubt as to our common intention.

'A sixth sense when it comes to knowing . . . what I like.'

A far-off ringing breaks into my reverie.

'*Mum!* Answer the *phone!*'

I circumnavigate the table and pluck up the handset, which by some miracle is still in its cradle on the occasional table to the side of the inglenook.

'Hello, it's me, Ralph,' my husband informs me.

'I know,' I say. I can't put any oomph in my voice. I sound flat.

'Look, I'm getting the 17.16 from Waterloo instead of the 17.47, as – well, I'll tell you when I see you. I've got . . . news. I want everyone to be there, when I tell you.'

There is a strangled note to this, as if he's undergoing a full prostate exam while he is talking.

I clasp my hand over the phone, even though there is a mute button on the BT handset, along with many other functions I

43

have never bothered to learn how to work, as I always throw away immediately the guarantee and the instructions for any new appliance, on principle.

'Team, it's Dad,' I say. 'Guess what. He's coming home. Says he has "news".' The only person who looks up, loyally, is Posy, who beams, and says, 'RT!', which is what she says when she likes something.

I look round the kitchen. The blue gingham curtains flapping at the window. The Cornishware on the dresser. The daffs in a bright-pink jug, the four-oven Aga the colour of clotted cream, the flagstone floor decorated with five pairs of school shoes and one chewed slipper, the oak table. The wonky mantelpiece over the gaping inglenook, where the home fires burn . . .

I replace the receiver and stand there.

Whenever I close my eyes, Farouche swims into vision, and I'm back on our nest on the fur rugs in the gazebo, so I try to keep them open.

I try to stay in my real life when I am already somewhere and someone else.

'Dad must have bought the quad bike, then,' says Posy, as she clicks out of Vine and into Facebook and opens a Snapchat, holds her thumb down, and then laughs.

'We're not getting a quad,' Cas reminds her. 'They're too expensive.'

'And dangerous,' says Mirabel piously.

I gaze at Cas's unruly head of chestnut curls and wonder what's inside it. I mean, if I'm having filthy thoughts about a woman and I'm well into my forties, what on earth must it be like for him, at his age?

As I start making supper, wondering whether Ralph has capitulated and bought the quad bike, the telephone rings again. It's Rose, of course.

She wants to post-mortem the Biennale dinner. For obvious

reasons, I don't. What if Rose got wind of my – I realize I have to find a mental compartment for what I did with Farouche last night, and lock it tight.

'Hi, Rose, I was going to call *you*,' I say, jolly-hockey-sticks voice, as if everything is normal.

But it's not. I need my next hit. I've never been much of a drinker. Don't smoke. Never taken drugs. Certainly, nobody could ever accuse me of being a workaholic. But Farouche. This is new. This is absurd.

I'm sure the French have a word for it.

'So d'you think Ralph really has got news, as in news news?' Rose says, after I've gushed enough about her party. ('And how did you get on with Farouche?' Rose asks. 'Who?' I reply, heart beating wildly, as if there's a thrush trapped under my left ribs. 'Farouche? Oh yes! She was lovely,' I say, moving on, trying not to ask more about her.)

'D'you think it's that he's bought Bubblegum – d'you reckon? – as a surprise? Is it your wedding anniversary?'

After a puppy, the children's next dearest wish is for a beach hut where they could smoke dope and have sex away from us, and there's one up for sale, in bright pink, known as the Bubblegum Hut, which we all lust after, from a distance.

'Very much doubt it,' I reply. As if we could afford to drop a bundle on a beach hut. And Ralph and I have a firm tradition of forgetting our wedding anniversary every year.

I open the foil lid of the fish pie with one hand. Underneath, there is pallid potato, yellow cheese, green parsley, black pepper.

'Thanks so much again for last night,' I say, and a shaft of longing pierces me. I wish I could press replay. Do it all again. But it's gone.

'You are amazing, Rose. Amazing. But listen, I'd better go – make supper.'

'Oh, and what are you making?' she asks competitively.

'I'm doing home-made fish pie' (I omit to say it is bought from her very own Court Place Farm Shop) 'with veg, and then honeycomb ice-cream' (also from her Farm Shop).

All four children stare at me like cows in a field, in dumb accusation, so I make a great show of picking up the trug from the windowsill and a pair of secateurs.

'Oh, come on,' I say to the four of them after I hang up. 'What's the problem?'

It's terrible when your own children judge you. And find you wanting.

'And we're having spring greens, so bad luck.' I do not have to say 'from the garden', as we have them at every meal, apart from breakfast.

'The problem is, Mum,' Cas says as all the others groan at the mention of spring greens, 'that lying just comes so naturally to you.'

I had to go upstairs to write, in bed.

So. I mean, Jheeze.

Dad dropped the L bomb.

We're going back to London – YAY! He's heading up the team at some new company I've never heard of (I didn't even know his oil and gas company newsletter thing had been bought. Think Mum did, though).

Yup. He's got a big new job.

Dad dropped the bomb after supper – Mum was just dishing up when he arrived – late, as he had missed the train – and then instead of sitting down and carrying on talking about it 'as a Family', he put on the *News at Ten*, something he would still do even if we were under nuclear attack from Martians.

Like all old people, he likes to listen to the BBC news several times a day, despite the fact that 1. you can watch it online any time you like, and 2. they always repeat the same bulletin word for word.

For some reason, old people seem to like this. They must find repetition soothing, like babies.

As soon as Dad starts muttering about 'just catching the headlines', I grab my laptop and iPhone, say 'love-you-bye' and get out of there.

Now, I'm lying underneath the rattling window as the wind howls over the hills and an owl hoots in the barn.

So this was *our* news.

Bong!

Dad pushes open the front door, drops his man-bag, comes into the kitchen.

Dad: 'I have something to say that affects us all.' Sometimes he sounds like Winston Churchill during the Blitz.

We are all praying it can't be that Mum's pregnant yet again, as she's way too old for Dad's magic seed (family joke) to fall on fertile ground, I fear.

Bong!

Great-aunt Grizel's died (that's not news, knew that already) and has left some money (that's news), not very much but enough for us to find somewhere 'modest' to live in London so we can 'all be together'.

Bong!

He starts on about the offices on the Strand, and fracking in the National Parks, and ownership of rights under private land.

Mum: 'Slow down, darling. You know that, try as I might, I still can't manage somehow to read a whole article about fracking.' Then she puts the fish-pie foil dish to dry on the Aga lid rather than throwing it away; she's very distracted at the mo.

Bong!

And, guess what, he's found a house – back on our *old* garden!

Bong!

Only it's not a whole house, it's not our old house, and this new place was 'formerly council-owned' and a maisonette.

Dad: 'There's a mother and son in the basement, we've got the two floors above, so quite big. In fact, I met them, Cathy and Sid. Didn't catch their surname. (Surnames are important to Dad.) Very nice. Quiet.'

I thought Mum would be pleased, but she went silent and started scraping the plates into the compost.

Dad dug in his bag and handed us the particulars. 'Stunning, spacious Victorian double-fronted villa in sought-after Queen's Park location, the dream family home.'

Me: 'That doesn't look too bad.' It looked really nice!

Dad: 'Oops, no, not that one.' Irritated voice, as if our fault he'd given us wrong one. 'That's a huge house in Queen's Park we'd all love – especially Calypso – that we, unfortunately, can't afford.'

Mum had started looking at the Queen's Park house we can't afford, though. Entrance to gabled front. Front garden and bay windows on the first and ground floor. Set back from the road, and behind a low wall and a hedge at the front. A proper house. Dad at last finds the right particulars on two sheets stapled together and hands them to Mum.

48

Mum: 'Well, I can see there's one good thing about this Lonsdale Garden Court place.'

Dad looks relieved.

Mum: 'It's got off-street parking.' Mum's always very keen on free parking.

Says the reason America is the world's most powerful nation is because you can drive your huge minivan to literally anywhere, 'the drugstore on the corner or Walmart', and there will be somewhere to park, so people buy more stuff and get out more.

Dad: 'I only see Garden Court as temporary, darling. We need a base, it's back on the old stamping grounds for you – the communal garden – and all our friends are still there. Well, *your* old friends.'

Dad only calls people friends if they were at prep school together in the middle of the last century.

Mum: 'But the children can't all have their own rooms.' Studies particulars briefly.

Dad: 'Don't worry. If the children don't like it they can go to boarding school. Like Cas. They live on Instagram or Twitter, anyway, so they shouldn't care, in theory, where they actually sleep. It's irrelevant.'

Cas: 'Dad! Don't be mean. You know we like it here. And we don't need a garden. Notting Hill is so over, anyway. Whenever we go it's full of old people. If we have to move, why can't we move some-where like Hackney?'

Cas is convinced that there is more cool in one manky pub in Hackney, or one multi-storey car park in Bermondsey, than in the whole of Kensington.

Dad: 'And in terms of square footage, it's not that much smaller than our old house.'

Mum: 'Quite a small sitting room.' Little voice.

Dad: 'Well, we could always **knock through** if we like it and decide to stay. And if you look here' – he jabbed at a bit of the floor-plan – 'this bit by the side return will make the perfect space for a small garden room or conservatory or whatnot. We'll just *pro tem* get a bigger mortgage.'

I looked at Garden Court, and it looked OK – not too old, almost modern – but it didn't have the sweet face Home Farm does. Garden Court looked blank. A bit sad. Like council flats.

Dad: 'I did tell you, everyone, that during the years we've been in Dorset we've got poorer and everyone else has got richer and richer.'

Dad's never been a glass-half-full or a glass-half-empty person. There's never been anything in the glass at all.

'The wealth gap as defined by the Office for National Statistics between the Flemings and the residents of London W11 is at an all-time high. Even with the legacy from Great-aunt Grizel. It wasn't much, but better than a kick in the teeth, anyway.'

Posy: 'Can't we go back to our old house?'

Mum. 'You heard what Dad said, Po!'

Dad: 'Not as things stand. I refer you to the answer I gave a few moments ago.'

Then, to summarize, Dad tried to explain all about the new fracking technology and how it could be very profitable and very safe or, on the other hand, it could be very profitable and very dangerous.

Mum: 'But could fracking potentially make us, as opposed to the UK economy, rich, then?'

Dad: 'It's more complicated than that, love. In England, unlike in the States, you don't own the mineral rights underneath your land. The state does. But it all depends . . .'

At that point, I stopped listening, because then Mum and Dad started talking about schools, and I've left school.

We can't be that poor because Mum said, 'Does that really mean Cas can go to Canford (boarding school) next term, then?' and Dad said yes, and Cas whooped – he's longing to board – and Posy will go to some Academy place in London.

Dad: 'If Harrow Academy's good enough for the children of Cabinet members, I suppose I have to accept it might be good enough for mine.'

If Dad has already looked into schools, this must be serious.

And Lucian's going to Ponsonby Prep, as Harrow Academy doesn't have a place since half the Cabinet started sending their kids there.

I thought Mum would be pleased as tbh she's always moaning about being bored and getting fat and not having any friends.

Dad: 'Well, darling, you've been moaning about being out of the London loop and how you've been missing journalism since we've been in Dorset, so now's your chance to get back in the saddle. You should be pleased.'

Mum, for once, says nothing. I think she's scared. Dad clearly wants her to be a laying hen again, and since she left London, basically, newspapers have gone to shit. Like, you have to pay – I mean, none of my friends has ever read one and never will.

Fifteen minutes later, Mum comes back in from the compost heap. Found her on the landline in the hall. Sounded like she was leaving a message. Mum was obvs trying to be discreet. She was using the landline, even though she could be in the kitchen, sitting in the inglenook on the little rickety bench with the handheld, in the warm, which is what I do.

Mum: 'It's me. Listen, you can't call me on the mobile number I gave you,' she was saying. 'It doesn't work in Dorset. Email me, instead? I can't talk for long, but I just wanted to hear your voice. It was' – Mum breathes in this horrible way: pervy – 'amazing . . . meeting you. Oh God . . . I don't know what to think. Just wanted to tell you, actually, that we're moving to London so –' Then she sees me. Goes red.

Mum 'Oh gods' again. At the sight of her own daughter. Sharp intake. 'Sorry . . . Ciao!' she goes, then smacks down the receiver. Darts into kitchen.

WTF?

Ciao?? Who says 'ciao' any more?

@posyfleming RT God Bless Little Maddy wherever you are xxx

Clare

Lonsdale Gardens

I love the 9 a.m. morning rituals, as closely observed in the neighbourhood as the Japanese tea ceremony in Kyoto.

Monday: PT with Hunter; Tuesday: dance at Santhosh; Wednesday: zumba at Emma Freud's; Thursday: Powerplate at Powervibe; Friday: Yogalates . . . But I need to head home after drop-off today.

I can't make Santhosh – that's Sanskrit for 'happiness', of course – today. I have other plans.

I turn left at the school and walk along the now empty pavement. The paps have moved on, in search of Cara, or Rita. I have to make a quick pitstop at the Giving Back Centre. There's just time before my summit with Donna Linnet, house healer.

I stand on the pavement and look up at the façade, where men in overalls are stripping off old render and taking it back to the brick, prior to turning the building into another monument to Michael Alexis's minimalist urges.

Trish Dodd Noble showed us, i.e. me and Gideon, the Alexis plans: he's retained the bare bones of the double-fronted Victorian mansion but is stripping back some of the over-fussy egg-and-dart cornicing, coving and other extraneous detailing – all the features, in fact, that estate agents like to flag up as 'a wealth of period detail'.

The dove-grey, smooth, poured-concrete ramp up to the wide, double-height entrance is already in, taking the visitor straight into the galleria-stroke-atrium, and then, on the dot of 9 a.m. – as arranged – the van arrives from the South Bank. It parks right outside, on the zig-zags, and I stand and watch as the piece Gideon and I have donated to the GBC – a Tracey Emin neon sign saying 'This too shall pass' in bright pink cursive – is carried out of the back of the van, swaddled in bubble wrap, by two men in black overalls.

I follow the sign into the GBC up the poured-concrete ramp, my heart full. Say what you like about Trish – and many do – but she seems to have pulled this off. Her dream of creating a community hub, a place of inspiring stories, where all people, from all walks of life, can be their best selves, is about to come true.

I pause and read the names of donors which Michael Craig-Martin has rendered in one of his squiggly computer paintings on the wall straight ahead of me, and my eye runs down the list of names, which are ranked in order of date – but not size – of donation. (The meeting to determine that lasted over two hours.)

The Kasparian Foundation
Sir Paul and Lady Ruddock
Brent Hoberman
Sir Michael Spencer
The StClair Family
The John Lewis Partnership
Richard Curtis, Emma Freud and Children
Tesco
The Ponsonby Prep PTA

My eye runs down the list, wondering if she's there. The GBC has just received the biggest, chunkiest donation to date, and some donors prefer to remain anonymous . . . but clearly not her. There she is. It was such a surprise that she wanted to commit, and so much – a whole separate donation from the solid *famille* StClair cheque, too.

But there it is: her name.

Farouche – just above:

Nokia
Vodafone
Sir Denys and Lady (Terri) Bradshaw
Soho House Group

And:

Trish and Jeremy Dodd Noble.

I know that the Dodd Nobles could probably have funded the whole thing from their current accounts – Jeremy's pay-off from Nokia was historic – but, despite the generosity of the above, they still managed to wrestle at least half the capital cost of the project from the council.

So the hard-working rate-payers of the borough will subsidize the yearning of the idle rich to self-actualize.

Yes, everyone in the Royal Borough is stumping up, so me and my friends can, if we are so inclined, learn playwriting with a young woman in DMs and with purple hair from the Royal Court; we can learn about the power of our vaginas from a feminist collective in Shoreditch; we can go to a first-novel clinic with Hanif Kureishi; or how to Make Our Own Christmas Decorations with Kirstie Allsopp; or how to make a yarrow poultice for post-partum piles with West London's resident White Witch of Home Remedies, Sof McVeigh. Which is wonderful.

I point to the spot in the *atelier* area of the atrium where we want the sign to go, as a message to all of those who come here in search of renewal, improvement and refreshment on life's path. It's a wonderful, calm, white, chapel-like space. I leave them to install the installation, and I take the lift up from G, past 1 (the Café, with break-out spaces and pods), past 2 (studio and workshops), past M (Mezzanine), to 3 (Media Suite and Theatre, doubling as a cinema, where the seats can be removed for large events like fundraisers and parties).

The carpet is being laid, which is so exciting – it's the gold hessian a hundred per cent wool carpet that Trish spotted in 5 Hertford Street in Mayfair, which is expensive, but so hard-wearing, and as Trish's motto is 'You get what you pay for,' of course she's ordered nothing but the best – but then, as Gideon observed, in fact, Trish is getting what everyone else is paying for.

He always cuts through to the nub of things. 'It's extraordinary. In Notting Hill, as in the Bible, it's not enough that to those that have shall more and more be given. From those that have not, it must also be taken away.'

I take off my biker boots and pad across the floor. They've put down the underlay, so it's like walking on a travelator. The Tracey Emin will be up by the end of the day, and the carpet down, so with a fair wind, it's all coming together for the Gala Opening. (Trish is bidding for someone like the PM to open it; he's top of her hit list, anyway!) It *is* exciting.

I head back home and, as I pass the huge villa, a former council-owned hostel of some sort, between the school and the GBC, I wonder who's bought it and when we're going to find out (Ponsonby's bid was rejected by the council, so a medium-sized oligarch is my guess), but don't stop. I have to be quick, as I want to pick up some citrus, blueberries and roasted Spanish almonds from the Portobello en route, to graze on as we sip our green tea.

Home, it's quiet. Aida is out.

I remove my shoes by the front door, sighing as I lean over.

I go down to the kitchen, which is quiet, apart from the throb of the dishwasher, and reach up to the cupboards to get down heavy, hand-thrown cream china cups and set out the fruit and nuts on a cream plate, then fill a little flask with milk in case Donna wants builder's tea – it looks welcoming – and a larger one with water.

I check the blackboard to the left of the stainless-steel fridge, where there's a separate entrance to the house, and where Joe's clutter – footballs, scooter – hangs from industrial meat-hooks and his shoes are slotted in pairs in wire racks. I go over to hang up a stray sweatshirt and, as I do, I cast an eye over the grid of after-school activities.

I've cut them down to the bare essentials, and keep Saturday free, of course, for tennis tournaments, and maybe, one day, cricket matches.

Monday:	Cricket Nets – Lord's
	Kumon
Tuesday:	Chess
	Piano
Wednesday:	Swimming
	Mandarin
Thursday:	Tennis
	Poetry
Friday:	Wu Shu Kwan
	Art Club
Saturday:	Free time
Sunday:	Meditation & Stillness
	Museum/Gallery

It's just so important for children to have time to stand and stare, I always think.

I like to carve out time for Joe for stillness, for discovering things for himself. I like to make sure he's not over-scheduled, like so many other kids. Of course, results matter. But educating the whole child is far more important.

I pick up the chalk and underneath the seven columns of his weekly timetable Monday to Sunday I write, 'Life Skills/Half term' as a *pour mémoire* in the area for extras like 'orthodontist' or 'sleepover Friday @Raphael's'.

I replace the chalk on its little ledge, underneath the blackboard, resisting the temptation, I realize, to hurl it across the room as I recognize the extent it has fallen to me to be both mother and father to 'our' child.

And I have to buy in where Gideon has sold out.

This is why I think I will enrol Joe in the How To Academy half-term Life Skills camp. After all, it's only £450 for a two-day course, so a small price to pay for Joe to begin to learn what it means to be a man.

The doorbell rings a few minutes before nine thirty, and I slip silently up the stone steps in my cashmere socks, holding on tight to the banister even on the way up to let Donna in, and the last time I saw her flashes across my mind.

Of course, we completely remodelled this house when we bought it from Mimi and Ralph Fleming, back in 2006, when I was pregnant with Joe.

Donna had told us that in order to conceive we needed to keep the Victorian shabby chic and as many soft furnishings as possible. We even put some paintings up on the white walls, and I stuck some family photographs around.

But it wasn't us. And after Joe was born I had to tell Ralph, Joe's donor father, that we'd basically erased all traces of the former Fleming family home. It made the situation easier for Gideon, too, obviously, as there was no way I could erase the trace of Ralph: his DNA was occupying more space in the house and in our heads every day, in the shape of Joe.

I open the door with a warm hostess smile.

But it's not Donna, in droopy pastel linens and Birkenstocks, as I expected. Patrick Molton in a suit is on the doorstep. Looking as if he's just jumped out of the shower, all shiny and slicked down and smug. And he's holding a bunch of flowers.

I stand there, and I can't help myself.

'Oh, yes, so you really think a quick bunch of flowers would do it, Patrick?' I snap.

I can't forgive him for the fact that he started his work without placing movement monitors on both our houses, and now, of course, our drawing room has a hairline crack in it and I'm sure the front door is sticking, too.

He puts the flowers in my arms. I have no choice but to take them. At least it is a reasonably inoffensive posy, of whites, pale greens and pinks, from Paula Pryke.

'Thanks,' I say gruffly, and then I notice over his pinstriped shoulder that Tiggy, the new Marguerite, is sitting in the car outside Patrick's new, and the Forsters' old, house.

Even though she's watching, I gesture with the bouquet at the motorcade of lorries and the skips, like a line of stationary tanks, at the suspended parking bays and all the hoardings screening off the building works disfiguring what used to be such a pretty, quiet, tree-lined street where parking used to be so easy.

I thrust the bouquet like a stabbing sword specifically at the huge, glossy hoarding emblazoned with the words 'LUXURY SUBTERRANEA' and the builders' Portaloo, within yards of my front door, from which a Pole in rigger boots, jeans and a grubby white T-shirt with a bottle of Heinz on the front and the logo saying 'I put Ketchup on my Ketchup' is emerging, pulling up his flies.

'God, Patrick, thanks for the flowers, but how many lorry movements a day? Constant noise,' I say, having to raise my voice against the blare of Polish pop radio. 'Drilling. Whole house bloody shakes.'

I feel like crying.

'It's all been awful. Gideon's ... moved out,' I carry on. This isn't strictly true, but it will do no harm: after all, Patrick tricked us. He said the work wouldn't be extensive compared to most sub-basements, and he and Antigone, aka Tiggy, would 'bivouac upstairs'. Actually, I don't mind Tiggy: she has a son and she's better than Patrick's previous: primary-school teacher Anoushka. For a while he actually had a girlfriend – a lap-dancer, inevitably – called Krystle Knight.

Gideon couldn't help pointing out to Patrick that he had a girlfriend who'd picked 'Kristallnacht' as her stage name. But, anyway, after Anoushka came Kristallnacht, and after Kristallnacht, now Patrick has settled down with Tiggy, having claimed that he'd had 'all the action he could handle', despite his earlier bragging to male friends, when wives were safely out of earshot, that he was 'pulling twenty-five-year-olds' and 'really enjoying the sexual variety'.

I do find it extraordinary that, after a certain age, very rich men insist on judging the measure of their own attractiveness by the youth of the women they manage to date.

And that men in their sixties, even seventies, still manage to straddle the age gap so that they have one foot in the grave, another in a nightclub. But there we go. I suppose Patrick is what some call 'technically very handsome', in other words, good-looking but, somehow, not sexy.

I look at his scrubbed face, which is pleading with me not to be cross with him, and I suddenly have a memory, of that afternoon last year, when it was so hot I was lying out on the lawn in the communal garden, on a Welsh blanket, reading my book-group book, *The Goldfinch*, and I became aware of a low, thumping sound accompanied by animal shrieks. The barnyard noises were emanating from the Molton house next door, from the bedroom window, which was open.

I could distinctly hear Patrick, using a strange, growly sex-voice, saying, 'Yes, baby, go on, baby,' and the sound of a headboard thudding.

What was so awful was that there were small children playing outside, either on their own or with weekend nannies/housekeepers, and we all exchanged glances and wondered whether we should move, but before we could the shrieking reached a climax and then there was quiet, blessed quiet, and then we heard a terrible bellow from Patrick – like a bull being gored – and we thought, Phew. Thank God that's over. The nannies resumed texting and chatting and opening little Tupperware boxes of green grapes and complaining about their employers.

I got back to my Donna Tartt but, five minutes later, we heard shrieking again . . . and then the headboard thudding . . . and we all burst out laughing. But the third time it happened we all just picked up our things and moved away, just as some noisy slapping had begun and I could hear Patrick saying, 'You ready for me, baby?' then moaning, then saying, 'Are you ready for more of me, baby?'

I lose my cool again as the scene replays in my head.

'Your works are bloody noisy, Patrick, all of them!' I glare frostily. 'We can't hear ourselves think! And there's a crack in the party wall, and I'm sure the kitchen floor is cracked, too. Do you want to see? I think you should. I know it's covered by the party-wall agreement, but still.'

He gives a panicked look and I know that I should probably dial it down a little, otherwise we'll only be communicating via our lawyers, too, like so many Notting Hill residents, and that gets nasty, not to mention expensive.

But I have to make my point. Our stone floors are famed

throughout the world of interiors, as they are laid with hand-hewn, fudge-coloured stone. I open the door, step back, inviting him in.

I am so fizzing with it all, the trickery of the dig, and his perfidy. You can't trust anyone around here. Least of all your neighbours.

'Thanks, Clare, I will, next time, but Tiggy's in the car,' he says with relief, 'and we've got an appointment.' At this moment Donna comes round the corner and is almost upon us.

My blood runs cold. An antenatal?

'So I should go.' He nods to Donna, who is standing, tact-fully, a few yards away on the pavement. 'The local angel-channeller or house whisperer or whatnot has arrived.' He backs off, down the steps, and Donna steps in instead.

I let out a big gust of a sigh as they leave, and turn to Donna.

'*Namaste*,' we say. We hug, and as we come in close I catch a faraway whiff of patchouli.

Donna steps inside and pitches forward, frozen.

'You OK?' I ask. 'Can I get you anything?' I am beginning to regret her visit already. Patrick has churned me up.

'Oh, oh – it's just – I can feel it, here, in my stomach,' she says, patting herself.

I hang her coat and bag alongside my Burberry trench and Mulberry satchel, on the pegs. 'I hate any sort of clutter in a passageway, too,' says Donna. 'It disturbs the flow.'

Then she does it again. Stands stock still, as if she inhabits another dimension. She closes her eyes. Then she opens them, and makes searching eye contact with me, as if reading me.

'Shall we go down, grab some tea,' I say, unsettled. 'Oh, and Donna . . .' I gesture down. 'Your . . .'

Donna bends down and removes her shoes, and we descend in our stockinged feet to the kitchen.

Donna prowls around the room. She circumnavigates the

oak refectory table, with its benches, and then she glides into each corner of the room in turn, from the street side to the garden end of the kitchen, where she stands still for a moment, then gives three sharp claps.

She cocks her head on one side as if listening to a distant echo, then nods. She reminds me of a GP doing an external exam of your inner organs, when they knock on your tummy in various places, then look pensive, as if waiting for an echo only they can hear.

I click-click-flame the gas on the range and slide the already boiled kettle on for a few seconds, to bring the water to piping hot again.

'Donna,' I counter, as I pinch some loose green tea into an iron Tibetan teapot. The clapping has annoyed me. 'Why the clapping?'

'To disturb any bad energy.'

'I know what clapping is supposed to do, but it's not the house that's unhappy, Donna.' This comes out sharper than I intended. 'This time, I just, wanted . . . you to come so we could talk about nutrition, and my strategies to optimize conception.' Reflexively, I take out my iPhone and check Fertility Friend, my ovulation app, for the sixth time that day. In theory, I am releasing an egg in ten days.

'Anyway, tea?'

'Lovely,' says Donna. 'And Clare, you know – I know you know – that you mustn't hold in your anger, it's bad for your liver. Are you doing yoga?'

I nod.

'Let me tell you a story. I went to this new hotel, this gorgeous boutique hotel on Holland Park, next to the Beckhams'?'

I place the teapot on the table.

There is a pause while I let it brew, then pour it out into our cups, the liquid steaming in the golden morning light, here in my lovely house on a perfect Notting Hill communal garden.

'As soon as I stepped over the threshold, and let me tell you it was done up to the nines – the level of finish was something else, the staff were all trained in New York, by Keith McNally – and yet, and yet.'

She blows into her cup of tea. 'I could hear them. I could almost feel them.'

'Sorry, what? You could feel and hear who?'

'The trapped souls – screaming to be let out.' She sips. 'They're screaming because the spirits hadn't *transitioned*.' She sips and smacks her lips, as if filling me in on last night's episode of *The Archers*.

'So I went off and I did some research, and bingo! Came back, and I told the owner, Sofia – you know Fia, lovely, five kids, she has that house on Dawson Place with the squash court and the tree house, married to, you know, that guy who owns –'

'I don't know her, but carry on,' I say, cutting her off. Donna's on my time, and she's no longer as cheap as she once was.

'So I came back and told her that her new hotel was on top of a medieval plague pit.' Again, Donna speaks as if this is quite a bog-standard development. 'And so needed proper, deep *cleansing*. Or else she needed to move, sell up and start again somewhere else.'

'You mean like pressure-washing?' I ask.

'No, not that: the energy lines were blocked, it was like a lorry jack-knifed on a motorway – I had to clear the blockage, like you do with acupuncture. Start upstairs?'

We climb to the top of the house, Donna puffing slightly, as if I am making her work, to the nursery floor, which Gideon has opened up to the skies with a glass roof, and roof terrace, but Donna scopes this in silence and without comment descends to the first floor, where there's the wet room and the master bedroom suite.

Donna's breathing suddenly seems very loud as we stand together in the bedroom. It is somehow odd to be up here, with her, the double bed, primly made, with two white pillows at each head, so near. It's hard for the thought of sex not to cross your mind when you're in a bedroom. Even with an estate agent. And, for Donna, sex is a key life force, so I tense myself for the inevitable.

'And how is your –' She pauses, raises her right hand, as if stopping traffic.

I know she is going to ask me a question that's going to make me feel terrible, about marital bed death.

'Intimate connection with Gideon?' she asks. 'After all, this is' – she gestures around the monastic chamber where I have slept alone for weeks, my orifices penetrated only with silicon earplugs – 'where it all goes on!'

I collapse on the bed. Trying to contain my irritation. Donna knows the problem isn't Gideon's sex drive. It's the fact that I couldn't conceive for hundreds of cycles, and it turned out to be Gideon. We don't use the word 'fault'.

'That's not the issue,' I say. Donna is one of the very few people on the planet who knows that Ralph is Joe's real, or biological, father. Not that Ralph sees it like that.

'Clare,' says Donna, 'I know the situation. We go back. If you tell me what it is you *really want* I can help you.'

Her eye is roving around the room, which is completely empty of any adornment or picture. The built-in cupboards across the length of one wall lack door handles – you have to push them and they spring open; it's one of Gideon's many signature features. In terms of stuff, there's just an iPod dock, like a block of concrete, the domed sunrise bodyclock and a B&B Italia modular chaise longue covered with the heaviest white linen, on which I now rest my socked feet.

'Hold on, I can't see your meditation gong, or your electromagnetic screen,' Donna says, her head swivelling like a Thunderbird puppet's. 'You have to disconnect to connect, you know. Have you put it away?'

Her eyes widen when I reveal we don't have either: of course, I meditate in here, every morning, and chant some of my mantras, such as 'I love and support myself.'

'Oh my God,' she says, with urgency. 'I'll ask the Bradshaws – you know Terri and –'

'I know Terri and Denys,' I say. Indeed I do.

'I'll ask them where they got theirs,' says Donna. 'I mean, have you seen Terri recently?' Donna becomes instant best friends with her clients, and goes on about them, even though she is supposed to maintain confidentiality. 'Married for, like, ever, fantastic connection, she looks *amaaazing*. She was telling me that since they got the screen she and Denys have –'

'It's OK,' I say. 'I know.' There's no one left in the Western world who is not fully aware that Terri is in her animal prime of life.

Annoyingly, it is Donna who glances at her watch. As if I am low down the client food chain.

'Next time, I'll bring some tools, clear the bad energy in here,' she says, which is annoying. Nobody likes to think they generate bad energy in the bedroom. I find this tactless, so cover the moment by standing up, then smoothing the bed back to a snowy, royal-icing finish.

'*Next time?*' I say. After all, she's only been here half an hour, that's £150, and she's done nothing apart from namedrop.

I stride to the window and look out across the garden to hide my annoyance.

'Don't you have your tools with you now? Like a plumber? What are they?'

'Yew branches. Copper rods. Salt crystals,' says Donna, as if everyone knows the approved kitbag for releasing trapped souls from medieval plague pits. 'Or, sometimes, just playing loud music works. You have to feel your way.' She pats her stomach again, to remind me that this is the seat of her capacity for divination.

'Donna, listen,' I say. She joins me by the window. We stand together and watch Lionel wheelbarrow a load of cuttings from the border opposite down past the playground to the shed – which is not any old common-or-garden shed but bespoke and designed by legendary local architect John Pawson.

'This isn't so much about the house. I thought I explained, in the email? Not house. Baby.'

Donna gives me a long look. She holds her counsel. Waits for me to continue.

'A baby brother or baby sister for Joe,' I say, as if there were more options available. 'I don't want him to be an only child. And, ideally, I'd like Ralph . . .' I trail off.

My eyes fill with tears as I think of Joe, an only child, and Giddy banging his interns in Shoreditch, and probably someone on the garden, too, as I sleep alone in the snowy and pristine Savoir bed. All the other mothers I know have at least three children. Four was compulsory in the nineties. Even Mimi Fleming – no role model – has four.

And the most powerful NHMs – Notting Hill Mummies – have five, as five is the new four, just as Thursday was the new Saturday for going out on a big night and now, suddenly, Wednesday is the new Thursday.

It's so hard keeping up round here, with everyone, on everything.

'Donna. Please. I need to make this happen.' As I speak, I am watching two little girls in floral smocks and yellow wellies

66

running across the lawn to the playground at the end, both aged around three, and two nannies trailing after them.

I turn around to see Donna standing in the middle of my bedroom with her eyes closed, as if tuned in to a higher authority.

'Yes, I can hear, I can hear,' Donna murmurs. For a terrible moment, I think she might start speaking in tongues.

She opens her eyes and stares at me, where I stand at the window. 'You have to go, to leave . . .' She gestures around. 'Gideon . . .' She shakes her head. 'Gideon . . . you're right. He's nowhere here. He's already gone.'

This is interesting. Finally, an independent, outside authority – Donna Linnet – has authenticated my innermost fears, and desires.

'And the Flemings?' I ask. 'What about them?' This was their house.

'This much I know,' says Donna. 'Listen to me. This is the ancestral home of the Fleming family,' she says.

'Actually, they have what Ralph calls a seat in Scotland,' I correct her. 'But you're right in that this is, or was, their *London base*,' I say, but my skin has come out in goosebumps, because I know what she's going to say next.

I've had the plan – well, for years now. I've tried it once before, to action it, and failed, but that was during a hard time for both me and Mimi. Years have passed. I could fail again, but this time I can fail better.

'You're right that the key to this is Ralph Fleming, Clare,' says Donna, speaking normally now and, thank God, with her eyes open.

'It's not going to be easy. And don't expect miracles. He's a tricky customer, and I'm surprised you ever swung it the first time. So brace yourself,' she warns. 'It may never happen . . . but I gotta feeling.'

I make a mental note to send an email, flagged 'Urgent', to the Wigmore Fertility Clinic, to whom I have been paying storage fees of £65 a month for eight years.

She comes over and puts her arms on my shoulders, and it's then I feel it, as she touches me, the energy running between us, her healing power, as if I've been jammed into a live socket.

She hugs me tight so I can't breathe, then pushes me away. 'And exhale,' she says.

I let out my breath in a shuddering pant, and when I open my eyes the world seems more focused, clearer and crisper, after months and months of buffering and weak signal. I can see the sky. It's such a relief, when you allow yourself to be a human being. I smile at Donna, and my cheeks almost creak as I show my teeth, it's probably been so long since I smiled at anyone.

'Good girl,' says Donna, and gives me a pat.

PART TWO

AUTUMN

From: MimiFleming@gmail.com
To: FarouchedeG@wanadoo.fr.org

Date: 13 September 2014

I'm here, I'm back. Notting Hill.
I want to see you, but I'm scared. You're ten years younger
than me.
You eat tomatoes like apples.
You smell like heaven on earth.
At Harrow Academy, there's a sign on the noticeboard saying
'Are you Lesbian, Bisexual or Not Sure?'
Ha!
I can't stop thinking about you. When I asked what you'd been
sacked for, thinking you were going to say 'smoking', you told me
what it was really for. Did you *really*? How many sixth-form girls,
did you say?
I was shocked.
Where are you? London, Paris or Venice? What about your
husband, who annoys you? (Show me a wife whose husband
doesn't annoy her.) What makes you think yours is so much more
annoying than anyone else's? What makes him so special?
When can I see you?
Mimi
xxxx

Mimi

Lonsdale Garden Court

I'm going through the motions and I know it. I wonder if anyone else can tell.

School run, children, cooking, writing to Cas at Canford, sending needy notes to previous contacts in journalism. So many of them have switched to beauty PR, or they're making gluten-free baked goods, or they're training to be psychotherapists, so not much luck so far.

And still no answer from Farouche.

Nothing. Not a bloody sausage. How could she? Where's she gone?

So I hate my life a lot right now. Hate the maisonette, which is total fucking chaos, like the rest of my car-crash life.

I find I'm stopping in the middle of things, lost in thought, talking to myself, talking to her, and it's as if I'm trying to explain what's happened to me *to a reporter from the Daily Mail*.

As is well known, the paper's main aim is to tell its readers what its prejudices are and then proceed to reinforce them. The paper does not merely believe in open *Schadenfreude* whenever a celebrity comes a common-or-garden cropper in some way. It also seeks to expose adultery or infidelity by any public figure so that the whole nation can enjoy a collective spasm of Shaggenfreude, too.

I didn't intend this to happen, I never planned this. I go around, trying to account for my feelings, for my affair with Farouche (so far: sum total of encounters two and a half, if you count the session in the gazebo at Rose's, which I most certainly do).

She's my main preoccupation. I admit she takes up far more headspace than the shambles that is Lonsdale Garden Court, where most of our stuff is still in boxes piled up in the 'study' at the end of the hall passage, and I don't have the energy or slightest urge to unpack them, as there's nowhere to put anything.

Even though we chucked several skips' worth of what Ralph calls our 'Lares and Penates' and I call 'our worthless crap' out of Home Farm – like all the children's videos, and my Le Creuset collection, which, as my husband pointed out, has not been used since we received it as a wedding present twenty years ago. But try throwing *anything* away in front of children. They want everything to stay the same. If only you don't throw away the pee-stained, rusting hamster cage, or Calypso's rubber-chew chicken, they must think, you and Dad will stay together always, as these frightful things will remind you of each other.

'Mum, I can't believe you're giving them away,' Posy almost sobbed, back in Dorset, as she chucked dead felt-tips and glue pens into a box in the kitchen, while I made a Matterhorn out of saucepans in the middle of the floor.

'What if one day you wanted to make, like, a lamb *tagine* (Po is an avid watcher of *Masterchef*) or a *kickasserole* . . . for a *dinner party* . . . like, for all the new friends you might make at *Harrow Academy?*'

Long pause, as I contemplate the non-existent chances of any of the above ever happening. Ralph hasn't made a new friend since he was in short trousers. And I, in this age of Facebook friends, can't begin to process the ones I already have, let alone trawl the school gates for fresh meat. And I gave up giving dinner parties in 1995, shortly before the terrifying advent of the 'kitchen supper'.

The twisted cassette tapes of Stephen Fry reading Harry Potter, mostly backwards – stuff like that – went. But we brought, of course, all the Fleming family furniture: the embroidered footstool emblazoned with the family motto, 'Dominus Providebit', or 'the Lord Will Provide', the sofas, the armchairs, the oak table in the kitchen, the paintings, as we loved them and couldn't afford to replace them. It all looks OK; the maisonette is . . . fine. (It's the only place on the communal garden where you can't see Lonsdale Garden Court.) But.

But.

Oh hell! I look at my iPhone, and it's updated without an email response from F, and it's Lucian's second day at Ponsonby, and I'm late, it's too late to go on foot, so I shovel him out of the house with all his stuff into the car, shout at Mirabel to get in (she wants a lift) and manage to leave by 8.20 a.m., only to hit one of those temporary four-way traffic lights on the junction of Elgin Crescent and Ladbroke Grove.

So we all sit there, me trying not to fume and swear and make everything unpleasant.

I even switch from the all-female line-up on the *Today* programme (sometimes, Ralph asks, 'Oh, is it *Woman's Hour* already') to Radio One to lighten the mood, while Lucian keeps going, 'Will we be late?' and taking off his grey flannel cap and burying his head in Calypso's fur and being brave, and then we *finally* get to Ponsonby Square.

This is new since my time. Somehow didn't notice yesterday. A pack of photographers in jeans and parkas on the pavement opposite the school, in a sort of press pig-pen.

Mirabel says, 'Fuck sake.'

She is not at Harrow Academy. She is not at school. In the parlance, she has 'fallen out of mainstream'.

She's talking about doing a creative-writing course at some sixth-form college and, as things stand, our daughter is a NEET

– Not in Education, Employment or Training. She's signed on. Ralph says that this is shameless, but I tell her it's 'brave, and why not, darling?' and she says she doesn't care what me or Dad thinks.

'Mum, chill. Face it. You and Dad just can't admit I'm just like every other female I've ever met in Notting Hill. Trapped on benefits. I have the Job Seeker's Allowance. They have husbands. You have Dad bringing home the bacon, paying taxes. What's the difference?

'Fuck sake!' Mirabel goes again as we approach the school gates.

There do seem to be more cars than usual.

'What are you fucksaking about now?' I ask.

'Mum, look – there! The paps! That's the supermodel Belle MacDonald, innit?' she says, pointing and twisting round as we drive past.

'And isn't that Oksana, the Russian one –'

'But Belle . . . she can't still be a mother here!' I say, almost in wonder, trying to see. All the women on the pavement outside the school are like gazelles, with high heels, tumbling hair and taut, shuddering thighs.

'She was here when I was last a mother here. She must be on child number . . . Oh Christ!'

As I approach, the morning bell sounds and the crowd on the pavement surges forward like a wave breaking on a Cornish beach.

I loop round the square in my muddy Subaru, shouting, 'Sugar!' as I can't find a pay and display: all taken, Vorsprunged by fucking Porsches and those new 'Minis' the size of tanks, and Range Rover Evoques and Priuses.

'I knew leaving Dorset was a mistake,' I blurt out babyishly. 'I don't think your father realizes that as long as I can't park in the borough life is all but impossible.'

I am still waiting for my ResPark to arrive by post. I literally can't believe how hard it makes life. In fact, the *only* thing about Lonsdale Garden Court is that some previous tenant had the sound good sense to rip up the front garden and put in hard standing, so at least we have OSP at home.

In the end, I make Mirabel sit in the car and I nose into a pay-and-display bay behind a tiny car, like a baby's toy, painted in fluorescent orange. It is covered with cartoon writing saying 'Happify Your Life!' and that the car's called 'Twinkle', both of which messages serve only to fill me with murderous rage.

I flick the hazard lights on, get out and run up the steps, and the door opens and out comes this man.

When I see him, I reckon he must be a father at Ponsonby, too, so I stop hurtling through the double doors, dragging Lucian.

I stop on the steps, hold the door and smile. You don't often get to share the same airspace as an attractive male, and when it happens I like to milk it for all it's worth.

'Come *on*, Mummy,' says Lucian. Lets go my hand.

The man stands there, too. Lucian has scooted down the hall to his classroom, where the tall, blonde teacher in pink jeans, Tod's loafers and a crisp, white shirt, glowing with raw health and shiny morning face is already hugging him and helping him with his bags and instruments.

I wonder if I could have that thing – that I'd had three times in my life, again, i.e. once with Ralph, and then with Si Kasparian, and once with a woman, Farouche.

I wonder if I can ever have that thing again with a man.

So I swing into seduce mode.

I give him The Look, in other words.

He looks maybe a teensy bit startled – it can be a bit disconcerting if you're not braced for it, Ralph admits – then smiles back. He looks a bit like a very handsome hyena when he does this, with his canines gleaming white in his brown face and his mop of gold-streaked brown hair.

I glance over my shoulder. I assume he's smiling at the pretty blonde teacher. But the corridor is empty.

Unlike every other woman I've seen so far in a three-mile radius of the Electric Cinema, I am neither thin, nor rich, nor hot. None of the above is ever going to change now, but he's still smiling at me.

We move together out of the doorway as if executing a simple routine off *Strictly* and stand in the hall, next to the photo gallery of valued members of staff, with their names, and the character-building Eleanor Roosevelt quotes stencilled on to the walls. Behind closed doors we can hear the excited cheeping of children.

'Do you come here often?' he says.

I wish I wasn't wearing the fleece I wore to take Calypso to the vet. I start brushing off the hairs automatically.

This isn't a pick-up line, I tell myself.

After all, he's an English father at Ponsonby Prep. And Englishmen make passes by accidentally falling into your lap as your taxi bowls round Hyde Park Corner at midnight. Or by staring at your breasts when they talk to you. Or by striking your bottom with their ski-pole as you stagger off a button lift at the top of a freezing mountain. And the closest they get to a declaration is muttering, 'I've grown accustomed to your face,' like Professor Higgins.

'Well, yes. I do! Come here often,' I babble. 'Well, actually, no, I used to. But now I am again. So I will be. Yes,' I conclude with triumph. 'You?'

'My first time, second day, if that makes any sense.' He gazes down the passage, wistful, a little lost, as if willing his beloved schoolboy son to reappear.

I can definitely hear a trace of a non-public-school back-ground in his voice. 'Feels weird.' He sighs. I wonder if he is a single father. 'Maybe we should have coffee, if you're not too busy?'

'Ha ha,' I giggle lightly, wondering if 'busy' is a tease.

Ralph has this theory that NHMs – and he includes me in this category, which is so unfair – go from Beautcamp Pilates to zumba to reflexology to hairdresser via ladies' lunch at E&O and designer boutiques, a smash and grab on Selfridges, followed by a little tea in the Bulgari in Knightsbridge 'to recover', that they are a breed who regard their day job as spending their husband's money, and the definition of being faithful as not shagging their personal trainer – not in the marital bed, anyway.

But I do glance at my watch. Mirabel is in the car, defending it from the traffic wardens.

'I can't today,' I say, allowing a note of regret. I smile winningly at him. He is, after all, very handsome. And he's younger than me.

I am cougar! I tell myself. Men, women, younger women, younger men . . . all are possible prey!

I am *force* of *nature*!

'But later in the week?' I say. 'Maybe?'

'Gimme your phone,' he says. 'I want to give you my number.'

I dig into the pocket of my padded husky from New Look. Realize I've left my phone in the car in my It bag of the moment, a free hessian Bag for Life from the 2010 Cheltenham Literary Festival.

I withdraw a folded piece of paper. I write my number on it and give it to him.

He looks at me with a grin and pushes up the sleeves of his jacket, as it's quite warm, still, for September.

The base colour of most Englishmen's skin is red. But that

of Italian and French men is the shade of *pain* Poilâne and turns a toasty brown in the sun.

He is not wearing a wedding ring.

'So who *are* you?' he says, gratifyingly, as if I am in some way mysterious, when I am plate-glass transparent.

His eyes are green against his brown skin, and his carefully chosen green T-shirt makes them look even greener.

I tell him who I am. It doesn't sound very exciting.

'Well, I'm Julien with an "E" StClair,' he says. I immediately worry that at least once some cake decorator squiggled in icing on the top of a birthday cake 'Happy Birthday Julian with an E'.

'Goodbye, Julien with an "E",' I say, and as I walk down the steps I am already wondering when I am going to see him again and realizing that if he is a Ponsonby Pop there will be two opportunities a day for . . . innocent flirting.

I am so relieved I find a man almost attractive again that I'm almost mown down by a supermodel in a Hummer as I skip across the road.

I get into the car, put the key into the ignition and drive off, and Mirabel is whining about me taking so long. My telephone whistles. Text.

'Darling, can you find my phone?' I say, driving.

Mirabel delves into the hessian bag and reads out the number.

'What does the text say, though?' I ask.

'Dunno. Don't understand. Some random has just sent you a text.' Mirabel pauses. She peers at my iPhone screen. 'Mum?' she is holding my iPhone up to me so I can read the screen.

I almost plough into a line of parked cars as I realize what's happened.

I must have written my number on the A4 sheet upon which I had inscribed my 'To Do' list. I've literally never made a list before, and I have a pin-sharp memory, unfortunately, of what is written on that sheet.

> PITCHES – praps long-form piece called To Notting Hell and Back abt changes to the hood. New Yorker/ Atlantic Monthly/LRB?
> BT re: broadband
> Re-register at Holland Park Surgery
> Mirena??
> Book Strip for full body wax/inc. tache
> Start website/Pelvic Secrets

Mirabel holds up the phone and looks at me, willing me to explain. But I can't. I'm driving. And blushing. Not about the waxing bit. Since I've returned, I've noticed that hair removal is a thriving, medium-sized British industry. There's a rash of parlours offering manscaping, or the trimming, styling or removal of the lady garden, and even grooming down there for *men*, as if this is as normal as going to the dentist.

I don't really care who knows that Julien with an 'E' knows I don't merely 'work a seventies vibe' (© Gwyneth Paltrow), as it's gone Mr Tumnus the faun down there.

I'm not bothered about the tache or the Pelvic Secrets stuff.

In fact, it was Mirabel who discovered that I can't have my own website www.mimifleming.com, because there's another Mimi Fleming, with a range of DVDs called 'Pelvic Floor Secrets', which explains why I get emails from PRs saying, 'Hi, great to e-meet you!' and telling me they've sent me the 'soft invite' for the launch of various incontinence treatments and products, all of which the children find revolting and sad and gross, as if they will never grow old as we grow old.

Yes. My name and byline are already occupied by a doppel-gänger who is, glamorously, a pelvic-floor guru in Bucking-hamshire. I have been brand-jacked by a younger woman with a steel-banded perineum whose sole mission in life is to get everyone totally down with stress incontinence.

In fact, the only aspect of the list I mind, of course, is that Julien knows I am so delusional that I think I could ever, in a million years, get anything printed in the *New Yorker*, when my byline was last printed in the *Godminster Evening Echo* in 2012, and that was above an account of de-stoning damson jam at the rolling-boil stage.

And I haven't written for the *Mail* since they put that head-line on my last feature. The feature was about juggling and having four children – I know, I know: but the *Mail* are the last remaining payers, and needs must.

When I opened the newspaper the following day I read a banner headline screaming, 'Why I'm *so* glad the tide is *finally* turning against working women!' over my own byline and a huge photo (the paper insisted on photographing me in a floral wrap dress from L. K. Bennett, nude heels – also L. K. Bennett – and tights, and said they would spike the piece unless the children – all four of them, naturally – 'posed up' alongside). As Ralph agreed as he studied the gory pic, I looked like a madam from Tashkent and the children looked like my grandchildren. It was a definite low point in my pro-fessional life.

I stuff the mobile between my thighs.

I keep my eyes on the road as we edge our way past the school again, past the plane trees with trunks of variegated patches of green and yellow bark which look like expensive camouflage trousers, and indicate right to head down past the stalls and the jumble and the silver, towards the fruit and veg end of the Portobello Road.

Then I almost crash again.

I've just remembered who Julian must be, dur, is. I mean Julien with an 'E', who's sent me a text saying, 'This is me,' presumably so I can create a new contact with all his details.

He's the husband of the woman I fancy the pants off – well, I would if she ever wore pants, something I've seen no firm evidence of yet.

@posyfleming Have found best ever haberdashery for sewing bee Golborne Road #bobbinsrock

I find a pay-and-display bay on Westbourne Grove, and hurl in two, then three, then four pound coins, to pay for an hour, then chuck in another two, just in case. I march past Tom's, past Joseph on the corner, averting my gaze from the window display, shaking my head at the man who stands in the doorway like a carpet seller in a souk, smiling at me, as if hopeful that I will yield to his charm and come in and spend £850 on a dress that looks like a white felt apron cut with sheep shears. I skip past him, down Colville Road, past the Myla lingerie shop, past Gail's bakery.

First Tuesday of school in September, and the sky is blue and pinging. I reach the junction with Portobello Road, the market to my right, the Electric Diner and Brasserie and Club on my left. There are no spare seats outside or inside, as this is a popular joint, a very up sort of media place where everyone says yes but yes means no, the sort of place where you have breakfast for the sake of saying you had breakfast there.

As I pass, I assign identities to the customers with their platters of orange-yolked, farm-egg omelettes and thick-cut, peppered, maple-cured bacon. That table with two men and a woman in a dress with the coffee and rye toast? Two television producers from an indie making a pitch to a Channel Four commissioner. The table with three young women and an older guy is a businessman with his PR team; then there are two matching singleton men but on different tables, both peering into their iPhones, with their trendy reading glasses pushed high on to their foreheads, making a man-made caesura between their stubbly faces and their bald pates, where nature has erased the one that was there before.

This is my favourite time of year for the Portobello – the time when the new crop of back-to-school Cox apples comes into the market and Len and Pete, uncle and nephew, have them speckled and stalked, nestling like crown jewels on green tissue paper in small boxes.

'Hey, Len,' I say, stopping at the stall. I am the only customer. 'How are the Coxes this year? Can I get a couple?' I select two of the best ones. The sweetest aren't always the reddest ones; they're the ones with brown scars on their shoulders where the birds have pecked.

'Remember me?' I say, as I refuse a bag, bite into one apple and drop the other into my hessian sack.

''Course I do, darlin',' Len assures me. 'Good to see an old face.'

Then he points to the jar containing the day's takings so far. A few pound coins and shrapnel.

'The locals don't come any more. The street's gone,' he complains. 'Everyone has their groceries delivered. It's quiet. And all these double basements, round here, it's mad,' he added. 'People aren't troglodytes. Why don't they just buy a bigger house?'

Since we've been back, we've noticed it, as Len says: one house in four on most streets has a boxed-off hoarding and a conveyor belt carrying dark-brown spoil in juddering peristalsis from the bowels of the earth. 'And now we've got a Tesco, a Sainsbury's, an M&S and a Waitrose, all within spittin' distance. Means the market's dying on its feet.'

Then he goes to the back of his van and returns with another box of Coxes, which he puts next to his scales. 'It might pick up come Christmas.'

'Hope so, Len,' I say, and press on towards the Westway, as I need the exercise, at which point I'll do a U-turn and loop back and come down to my final destination, the Tea & Coffee Plant, to pick up Ralph's leaf lapsang souchong.

I'm at the top end of the Portobello Road now, wondering why all the India shops selling cushions embroidered with coins and Afghan slipper socks smelling of sick have been replaced by boutiques and coffee shops and fro-yo parlours, as if all anyone wants to do when they come to Notting Hill is eat and shop.

I pause outside a grimly minimal coffee place with a polished concrete floor called the Talkhouse.

There's a glistening, sugar-sprinkled display of golden fried doughnuts clustered behind a glass wall and, behind the counter, the grooviest coffee-making system currently obtainable: an old-fashioned drip machine.

I go in and stand there, my mouth watering.

There are a few customers towards the back, working on MacBooks, and Al Green is singing about how he's so tired of being alone, and it's so cool and hip in there that nobody meets my eye or takes my order.

So I call out to a man with red hair and a luxuriant red beard in an apron who is ignoring me, as if ignoring customers is part of his job description.

'Yo,' I say, semi-ironically, as if I'm down with the whole hipster vibe and I'm actually from Dalston. 'An extra-hot, two-shot, semi-skimmed flat white, please. Bro.'

He doesn't move. Instead he starts, very slowly, twisting a rag around the milk nozzles on the top-of-the-range coffee machine. As if considering my request.

'Sorry, you can't,' the barista says, as he starts frothing milk in front of me in a metal jug. There is a large industrial Italian espresso machine as well as all the fiddly cold-brew and drip laboratory equipment.

'Why not?' I ask.

'Well, for a start, at Talkhouse we only serve coffee warm. Not hot. And never extra hot.' He talks as if I'm a total hick when it comes to the new coffee culture. 'And, second, we only use full-fat milk,' he says, and goes on to tell me at length that to drink it otherwise would be 'disrespecting the bean' and 'failing to honour the milk from our own farm'.

I keep my iPhone running on record, as this is proof that coffee fascism has reached commanding heights and is all good copy for my long-form piece about the rise and fall and rise of Notting Hill, and leave with a pointed 'Thank you'.

Coffee-less, I stand at the top of the Portobello Road, looking down past the stalls, some selling batik playsuits, army surplus, bootleg cosmetics, home-made soaps, olives and feta in wooden tubs, flowers, CDs. Under the flyover, I can take away Thai or falafel or Mexican.

I'm in exactly the spot where Martin Amis once said that, if anything bad was going to happen, 'it would happen under the Westway.'

'Well, Mart, it's happened,' I say out loud into my iPhone. 'The bad thing you predicted has happened. It's no longer scuzzy or even dangerous up here, under the Westway, where rastas in natty dreads used to sell weed and gang members shank each other with blades. There are no beheadings, even, you will no doubt be disappointed to hear. No, the bad thing that's happened is that everything that made Portobello "badass"' – I place inverted commas around 'badass' with my voice – 'has gone for ever, vanished, never to return, and chi-chi artisanal bakeries and coffee places selling cronuts and pistachio-filled croissants, and an outpost of Soho House selling Italian fennel sausage pizza at eight pounds a slice have taken their place.'

I canter back down, away from the Westway, past the lady with the blowdry who won the lottery but still runs her flower stall every day, just as she used to before she was rich, so her life remains just the same as it always did, only with better hair. And then I stop in my tracks. I somehow missed it on my way up.

There's a pound shop on the Portobello.

Ralph is right, then.

As the very rich have become even richer and the poor poorer, so the very top and the very bottom of the market are the only ones thriving. The local economy is made up of Prada at the top, Poundland at the bottom, and nothing in between.

I say this into my phone, then go into my emails to check whether I've had a reply. From Farouche. I haven't. I haven't . . . But I do have this.

From: Clare@claresturgis.com
To: MimiFleming@gmail.com

Dear Mimi

Lovely to see you, if briefly, at the school gates, and so clever of you to get a place for Lucian. I do think Ponsonby is so much more nurturing than Wetherby, and the early-years well-being curriculum is genuinely groundbreaking. Now, I'd love to give a dinner – very casual, I promise – to welcome you and Ralph back to the garden! Just old friends/neighbours. I hope you're free next Wednesday?? Eightish?
XXClareXX

My mobile rings just as I am approaching the Tea & Coffee Plant and tapping out a guarded reply to Clare.

My screen says 'Unknown'.

'Yes?' I say.

'It's me!' someone says.

Why do women do this?

I assume it's a wrong number, but the voice goes on.

'Olivia! Olivia –' I can't hear her surname; she either swallows it, or fails to give it. 'Remember? From the *Telegraph*!' She chirps a bright, I-give-great-phone-type of professional female voice that warns any resistance will be futile.

'Are you in Dorset?'

'No, I'm back in London,' I say.

Someone says, 'Excuse me, love,' and I realize I am blocking a man trying to unload a canister of Ethiopian goat curry from the back of a van to pour into a wide, steel saucepan set over gas and flog in leaky punnets to tourists.

'Great, great. Now, is this a good time?' Olivia goes on, as I move upwind, away from the smell of curried goat.

I admit that it is – it's not as if I have a job – and duck across the road so I am standing right outside the Tea & Coffee Plant's three outside tables: high ones, at which various long-established local fellow loafers and distinguished idlers are already perched.

'We were wondering if you were in the market for doing anything?' says Olivia. 'We've got a thought, but it's a bit complicated over the phone, so maybe you could come in for a chat?'

'Sure,' I say, too quickly. When I last spoke to Olivia, she had progressed from being an intern at *Tatler* to i/c the *Telegraph*'s annual spa supplement, a vehicle for advertising, which involved sending a hack to the Seychelles to write a 200-word piecette and, sometimes, even paying them for it. She was one of the most popular female journalists in Fleet Street as a result.

'But not the *Tel*, I'm on *Newsnight* now,' Olivia continues with a modest titter.

Newsnight?

How could . . . little Olivia fairly long name, oh yes, Feather-stonehaugh, be on *Newsnight*? It was like David Cameron becoming prime minister!

'There's a package we were hoping you might be involved –' she pauses, as if she doesn't want to give anything away on the phone – 'in the preparation of,' she says. 'It's a little delicate. The editor's super keen, though. Josh Kurtz?'

I make noises to confirm that I am aware of the young gun's position at the helm of *Newsnight*.

And then, as I stand there, I hear a piercing voice I'd recognize anywhere, and my phone buzzes. A text.

'Yah,' Olivia goes on. 'You know. He'd *sooo* love you to be *looped in* on this. Could you come to NBH for coffee? How's tomorrow at eleven? Good! I'll make sure there's a pass for you at Recep.'

I say goodbye and am now reading a text that has whistled on to my iPhone from Julien in answer to mine to his.

And then I hear the voice again, louder, an American voice, pealing out above the sounds of Len in his stall crying, 'Best English *Coxes*,' and flat-capped, broken-nosed Pete shouting contrapuntally, 'Last strawberries of the season, *last straws*,' and bosomy, blonde Cheryl in her stall giving change to a little old lady in a mac and handing over a blue plastic bag with leeks branching green from the top and saying, as she hands over the seven pence and pops it into the old lady's open purse, 'There you are, babes, have a lovely day now in this sunshine, won't you?'

'Hiiiii!' says Sally Avery, zipping towards me up the Portobello Road, not looking at any of the fruit or veg, or at the hipsters wandering towards their independent production companies holding soya chai lattes, or at the mothers on their way to play dates with buggies.

'Heeeyyy! I heard you were back,' she yells at me, 'which is so *great*. We must give you a *dinner*.'

'No, no,' I respond, thinking in panic of all the reciprocal dinners I will have to give in the small kitchen-dining room at Lonsdale Gardens, which will cost me the price of a small car. I can't keep saying yes.

'*Yes, yes!*' Sally says. 'I'd love to give you guys a dinner in your honour. It's been a ways too long!'

I'd forgotten that there were not two but three sexes in Notting Hill. Men. Women. And American women.

Sally Avery is wearing Lycra three-quarter-length leggings, a tight running top with a neon trim in a special sweat-wicking fabric and complicated trainers with socks with neon bobbles peeking out cheekily over the heel, in a cute cotton-tail way. On one wrist she's wearing a Buddhist mala bead bracelet; on the other, a high-tech band that uses skin conductivity to record calories in and out, heart rate, sleep and steps.

Her whole outfit, and her demeanour, all convey one simple, basic message: life is a highly technical competitive sport.

But I can't deny that Sally looks sensational.

I log on to her high, round breasts, full and slightly straining the lightweight fabric of her top so that each nipple is plainly visible and perfectly centred in the middle of each perfect globe, like a buzzer on an old-fashioned Georgian doorbell somewhere like Bloomsbury.

Her freckled skin, burnished by 'summering' in the Hamptons or Nantucket, or wherever it is the Averys have their 'cottage' (i.e. a twelve-bedroom beachside mansion with more amenities than a golf club and the All England Club at Wimbledon combined), has an endorphin-high sheen, her eyes are like shiny, blue marbles, and her lips and cheeks pink, pumping with oxygen-rich blood.

Sally doesn't seem to mind my keen gaze travelling her taut figure, and we fall on each other like old friends, which is what we are.

We hug, and hold each other close. We inhale each other's scent. We caress each other with our hair, and at one point she holds her cheek against mine and I can almost feel the blood pumping in her smooth, unlined neck.

Sally disengages from my hug first – I think I may have passed out in her iron grip, from the constriction of blood supply – and leans out, holding me by the shoulders, giving me the once-over.

Suddenly, I find myself shrinking under her inspection. I remember she once ticked me off for wearing wellies in the Portobello Road, scolding me loudly in front of the ratty-haired, panda-eyed fashion stylist at *Vogue* who was within earshot: 'You're not in Dorset now, Mimi.'

She somehow manages to stop herself from saying whatever is the opposite of 'Hey, you look great, have you been working *out*? Or lost *weight*, or been to a *yoga retreat*?'

Sally knows, and I know, that I look like a woman who's been entombed in a sleepy, shaggy West Country hamlet for the last five years, a woman who's bought all her clothes at the Dorset Show, at the stall where they do a brisk trade in steel-capped boots and canvas camouflage trousers, mainly to the sort of person who plans shooting rampages in his spare time.

'Anyways, I literally can't wait for us guys to *catch up*,' Sally says, checking the black, rubbery sports band on her wrist, which must also tell the time, as well as everything else.

'So you must be coming to the *crisis meeting*?' She nods towards the Tea & Coffee Plant.

She zumbas sideways into the crowded depths of the Tea & Coffee Plant, where a caffeine-addicted queue stands restively, twitching like racehorses at the starting gate, impatient for their hot drinks, nodding along to Daft Punk and scanning the shelves, where tea leaves and cocoa powders in clear plastic and coffee beans in silvered bags from every nook and cranny of the tropical world await purchase, as well as chocolate gingers, raisins in yoghurt and many other sundry sweetmeats.

It's at this second that I spot it.

Another nail in the coffin of beloved market – the shop next to the beloved Tea & Coffee Plant is a Whittard of Chelsea. 'Tea and Coffee Passion since 1886,' it says on the shopfront.

A Whittard! Yes, founded in Chelsea in the nineteenth century, but still part of the evil chainstore massacre.

Bang next door to the Tea & Coffee Plant, so hipster that there's a sign saying, 'We do not serve customers on mobile phones,' an edict the staff, who always look as if they've spent the last three days at an indie music festival in the rain somewhere in Suffolk, enforce with fierceness.

And on the other side of our beloved T&C, there's an American Apparel store and, next to that, a Santander bank, and next to Santander, a Costa Coffee.

It all makes sense.

The crisis meeting must be about saving the Portobello Market from the march of bland retail.

I stand and sniff, inhaling the familiar smell of the Portobello: the German Wiener van's sizzling, big, shiny, pink frankfurters; the roasty-toasty aroma of grinding beans, the smoky top note of the squashy cigar-end in the mouth of the American writer in chinos reading his *Herald Trib* and sitting outside on a stool so he can smoke; a craggy man whose name I forget – Charles Glass? – but who I always say hi to; the rank tang of the dump truck that grinds up the street with its bow doors open while the dustbin men hurl in one-handedly black sacks of rubbish and reeking boxes of rotting fruit and veg . . .

Of course, we *must* save Portobello Market!

I turn to Sally. 'Of *course* I'm coming to the crisis meeting,' I say, resisting the urge to say, 'Crisis, what crisis?'

Sally then takes my hand and drags me towards a table of seated women, none of whom – and I would put money on this – have ever bought fruit or veg in any quantity at any of the stalls outside in their entire life, or carried it home on foot, or not without the assistance of at least one Filipina house-keeper-cum-slave, anyway.

'Guys, it's Mimi! Mimi, the guys!' Sally says, pointing at me.

Sally clatters a chair backwards and tips me into it, right in the middle of the group. 'We have Mimi on Team Trish!' Sally announces. 'Hell, yeah!!'

I wave hello, smiling, trying not to let them smell my fear.

So long as it's the Portobello, not another planning dispute, I'm thinking. Or something to do with the communal garden, the blood-stained arena for fights to the death over whether dogs should be on leads, or the willow tree pollarded, the play-ground re-barked, or whether to cull yet again the select list of outside keyholders who have access to the precious green sanctum . . .

Communal-garden politics and planning disputes are far more brutal than national campaigns or any mid-term by-election. They lead to solicitors' letters and spells of no-speaks that persist for years at a time.

Planning disputes are time sinkholes, they suck you in, and the problem is the people with the most money, the money to hire the experts, both within and without the council, who have the bottomless resources to appeal every decision, are the ones who always win.

And the little guys always lose. Everyone knows this, but has the fight anyway.

A selection of rehydrating coconut-water cartons, decaff soya lattes and green teas litter the table top, alongside the phones. I wonder whether to go up and get a coffee, but decide not to.

If I leave now . . . I might never come back.

So here we all are!

Trish, Virginie and Marguerite, who hail me eagerly as an old friend, for, after all, that is what I am, plus two women I don't know. And no Clare.

The younger of the two women I don't know has thick, ropey, long blonde hair and a clinging, delicate T-shirt of the sort that screams that it actually costs £200, and necklaces nestling in a spaghetti tangle between her breasts. The dyed blonde hair, hazel eyes, wild eyebrows, expertly maquillaged, look familiar, but I can't place her. She is introduced to me as Oksana Dunbar.

The other has jet-black hair scraped back from her brow like a prima ballerina, skin the colour of milky coffee, and she also looks vaguely familiar.

She is texting while furtively glancing at the comment pages of the *Guardian*, which she has on the table. She leaves her iPhone so I can clearly read that the last person she's texted, or has been texted by, is Alan Rusbridger.

I lean across the table and introduce myself, to this dark one first.

'Erm,' I open with. 'Hi! I'm Mimi . . . Mimi Fleming . . .'

Trish helps out. 'Mimi's on the garden, she was in Clare's house, and now she's back but in the ex-council-flat maisonette, you know, the building behind the compost heap,' she says helpfully.

'Oh, yes,' says the dark woman. Looks concerned. 'That's

the house that doesn't have direct access to the communal garden, isn't it? Poor you! It's terrible that council-house tenants don't have direct access.' She returns to her phone, which has bleeped.

'Yes, ha ha, we do have a garden key, lucky us,' I say, trying to get her back.

But Marguerite Molton is saying something at her end about a woman with breast cancer having a 'healing shower' in Phillimore Gardens, and Donna's name has come up, something about how your house itself can practise mindfulness as well as cleanse and recharge.

I have, I feel, had my chance with the dark beauty.

'Haven't we met somewhere already?' I persevere, in the hope she will tell me who she is.

In response to my bid for attention she picks up and checks her phone again, until I feel like pawing at her like a puppy for attention.

'Perhaps,' she says, while tapping out a text. 'But I'm horribly embarrassed to say it's probably because you've seen me on television. And I have a column on the *Observer*. Meredith Blacker?'

Her teeth are blazing white. Fair enough, I suppose, if she does do telly.

'Yes,' says Trish, with pride, as she turns to us. 'Meredith is very much our high-flyer.'

And then I ask Meredith where she's worked, in the hope that eventually she might ask me about me.

'After a career in terrestrials, mainly in newsgathering,' she goes on, as if she is in mid-job interview to be the new chairman of the BBC Trust, 'I now write a weekly column for the *Observer*, plus longer pieces for the *LRB*, so I'm a columnist, broadcaster, whatever.' She gives a light laugh, as if she is so multi-talented even she finds herself impossible to pigeonhole. 'And what do you do?' She looks at me with shiny eyes, showing interest, which is intoxicating.

I crank up and begin to tell her – changing from first into third gear as I amp up my small column on the *Weekend Tele-graph*, which I omit to tell her was asking people to supply the running order for their own funerals.

'I'm hoping to get back into journalism, actually,' I say, even though the game has changed. One used to get a decent whack for writing a shortish piece in an in-flight magazine, say, but now in order to make any money you have to blog – or is it vlog now? – for *Vice*.

But I feel licensed to press release myself, as she just has, and as I tweet out my paltry CV Meredith Blacker sips her coco water.

And it's awful. I realize I've lost her. So I decide to say hello to the blonde model-stroke-hooker, Oksana, but as she is replying – Oksana is filling me in on her art business-cum-fashion line – Virginie, it would be Virginie – says her name.

My head fills with a roaring sound. My heart leaps to my mouth. I wonder if I'm going to be sick.

'Yes, where ze 'ell eez Farouche?' Virginie is asking. 'Eez eet her morning with Hunter?' She says 'Ooon-tair' instead of Hunter.

'Speaking of Farouche – and say what you like about Farouche, we all do; I honestly have her down as a closet heterosexual – I don't know what she puts in it, but Frisson is freaking amazing,' says Sally Avery.

I ask what Frisson is, and everyone tells me, as if I'm the last to know, that it is Farouche's signature scent, her 'limited edi-tion love potion', available in only three stores worldwide, and people 'kill to get their hands on it'.

'And, have you heard, she's decided to let Sam Taylor-Wood-Johnson, or whatever her name is, go, and she's making the commercial for it herself. It's all top secret. Well, it was.' Sally giggles.

'Are you talking about Farouche, the artist?' I ask. 'French? Looks like Pocahontas? Long hair, bare feet, apartment in Notting Hill and one in Paris?' I hope my voice isn't giving anything away. But Virginie is a minx.

This stone-cold French superfox can read simple English hearts like a Ladybird book.

And now even Meredith is looking at me in an odd, speculative way, as if studying the tasting menu in a Michelin-starred restaurant.

'Yes, I suspect we are,' says Meredith. 'Farouche is a very important young artist. I went to the first night of her show at the Gagosian in New York, actually.'

Virginie puts a hand on my arm. 'No, Mimi,' she says, putting a serious face on. 'Don't leesten to Meredith' (although when Virginie says it, it sounds like 'Merde-eeth'). 'She's not French. She is *la salope* from *Knokke-le-Zoute*. *La méchante belge!*'

Then she cackles.

My heart is hammering. I don't care what Virginie says. She's just jealous. Doesn't like competition.

'Is Farouche coming to this crisis meeting?' I ask, trying to be casual, but another part of me is filing away the information that Meredith – this younger, more successful, skinnier and glossier writer-cum-presenter – knew Farouche *first*. 'If so, isn't she a bit late?'

'No Farouche today. She texted, but who needs 'er. Eetz so good to see you, too, Mimi,' Virginie says. 'Eetz been too long!' she says. 'Manay year, *non?*'

I grin back, my heart doing a jig of joy.

I don't mind that Virginie's forgotten that, in fact, we've seen each other twice since Ralph's birthday party in Honeyborne. The first time was at a Christmas party at Claridge's, when I was trying and failing to impress newspaper executives at a party: I was heavily pregnant with Lucian and Virginie asked me, '*Et, dis-moi*, do you know who the faz-er *eez*?' within earshot of Ralph.

And the next time was when we bumped into Virginie and her weedy husband, Mathieu, at Cheltenham Races, and that was only last summer.

I do not remind her of these two previous encounters. I am too happy.

Marguerite smiles at me, too, and as I smile back at the women, I note her lovely ivory face has taken on that melted-candle cast, so she looks beautiful in one way – if you half close your eyes and pretend she's another person – but in another way like a waxwork of her previous, younger self.

I gaze at my old friends and possible, potential new best friends, at their plumped, buffed skin, their floating hair and flashing eyes and dazzling, whitened teeth, and the words leave my mouth.

'I don't know *how* you *do* it,' I blurt. 'Have you guys *all* had *work*?'

There is a moment. This can go one of two ways. I have either insulted them – or paid them the most tremendous compliment.

Everyone looks at Marguerite. As if she leads on this one.

'Not . . . *as such*,' she says.

Trish echoes, 'Not work-work, anyway.' She says this as if there's work, and work. Like rape-rape. And some work is better than other work. And it's important to make the difference between the full-on Bride of Wildenstein (which is like real rape at knifepoint by stranger in dark alley) and everything else.

Meredith. Virginie. Sally. Trish. Marguerite. Oksana. All have taut, flushed skin and shining eyes.

'You can't look this good and have had *work*,' Marguerite explains. 'Now we have treatments, rather than procedures. It's much more . . . I mean, much less, invasive, these days . . .

'Now, the new thing is you want to *look like yourself*.' She says this as if this is a radical concept. I suppose it is when you think that Meg Ryan and Renée Zellweger look like completely different people.

Everyone nods, chirpily.

'You want to look like yourself. Just *on a really good day*.'

'Ah,' I say, as if satisfied.

I hear Trish whisper to Marguerite, 'What about that week in Lamu, when you thought yourself younger?' and Marguerite says, 'Oh yes, Trish, that's a good point.' And she turns to me.

'Another way to go is to think that age is all in the mind. I did this amazing course of neuro-linguistic therapy with a professor. It's a week-long residency, where it's not all about being as old as you feel, you can actually achieve age reversal mentally' – nobody seems to laugh out loud at this bollocks – 'you can be as old as you *think* you are.'

'How does that work, exactly?' I ask.

'What you do is visualize how you looked in your twenties, and it shows in your face.'

'I must try that,' I say, smiling around the group. 'If I may say so, you all look younger. Thinner. Fitter. Than you did five years ago. I'm fatter than I've ever been, and I've even got some grey hair . . .' I stick a finger into my parting. 'So well done.'

'You're not fat, Mimi, you're gooorgeous,' Marguerite says. 'But, if you want to know' – everyone gazes at her supportively, as if this is an intervention they've worked out beforehand for me – 'you eat two thirds vegetables, you have a Nutribullet breakfast, you don't eat meat, or anything white.' Marguerite told me eight years ago that she 'couldn't remember what brown rice tasted like'.

Yes, Marguerite Molton really kickstarted the gluten- and dairy-free thing round here. She'd had the whole family tested for allergies. When one Molton tested intolerant to one thing – let's say, wheat – she'd moved the whole family to gluten-free and on to almond milk, as it 'made the catering operation easier'. Ralph is not alone in assuming that this move was the trigger for Patrick to stop fucking his wife and start fucking the kindergarten teacher and spending a whole lot more time in New York and a whole lot less in WII.

'Or you do the raw diet,' says Trish, and we all look at her. Her skin glows. Her teeth blaze white and her thighs are so slim, crossed in her white, skinny jeans, that it's as if she's tied them in a careless reef-knot.

Ah, so this is why more women aren't on executive boards, I realize.

It's not because our heads are bumping against glass ceilings at all – it's because here we are, at a meeting in the middle of our busy days, and all we are talking about is what we put in our mouths and when.

As if reading my thoughts, Trish calls the group to order, with executive briskness. 'Guys. Here are the headlines. Do you want the bad news? Or the really, really bad news?'

She has our attention now. We all look at Trish, smartphones ignored for several seconds.

Then Meredith Blacker stands up. She swipes her carton of coco water from the table and holds up her iPhone as proof, and as if she wants us to read the message on the screen. We all peer at it, but as we are over forty now it is impossible to read without us finding our reading glasses in our various It bags (everyone else) or hessian Bag for Life (me).

'Meredith?' says Trish. 'What is it?'

'I'm terribly sorry, everyone, but the *Guardian*'s called me in to the leader conference,' she says. 'I've got to go.'

She pulls on a black cashmere coat with a ruffly collar – I glimpse the label (Balenciaga – black letters on silky white) – and grabs her Céline satchel, from which a laptop peeks from amid that day's papers. She leaves the café as the crow flies, so customers have to part to make way for her, and I have a sudden premonition.

It is of a black bird taking spooked flight from an open grave.

'Pity Meredith can't stay, she's a heavy hitter, but anyway,' Trish resumes, 'we have a real fight on our hands. You guys are not going to believe this.'

One of the baristas has turned down the banging music, the place has emptied a bit, the buggies have gone back for nap time and freelancers with MacBook Airs have taken their place. The mood becomes almost businesslike, and I remember – we all have *degrees*. Some of us have had millions, if not billions, under our management (Trish and Marguerite), have run their own poncy Peter Pan-collared childrenswear labels (Virginie), and presented hard-hitting documentaries (the absent Meredith). When they find an obstacle in their path – a teacher falling down on the job, a rejection from a sought-after school – my neighbours are highly trained killing machines. They are like ISIS warlords. They take no prisoners.

Trish hands round photocopies as if they were live rounds of ammunition to freedom fighters. 'Copies of a note' – she holds the original in her manicured hand – 'I found taped to the bottom of a lamp post in Ponsonby Terrace.' She hands one to me.

I look at the sheet. It is one of those planning-application things you see everywhere, all over the streets, taped to every other tree.

NOTICE OF PLANNING APPLICATION
PLANNING (LISTED BUILDING AND
CONSERVATION AREAS) ACT 1990

I glance over it.

At the bottom, there is a brief summary of the application: a date, a reference number, the mention of the 'North Area Team', the address of the development, which is 8 Ponsonby Terrace, London W11 2LQ, a summary of the works, which I don't really take in, and then the name of the applicant.

'Alpha Star?' I ask. 'Who's that?'

'Not who,' says Trish. 'What. It's a corporate envelope.'

I am trying to stay on task. Even though I have no idea what a corporate envelope is, the print swims, and I suddenly want a cigarette. I can taste Farouche's Gauloise Blonde again, and smell the tobacco on her hair.

Now I've heard her name it all seems real, and possible. All I can think of is seeing her again. Her skin. Her scent. I take a deep breath, as if I can get an intoxicating whiff of her.

I can't focus on anything.

Suddenly, Oksana stands up, looking white. 'I have to go, too,' she announces. 'Something's come up . . . the children.' This is odd. She hasn't even been on her phone. I just stare at her, and then smile, as if whatever she has to do is fine by me. She grabs her bag from the floor, everyone says goodbye and Trish promises to keep her posted, and of course Meredith, by email, and then she flees, her high-heeled ankle boots making a clopping sound on the stone floor.

Trish removes the sheet from my hands. 'So it appears this is what the council has done. Instead of selling the house between our Giving Back Centre and our school to Ponsonby, which had a bid in, they've flogged it to developers, rejecting the rival bid of Ponsonby Prep, which, as you all know, had a parent-supported, fully financed offer in,' says Trish, as if this is the worst thing to have happened since Hitler marched into Poland.

'Yes, do you remember the wonderful letter Richard Curtis wrote,' says Marguerite, almost dreamily. 'That wonderful line "You are not a private landlord, you are our town council."'

There is a sacramental pause at the mention of the blessed Richard, movie director, co-founder of Comic Relief, the patron saint of Notting Hill.

'But now, according to this document, the developers have put in not just for a basement. Not just for a double basement. A triple! Bang between us and the school! It gets worse,' Trish continues. She waves another letter. 'This was put through the door of the GBC. I found it yesterday after the Mind-BodyReset lunch for sponsors that some of you came to.'

'Wasn't it lovely?' says Marguerite. 'I must get the recipes for the frittata and those amazing Helmsley & Helmsley black bean brownies.'

'But guys, the *green-tea ones* from the Grocer!' says Sally.

Ignoring them both, Trish goes on. 'This letter is addressed to us, and it's the traffic-management plan for the Alpha Star development next door. Reading between the lines, it says that for the first year of construction disruption will be total and, owing to the number of expected lorry movements and skips, and so on, they will have to close the road. Close Ponsonby Terrace. From December – i.e. just as we open the centre. We have only ten days to object. If nobody objects, then the application doesn't even go to the PAC, the planning committee, and will be decided by pen-pushers, sitting at desks.' She pauses so we can all absorb the emergency and the full gravity of the situation sinks in.

We all give – in my case, token – cries of outrage.

'You're still a journalist, right? I heard you saying to Meredith?'

'Yes,' I say. Not knowing what else to say.

'That's great. 'Cos we need you,' Trish says, looking at me with fervour. 'Only you can find out who this lot are.'

I feel flattered. First, Olivia Featherstonehaugh wants me, and now the STD coalition, under Trish's leadership. I have been, clearly, undervaluing myself and my potential contribution to various important projects.

I mean, the others – with the exception of Meredith Blacker, who is overqualified at almost everything – they don't have my long years of experience . . . writing columns. And features.

Even if my columns and my features were mainly fluffy ones – that interview I did with Johnnie Boden, the piece I wrote about puppy-training classes with Calypso – but who cares?

It's great to think I've still got it or, at any rate, that some people think I have.

'OK, yup, no, I'm on it,' I say, and put my game face on.

Trish plucks her iPhone from the table.

I see her put my name in the Google search bar and, before I can explain about the other Mimi Fleming, she presses go.

She scrolls through the results.

I know, because I have self-Googled, that there's stuff from the *Telegraph*, and also photos of me with Con, my famous younger brother, who, like all men, and unlike all women, the older and grumpier and wrinklier he becomes, the more popular and revered he is.

But all this comes many thousands – possibly hundreds of thousands – of hits after the other Mimi Fleming, the incontinence guru, she of the Sunrise perineum workshops in Bucks.

I don't say anything, though, as there's no way Trish can confuse us. She's known me for twenty years, and the other Mimi looks nothing like me, i.e. she is blonde and gleaming and glowing, and wears a white wrap top and white palazzo pants in most of her pictures, as if to show confidence in her own urethra-tastic regime.

Trish replaces her iPhone on the table along with everyone else's. They lie there like guns on the bar in a Western.

'But Mimi, are you sure you have the time now?' She cocks her head. 'Aren't you busy? You should come and do your own Kegel class at the centre, you know. We'd love that. And so would our husbands, I bet, heh heh.' Trish chuckles.

To general disappointment, I explain I haven't become an incontinence guru, and as I speak I feel something else, something I haven't felt for a long time: the stirrings of that ancient urge, almost a compulsion, to make something out of nothing, i.e. to write a long article that will annoy almost everyone I know, for a small amount of money.

And as I look across the table at their taut faces, the plucked brows, I know what it has to be about.

It is such a classically wonderful clash, I think. The do-gooding, NIMBY yummy mummies, full of guilt that their banker husbands broke the City, but who carry on sitting at the best tables in London versus the faceless machine of brutalist developer capitalism.

I can write it in my head already. The headline, the stand first, the pull-quotes, the pictures of Trish and Sally, the quotes from the council and exasperated neighbours . . .

'We really need someone with your *Fleet Street chops*. Don't we, guys?'

I try to snap my attention back to them and away from my guaranteed British Press Award for this feature.

'I'm sure you get this *a lot*, but I think he'll regard this as a *special case*,' she went on. 'This is *different*. The Giving Back Centre really is a *good cause* and a community resource. He'll want his name attached to this one. Trust me on this.'

Trish is speaking as if *she* is doing *me* a favour, so I know what's coming. In fact, I have a little folder in which I keep emailed requests from people who think I can deliver Con to them to open their fete or address their guild's black-tie centenary fundraising dinner, 6 p.m. kick-off, in some stuffy basement banqueting suite of a hotel off Hyde Park.

'We were thinking, do you think your brother, *Con*, would help us in the campaign, and like, maybe open the Giving Back Centre, if there is a GBC to open?' Trish presses, looking me in the eye.

'Sorry, I'm in a muddle,' I say, stalling for time. 'Is the Giving Back Centre the same as the Making a Difference Centre, and also different from the Second Life Centre up at St Charles' Hospital?' I ask, wanting to be sure.

'It was called the Making a Difference Centre for a while, at the beginning, but then, for obvious reasons, we changed it,' says Trish.

'Right,' I say.

Trish continues. '*Con!* He's *just* so popular. So charming, so funny – a guinea a minute!' Everyone is beaming and laughing, as if Con's doing stand-up at the next table.

'Con charges a lot more than a guinea a minute,' I say. And then I just have to say it. 'But look – guys – the Giving Back Centre, formerly the MAD Centre, whatever, in Ponsonby Terrace. Of course I'm on board, to fight the dig, and so on. But it's not as if we live in a deprived area, socially? How are you going to make sure that those who need the centre are the ones who are going to use it? I mean, getting the ratepayers to subsidize pilates for the Real Housewives of Notting Hill . . . isn't such a good look, is it?'

But no one is listening to me; they are all still so entranced by the prospect of my brother Con rocking up and opening the centre, as if the mere idea of Con is utterly delightful.

'I mean, it would make the whole difference, wouldn't it, if he did, wouldn't it, everyone? Please, pretty please, Mimi,' Trish drills on.

'Of course I'll ask, but I do think you need to work out who or what the GBC is really *for*,' I say, finally.

Everyone looks at me as if I've done something awful, like said something bad about Judi Dench.

'But Mimi,' they cry, in amazement, 'it's for everyone!'

'It's for everyone, *for ever*,' says Trish, with finality.

I finally escape, picking up an extra-hot, two-shot, semi-skimmed flat white on the way out.

Boy, do I need it.

By the time I get back to my car, which, miraculously, hasn't been ticketed, as I have run over my allotted time by at least two mins, Trish Dodd Noble has already round-robined me, and Virginie, Meredith, Sally, Marguerite, Oksana . . . and Farouche.

The subject line is 'STD'.

Hey, guys,
Great meeting! Just thought I'd whizz round the minutes while
they're still buzzing from all that caffeine!

[None of us actually drank real coffee, but I let that pass and read on.]

To recap on what we agreed:

- Marguerite has been put i/c written submissions to the council,
  and is organizing the campaign of objections to the monster
  triple dig, getting as many locals to write letters as possible, so
  the application triggers enough objections to be voted for at
  the PAC.
- Sally is Trish's number two. Sally is in charge of the fabulous,

fabulous Solidarity Quilt. The solidarity quilt is Sally's idea, and is to be the 'emotional centrepiece' of the STD coalition for the Giving Back Centre.

- <u>Mimi</u> has agreed to 1. get her bro Con Malone to open the GBC Centre at the Gala Opening and 2. will support <u>Meredith</u> in the media campaign.
- <u>Mimi and</u> <u>Meredith</u> (Meredith, this OK with you? We do realize how extremely over-committed you are) are the investigative team, and will try to find out who or what Alpha Star are.
- Cheeky thought for <u>Oksana</u>? Ask Keith to stump up for the Stop the Digs (STD) coalition to hire its own planning consultant and structural engineer and solicitor?? Or too big an ask??

I propose we have another session before the PAC meeting later in the month to get all our ducks in a row. So . . . MTF.
xx Trish xx

Text from Mirabel:

Nice one trying to follow me on Instagram
#nevergonnahappen

I have several further emails, which reveal my shopping habits as clearly as an MRI scan:

- Scotts of Stow
- Lakeland Plastics
- One from a travel PR, telling me she is moving company, beginning 'Dear [First Name]'
- A Google Alert telling me that the other Mimi Fleming is offering a 'Pelvic Floor for Mums' class
- And – oooh – an email from Rose! Unfortch, as Mirabel would say, it's catchlined 'Amazing news!'

I sigh. Can I take any more success or good fortune from Rose?

I almost prefer to read those endless emails from contacts who've been hacked and then the hacker sends out spam to all their contacts in an email catchlined 'Bad Trip' and saying that someone's been mugged in Kharkiv, Ukraine, and needs £2,500 to pay a hotel bill and make the plane.

'Bad news' is always so much more rewarding of attention than 'Having amazing time!'

I quickly scan the email from Rose, which is copied to her scarily efficient PA, Gerlinda.

Dear Mimi, I called you at home, no answer and your mobile went to voicemail, so sending this in hope. Longing to speak and hear all your news.

Before you left Dorset, I think I mentioned that I'd been approached by BBC2 to present this series – working title 'Farm to Fork'. You were busy with the move, and probably didn't take it in. Well, it's been commissioned. And – this is where *you* come in – they love my idea that we film at *Home Farm*, which is still empty, isn't it? Or have you found a tenant now?

So I used your spare key, as you said I could, and showed them round, the Prod Productions people, and they went mad for it, so they'll pay, at least until the next series is recommissioned. It's win win, and means Court Place won't be cluttered up with camera crew.

And if we make Home Farm the centre of operations for filming, then we won't disturb Pierre, who's working on several major pieces right now.

Rose xxx

PS Really strange – I found a pair of pants with a Posy Fleming nametape in the gazebo. I've had them laundered and I'll send to you. Can't think how they got there, can you?!!

Mirabel's blogpost 15/09/2014 2.00 a.m.

So I'm walking down the Portobello, checking Tinder as I go, dodging men with boxes and women with buggies and comparing the prices on a punnet of blueberries at each stall. At the posh delis, like the Grocer, they're three quid. But you can get them for £1.50, but when you think that some families live on, like, £20 a week for food, it's still a lot, and you can see why they just go to Greggs on the corner for a jumbo sausage roll instead.

Mum's so down on Tinder.

Mum: 'Darling . . . it's bad enough having sex with someone you know and love . . .' (Giggles hysterically; ugh!) 'Let alone someone you've *only just met*.'

So, swiping through the next batch of guys within a mile radius and thinking, if this was Honeyborne, Dorset, there wouldn't even be one male I could sleep with for, like, a hundred miles.

'Getting girls to have sex with me is like spreading butter,' says Amir, 26. Amir is holding a baby. Euw. He's only 800m away from me *now*.

I can't help looking around when they're close by, to see if I can spot the dude.

Savage, 28 – swipe left.

Dread, 22 – swipe left.

Savage, Dread – these names for real?

And then I swipe and I see Sid. Sid is 90m away. But I know that already. He must be right here, right now, in the Portobello, working on his dad's stall. I slow down. I'm going to see him any second now.

I stand outside the Electric and check out the five pictures of Sid, 20, linked to his Facebook page. I look at them all. He is tall and dark and athletic, and he is, admittedly, wearing a baseball cap in one, but in another he is in QPR strip. We have (1) shared friend. I don't bother to check to see who it is.

Then I do something I've never done before. Sid lives below us in

Garden Court with his mum, Cathy, and they have this basement flat, so I see her in the street. Or the garden. I don't think they have access, like us, apart from with a key through the side gate.

I haven't spoken to Sid yet. I swipe right.

We match! He'd swiped right, too. We live, sleep and breathe only metres from each other, but a hook-up app has brought us together!

I am thinking, how romantic – I can even imagine it now, telling my grandkids: 'Yeah, we were living in the same building, so I wasn't even the girl next door, I was the girl upstairs, but we actually didn't properly meet, apart from passing in the hall, and stuff, or saying hi in the street when he asked how old Calypso was, and I thought, The hotness!, so yeah, it didn't really happen until we connected on Tinder' – and I'm just firing off my first message to Sid, and then, as I'm standing there, Clare, that emo woman who stole our house, comes out of the American dry cleaner's, carrying various garments in one hand and a navy bucket bag in the other, with a copy of a book called *The Mindful Baby* sticking out of the top.

Clare: 'Oh, hello! It's Mirabel, isn't it! You're all back, aren't you?'

Then she glances at the screen in my hand. Hashtag awkward!

So many things wrong there.

Clare: 'He looks nice. Is he your boyfriend?'

Me: 'Sorry?' Shocked to *core*. Awks, or what! One, you never, evah, look at someone else's phone like that.

And who says 'boyfriend' or 'girlfriend' any more? That's so nineties. You say you're having a sort of thing, or sort of seeing each other.

No way I'm going to explain Tinder or all that to an old lady, and I tell her I had to pick up, as Cas and Posy are at Harrow Academy and Mum's having her hair (in fact, her colour) done.

Clare: 'It is Mirabel, isn't it? Do you remember me? I'm Clare, I live . . .' She doesn't say 'I live in your old house', as if I will find that too painful. Then she asks me if I want to be a waitress at some dinner she's giving for Mum, so I feel trapped and say yes. I did it a couple of times for Rose so wtf and I need the cash.

Me: 'Nice to see you, too, and see you then.' Then I move off, as I want to check my phone. 'I'm just getting some stuff from Tesco, and the market, of course,' I add hastily, we all have to pretend we never go to Tesco, as all the supermarkets are putting the market out of biz, 'for Mum for our supper.'

Message back from Sid.

'Aren't you the girl upstairs?'

So I message him back and we start chatting. I pick up carrots, chicken parts – thighs and legs – from one of the halal butchers, the one after Tesco but before all the Spanish delis that smell of manure. Plus, sweet potatoes, so Mum can make her 'sticky chicken traybake' with its special secret ingredient (she drools elderflower cordial all over it).

As I lug the bags home, I have this feeling.

Sid. He'd never send me a dick pic.

I just know.

He's the one.

Twitpic from @posyfleming I <3> Calypso my dog in her knitted coatigan

Clare

Lonsdale Gardens

The stress!

However much help you have, however much money you drop on it, a dinner party is always, but always, a three-day event that you have to pretend has taken no time or trouble at all: it's an occasion that you host, even though you know most men only attend on sufferance. Even though I, personally, have to do hardly any of the shopping or the cooking, there's still so much else to do, even before D-Day minus one, i.e. the day before.

Casting it. Sending the *pour mémoires*. Recasting it when four people who have previously accepted with delighted emails drop out when they receive subsequent invitations. Planning the menu, mindful of any dietaries, while also remembering to substitute ladies' lunch staples such as beetroot, quinoa, spelt, kelp, and kale (all the comestible equivalent of Birkenstocks) with luxurious, gluttonous, fattening ones – double cream, red meat, cheese, like that Brie with truffles you can get in the French stall on the Portobello . . .

And then on D-Day: Lay the table. Polish the silver. Find the right serving dishes. Iron the antique French linen napkins from Summerill & Bishop – not the Peter Rabbit blue ones but the sophisticated pale grey-green ones the shade of ripening wheat. Make the flatware shine and the crystalware sparkle – yes, however much 'help' you have, the supervision alone of such tasks for a dinner party At Home is a full-time job.

I try not to ever say 'kitchen supper', not if I can help it, as it builds up too much expectation.

Kitchen supper – the Notting Hill Kitchen Supper (NHKS) – is the most elite and exclusive invitation of all, as it denotes real friendship, and intimacy beyond price. If you say 'Come and have scrambled eggs in the kitchen; the children will be in their pyjamas, kitchen supper, it'll be total chaos,' in Notting Hill, people expect the prime minister, or at least one member of the Cabinet, to be present. And to drink vintage claret, even if it is out of tooth mugs.

I'm upstairs, to arrange the flowers in the sitting room and light the fire, even though it's warm, but cosy is what people want at the end of the day.

They want cosy, they want comfort food.

'Breathe,' I say out loud to the empty sitting room, which looks lovely: creamy, calm, a log fire burning, the new Taschen books on the coffee table and white lilies in tall glass vases on every windowsill. All is spotless and in its place: what Gideon calls 'the right things in the right order'.

Serene. Unlike me.

So, who's coming? I run through it in my head again, and realize my mind's gone blank. Mimi and Ralph, of course. Sally and Bob.

Trish and Jeremy Dodd Noble. Keith Dunbar and Oksana. Virginie and Mathieu Lacoste were coming, but they cancelled. Marguerite and her 'plus one', who is tonight Julien StClair, as Farouche is in Paris.

'I don't care if he's a jihadi from the Islamic State of Birmingham who could be my grandson so long as he's male and single,' Marguerite had said to me, in delight, over the phone, when I told her, knowing how hard it is to find anyone male and single who is prepared to contemplate sitting next to a woman his own age and chatting even for one evening.

Since her divorce, Marguerite has been 'out there', i.e. dating again, and had one brief affair, I think, with a nice barrister called Edward, a couple of years older than her, whom she'd played tennis with a few times, up at the club.

They went to the south of France, stayed for the weekend in Vence and then . . . nothing. For week after week.

Instead of accepting the inevitable – Edward had moved on to a thirty-year-old who ran her own website streaming old arthouse movies – Marguerite thought he was pining for her. So she printed out all her iPhone pictures of the Vence weekend via an app, stuck them in an album and wrote captions all about the visit to the Matisse chapel or the restaurant in St Paul de Vence and said she had to see him. They met at E&O, where she made the presentation of their Special Album of Love, after which he ran for his life, and she hasn't mentioned him since, apart from to say that she's started removing all her hair 'down there', as 'men seem to expect it.' Poor thing.

She's jolly lucky I've wrangled Julien. And everyone's lucky that Julien is minus Farouche, the heart-stealer, who comes drenched in her signature scent, identifies the most vulnerable and needy person in the room, male or female – and sets about seducing them.

So add me and Gideon – graciously deigning to come to his own dinner party – that makes twelve.

He went a bit quiet when I told him so many were coming, including the Blackers, and oh my God!

Just realized.

If the Blackers are coming we're not even twelve – we're fourteen!

I race downstairs, barefoot, and re-lay the table, feeling a combination of anxiety that I could have forgotten – am I losing my mind? – and relief that I remembered in time.

Eli, the River Café chef, is at the range, searing the fillet. I always do fillet for lots of people – it's so easy – and grill vegetables and whizz up a bright-green salsa verde of garlic and herbs from the garden. John Armit has delivered the wines: the Pouilly-Fuissé is in the wine chiller and I've decanted the claret – three bottles of it, anyway – into the John Pawson decanters.

Harper & Tom's have delivered the flowers, Mirabel has agreed to be a waitress, and at least the girl did arrive *à l'heure*, very pretty in a black mini-skirt and a white T-shirt, over which she's layered one of Eli's white aprons. I'm not sure about the DMs, but I haven't asked her to remove them.

The doorbell. Back upstairs again.

'Mimi!' I cry as I open the door. She stands alone on the doorstep, looking unsure of herself, in a splodgy green, purple and blue tea dress I saw in the sale at Cath Kidston, lifted by some neon-pink espadrilles.

I'm in a white Margaret Howell man's shirt tucked into high-waisted Stella McCartney sailor trousers. I've slipped on the ballet pumps I buy in bulk from Capezio in the East Village.

We hug. Mimi brings out a bunch of yellow and blue irises from behind her back. I'll have to display them, even though they are completely the wrong colour for the house.

I stop myself from snapping, 'Where's Ralph?' as I take them.

He's the whole point of this evening. Tonight is the night for Stage 1 of the project.

'Am I early?' she says, not referring to Ralph's absence, so my heart misses a beat.

He's not coming.

'Is Mirabel here? I do hope so,' she continues, handing me a bobbly lilac pashmina that manages to clash with her espadrilles, as well as the flowers and everything in the house.

'Ralph's on his way,' she goes on, and I almost scream with relief. 'I mean, this is so sweet of you, Clare. I can't believe it. Joe in bed?'

I nod.

'Oh,' she says, looking disappointed yet relieved, as I clutch the pashmina like a baby's blankie, wondering where to hide it. 'But I can't wait to see what you've done to the house . . .'

It must cost Mimi a lot to say that. This used to be her house. And Joe is her husband's son. His biological son anyway.

Maybe . . . maybe, what I have in mind may just work. I tried before, and failed, but that was then.

As we're going downstairs, the bell rings again, so I go back up, still clutching the irises, and away we go. It's the Blackers. Mal's carrying two bottles of ice-cold champagne and Meredith is on her iPhone, saying, 'Sorry, I normally would be up for doing the discussion with Cable and Chuka, but I'm about to arrive at a dinner.' She smiles at me, showing very white teeth, and says, '*The World Tonight* again, oh well.'

I say, uncertainly, 'Well, don't you think you should . . .?' as I can't imagine turning down something so important, but Meredith barks with amusement. 'No, no,' she says, coming in and giving me her Balenciaga black coat with the ruffly collar. 'If I did every TV or radio interview, I couldn't ever go to a party! One's got to keep it all in balance. I've got to have a life. Haven't I, Mal?'

Mal gazes at her with pride. I open his cold champagne, and stick the other in the ice bucket I have ready upstairs.

At 8.50 precisely, when everyone else's arrived – Julien, the Averys, Marguerite – and downed at least two flutes of fizz, I order everyone down with a bright laugh, and as they mill around the candle-lit table I tell them to look for their place-cards, which I've had Joe inscribe with a Sharpie to give the dinner that intimate, personal touch.

I seat Ralph (spelt 'Ralhp') next to me during the dinner, on my right, while Mimi is on Gideon's, with Meredith ('Merdith') opposite Gids ('Daddy'), as he insisted.

He's been fascinated with Meredith – the Burmese blood, the ballet walk – ever since he heard from Jeremy Dodd Noble, who heard from someone who was a fellow Kennedy scholar with Meredith at Harvard back in the early nineties, that Meredith was GIB. Good in Bed.

I've always been puzzled by this. I long to know what men mean by being 'good in bed', a phrase that has always made me feel deeply anxious and inadequate. But Meredith's rep as a great lay precedes her everywhere she goes, and I don't deny it helps to make it all click tonight.

Everyone inhales my airy buckwheat blini and oak-smoked salmon starter with horseradish cream at top speed – people are so hungry by 9 p.m. midweek – and topic one is the mansion tax, and how people are going to avoid paying it, or whether a rerating of properties is on the cards.

Meredith seems to know all the inside scoop on this. She seems fearfully well connected. Then someone asks her about a column she did for 'the *Obs*' about predistribution.

All eyes are on Meredith as she explains the inequity of income distribution between the top 0.01 per cent and the rest. Gideon is gazing on admiringly, clearly thinking that she is very easy on the eye and no birdbrain, as well as being an ex-ballerina and, famously, GIB.

I hear him saying, with oil in his voice, as he tops up her wine, 'Thank God for you and Mal. I thought Notting Hill was over the day Bernardo Bertolucci sold his house to that Chinese hedge funder, but you Blackers' – he tips his glass – 'give us all grounds for fresh hope.'

But then Ralph rises in my estimation when he mentions the elephant in the room.

'What you say is all very interesting, um, Meredith,' says Ralph, 'and I'm sure Pulitzer Prize-worthy. But I just wondered . . . how do you square your enthusiasm for Piketty with your ownership of a private jet?' Bold of him.

'What's that got to do with it?' Meredith replies, as if she genuinely can't see any connection.

'Mal bought the PJ, anyway,' she goes on, as if lecturing a class of primary-school children where fifty-six different first languages are spoken, 'when he sold *his company*. When he sold his company *to Tetrapak*.'

'Yes,' grins Mal. 'I bought it. Way I see it, there's EasyJet, and there's Easiest Jet, which is having your own plane? Ha ha.'

'Yes, I can see it must be very convenient,' persists Ralph, 'but if you actually practised proper Pikettian predistribution you'd never have been able to build up your company in order to sell it and buy the private jet, let alone a large house – actually, make that two houses – on Lonsdale Gardens.'

There is a slightly frozen pause, as it is not done to point out any hypocrisy shown by high-rolling Labour voters like Meredith who pursue the creed of 'Do as I say, Don't do as I do.' I wonder if Ralph knows that not everyone in W11 is true blue; there are REVELs, too – people who are Rich Enough to Vote Even Labour.

'If you really can't see the difference, Ralph . . .' Meredith says, with a chill. I do hope we are not going to witness a Meredith Meltdown. I'm wondering whether to clap my hands and say, 'Pudding and then cheese, or cheese and then pudding?' and stage an intervention, but Mal gets there first.

'Ralph's right, baby,' he says. Then he turns to Ralph, as if settling the matter. 'Mer didn't want the jet.' He gives his wife a look of tender indulgence. 'The truth is, Mer actually prefers travelling economy, as she enjoys talking to people and finding out their stories – don't you, darling? And I literally have to drag you on board, don't I? It's my boy toy. And I think it's so cute' – he chucks her under the chin – 'when you write your column about the working poor or care pathways in a cream leather seat with a glass of champagne at your elbow. I find it sexy.'

Phew, everyone laughs, even Meredith at herself, and then the conversation becomes general, and moves on to splits and crack-ups: who has been in, who's out of the Priory, the new Priory in the City, and which local couples are divorcing. All the men focus on this topic, keenly.

'Thing is, only if you're really, and I mean really loaded, can you get it over with good and fast,' Keith Dunbar is saying.

'What does "really loaded" actually mean in terms of wealth?' asks Mimi, to general delight.

She's been off Broadway for so long – so long, she doesn't know that 'really loaded' means three digits. More than a hundred million. If you have less than a hundred – worth sixty mil, say – you're only two digits.

Keith was obviously glad she'd asked this question and, as the richest man present, had right of reply.

'A million these days is middle class,' he says. 'To be seriously rich, you need a billion.'

As Keith speaks, going redder, I wonder yet again about his cock. Keith's is reputed to be as super-sized as his bank balance – something I found out, curiously, from Marguerite, who has become considerably more ribald and direct since she entered the velociraptor ranks of Notting Hill Divorcees.

'Keith's not only VHNW,' she'd divulged over a soya flat white at Daylesford, leaving her perfect cube of Sicilian lemon polenta cake on the side, 'he's HLD,' and then she described the size of his enormous member, as if cradling a prize marrow, her white, delicate hands with their blueish, translucent skin outstretched over our table for two upstairs by the meat and cheese counters. There are never any men having lunch at Daylesford. They've tried to launch an evening offering that's more hearty, more gutsy, to reel them in, but Gideon has so far resisted my suggestions we go there and maybe have a date night.

He says that, like every other café on Westbourne Grove, from Ottolenghi ('too gay, too Israeli') to Granger's ('too Australian'), Daylesford is 'too much like every other place around here, a non-working women's club'.

'But how do you know?' I'd asked. VHNW, of course, was Very High Net Worth, and her hand gesture reminded me that HLD was the acronym for Hung Like Donkey.

If a man has a tiny penis, or a monster, women regard it as their sisterly duty to expose the plain facts that would otherwise remain hidden until it was too late to act upon the information. But this was news to me. Everyone in London knows that Alain de Botton is huge, as is Michael Gove and Matthew Freud, but now we add Keith Dunbar to the HLD list.

Keith's looking mottled, after putting away most of a decanter of claret on his own, and it did cross my mind that he might peg out at my dinner party.

'Rupert Murdoch and Wendi Deng. He did it *bang bang bang*. Over,' Keith is saying with vigour. He strikes the table with the side of his hand in a chopping karate action to accompany '*bang bang bang*'.

'*Bang bang bang* over, then it's *next*,' says Mimi. 'That is, you're a media mogul even if you're eighty-two and look like a fossilized tortoise like Rupert Murdoch.'

And when Mimi says 'next', Keith winks at Oksana. 'Not you, Scary,' he says.

There is a moment while everyone downloads the fact that his pet name for Oksana is 'Scary'.

'There will never be a next after you, I promise.'

At which Oksana puts her pillowy lips together and blows him a kiss across the plates smeared with the red juices from the beef fillet, the livid, Kermit-the-frog green sauce, the crystal glasses catching the candlelight, the silver pepper-mills. She looks satisfied, as if her pre- or mid-nup has been triple-locked by the most expensive silk in London.

I sigh and push my beef around my plate. I can never eat at my own dinner parties. But it's good. Everyone's talking.

It isn't exactly the Round Table at the Algonquin, but it never is, not at Notting Hill Kitchen Suppers.

You have Rich People's Conversation, which always boils down to 'the best thing I ever bought'. Followed by 'what I spent my money on next', with digressions for the highlights of the men's careers.

Then the men revert back to names of trending divorce lawyers, while the women exchange little-black-book data and release names of special, secret hairdressers, colourists or aestheticians, or personal trainers, tutors, marital counsellors and every imaginable sort of therapist.

I throw in the name of the woman who gives me internal facials to Oksana but, as I listen to the men, it becomes clear how much forethought the VHNW men have put into this, the most dangerous trade of all, which is swapping their wives for younger derivatives as quickly as possible and at the smallest risk to their bank balances.

'No, no, guys, you so don't want your wife being represented by *him*,' Bob is saying, mentioning a well-known QC.

Sally looks up beadily, as well she might, as her husband could be divulging that he's already done due diligence on a particular expert in dispute resolution when it comes to Big Money divorces.

'He's a black hole. Your current account'll plummet quicker than the gas on a stretch Hummer.'

Then Mimi raises a hand. Clears her throat.

'Erm, I just wanted to say, very quickly, how sweet it is of Clare . . .'

She rises to her feet, toppling a glass, which Ralph catches before it spills claret on my linen tablecloth, and Keith Dunbar cries, 'Good save!'

'It's lovely to be back in the garden, among so many friends. And to meet Keith and Oksana, who aren't on the garden – I am looking forward to inspecting Phillimore Gardens very much – and with whom I intend to become New Best Friends immediately. And it's even lovely to be back in our old house, which is unrecognizably smarter than it was when the Flemings inhabited it. There is no question,' she continues, blushing prettily, and now swigging claret from a refill, 'that Clare and Gids do things in a style to which I've never been accustomed and to which we Flemings can only aspire.'

Then she thanks me and subsides, to light claps. Only to rise again to her feet, like Glenn Close refusing to die in *Fatal Attraction*. She tings a glass.

'I forgot to ask. Does anyone have any useful intel as to the mystery new owner of the massive property on Ponsonby Terrace? You know, bang next door to the new menopause centre? Alpha Star? They've put in for this super mega-double basement – '

Trish takes over, having corrected Mimi on the GBC, insisting that it's not about merely mature wellbeing but life-skilling at any age.

'Yes, thank you, Mimi, for raising this,' she says. 'But double basements are so last year. This one's a *triple*.' Trish widens her eyes.

At this point, Mirabel emerges from the kitchen end of the room, as previously instructed, with the cheese board, which is a polished plank of hardwood in the shape of a paddle: I know it's more elegant just to have one, perfect cheese, but I've gone mad and there's a goat and a Vacherin and a hard cheese, and a slab of Gorgonzola, chalky white and yellow-cream against the vivid green of the strewn vine leaves, picked from my own garden.

There's no room on the table to put the cheese down, so Mirabel goes round and conversation pauses as everyone loads up on it, as if in for the long haul. I glare at Gideon, and he gets up and goes around with the decanter of claret and tops up the men, and Mimi, and people keep helping themselves to cheese, grapes and those addictive fudgy biscuits from Clarke's that are basically all butter, bound together by oats and sea salt.

Trish waits a moment – for everyone to apply more butter to their biscuits and pats of cheese – before relaunching. I wish I could stop her, as talking about planning is always a total buzz-kill. Gideon has taken out his phone. Oksana is showing Mimi pictures of the twins. Keith Dunbar has gone strangely quiet. Julien is whispering something to Mirabel as he carves himself a slab of cheese, and Bob and Sally Avery have a slightly detached air, as if talk of disruptive developments is so last year.

'OK, so this is the deal. A planning application with all the diagrams and floor plans has been lodged with RBK&C. But here's the kicker. It's all in the name of some shadowy corporate entity.'

'Hey! Is that allowed?' asks Bob Avery. He takes off his tie and unbuttons his collar, as if preparing to box.

After all, the Averys have serious form here. And I should know. I was the one, after all, who led objections to the Averys' so-called 'garage', which turned out to be a three-storey house, complete with underfloor-heated marble, broadband, chandeliers, French windows, as if a car deserved nothing but the finest five-star accommodation.

'Wow. If only I'd known,' Bob Avery continues, popping his rolled-up tie in the pocket of the jacket he's draped over his chair-back, 'that you could do your planning dirty business . . . without leaving any mucky fingerprints, then there might not have been all that local . . . unpleasantness about our . . .'

Everyone waits in anticipation to see what word he would use. 'House', or 'garage', or even 'three-bed Notting Hill new-build'.

In the end, he trailed off, which was tactful, as everyone knows two of his older student offspring are now using the so-called 'garage' as a £2 million grad-pad in W11.

'Ha ha, Bob, but back to the triple basement,' says Trish. 'Despite repeated FOI requests to the council, there is nothing so far on the site that gives away the name of the architect or the owner, or owners.'

'Freedom of information,' says Ralph, for Mimi's benefit.

Mimi pipes up in her professional journalist voice. 'But who on earth *is* the owner? It must be possible to find out. The Land Registry – dunno – Mouseprice? Rightmove? Isn't everything transparent now? I mean, doesn't the government read all our billions of emails –'

Ralph says, 'I don't think they actually read all of them, darling.'

'So shouldn't it be relatively easy to find out the ID of the new owner of a massive £15 million house in the Royal Borough? Shouldn't it? Or am I missing something?'

Mimi is like a dog with a bone.

'Do the plans give anything away?'

'The plans are all online, and I suggest everyone inspects them asap,' says Trish. 'We can't prove dirty dealing here. Or that money has changed hands,' she goes on, sipping water in a professional way.

So many social 'events' are like this. Business.

'The Ponsonby triple-dig,' Trish goes on, 'could affect adjoining houses and houses in the vicinity. Which are all on a slope. This is Notting *Hill*, hello? The road's likely to be closed for a whole year, which will not only screw the school and the GBC but also bar residents' access from the Kensington Nursing Home to their local shops, like Marks and Spencer.'

Everyone tries to look concerned about the plight of the distressed gentlefolk of Kensington and their restricted access to M&S Simply Foods, and the blight cast on the Giving Back Centre, and frown, as if hearing about another terrible Syrian war crime. But it's hard. The GBC, after all, is just another project.

As Gideon says, women who don't work, or the super-rich, not in conventional employment, don't have jobs: they have 'projects' instead.

Trish picks up her wine, then puts her glass down on the tablecloth. Trish's never been a big drinker. In fact, I suspect her of being a secret non-drinker, like me.

Mirabel is clearing plates, and everyone smiles at the sight of someone's child behaving appropriately and looking decorative, as if she is a credit to us all.

'So the status on the centre is this. After all our hard work, and fundraising, our blood, sweat, hot flushes, ha ha, and tears, we are facing having our first *two* years of operation ruined by major building works. *Really*. I could cry.'

Keith Dunbar puts an arm across Trish's shoulders. He doesn't speak, as if holding back strong emotion.

'You've all got to write letters and come to the meeting. Stop this madness.'

'Baby, you're being too emotional,' says Keith, in a voice-of-reason way. 'This is pure economics, baby girl. It's not personal.

Planning regulations mean you can't build *up*. So the only way is *down*,' continues Keith, emptying the dregs of another decanter into his glass and waving a hand. Gideon goes to the side with it and chugs in another £200 worth of Lynch-Bages.

'Maybe we should put an application in, Ralph,' Mimi says, as a joke. As if she doesn't live in a grotty maisonette. They don't even own the lower-ground floor on Garden Court!

'Last word on this,' says Keith, holding up a pudgy hand. 'My ex-bank manager left his bank and he's now head of a basement company. He starts on one in the street and he told me that, before the end of the project, every time, he's got four more in the same street.'

'It's like cigarettes. Everyone says they hate smoking, but as soon as someone lights up a cigarette and passes them round, everyone wants one.' Gideon is sending a text, which is odd, as he is in the middle of actually speaking.

The evening is going very well, I think. People have only checked their phones once or twice each.

'If your place does have dig potential' – Keith looks at Ralph, man to man, as if he's taking Mimi's comment seriously, and as if the Flemings were the sort of people who could 'bang up' half a million on a dig – 'then you should think seriously about doing it, as your house won't be worth £4 million, it'll be worth seven, maybe eight, and think what a difference that will make to your twilight years . . .'

Ralph grunts and says something about 'the unpredictable dangers of honeycombing the sub-structures of both the private and public realm with deep underground excavations so we get not so much London clay but a substratum honeycombed like a Crunchie . . .' Then he pauses and grins at Keith.

'But, actually, Keith, we live in a former council house, so I don't think we could add that sort of value to the property, anyway,' he admits, and my heart melts.

I love the way Ralph always calls a spade a spade. There are absolutely no false pretensions about him.

I drop my napkin and duck my head under the table, to do a check.

The first lap I check is Gideon's. But his feet, ending in the tan pigskin slippers he buys in bulk in Firenze, are planted on the stone floor. But there is one arched, elegant foot – in sheeny, black silk – in his lap.

Meredith has slipped off her Louboutins and is resting one foot in my husband's groin, and her toes seem to be caressing his cock, underneath his linen trousers.

That's all I can bear, so I break surface. 'Oh, I thought you'd gone,' says Ralph, when I re-emerge from my recce, slightly flushed.

This is the first time he's talked to me, and I know I have to move quickly.

This is the sign of encouragement I need. I remember Donna's parting words.

'Ralph.' I say it in an intimate, low voice. I put my hand lightly on his thigh, but only for a second, so it's more of a pat than a paw.

Mirabel is now helping to clear – Julien has jumped up to help – and the conversation has switched again, to what everyone's doing at half term, and the evening is moving like the life of a much-loved monarch towards a close.

At the mention of half-term it comes out that Notting Hill is migrating to Mustique for the week. Just as I've planned.

As the red wine flows and I whisper in Ralph's ear, I can see out of the corner of my eye that Oksana is becoming looser, more drunken.

She leans over and says to Mimi, 'It's been so lovely to meet you properly. We didn't really at the STD meeting – I had to go!'

I smile warmly at Oksana in approval. It's very important that Mimi and Ralph are incorporated in all communal local happenings, attend Garden events like Bonfire Night, the annual drinks and Garden Sports day, but top of the list is of course Mustique, half-term week.

If I can pull this off, without appearing to have had anything to do with it, I'm halfway there.

'But why don't *you* come to Mustique?' Oksana is saying, as if suggesting a quick coffee in Daylesford. 'For half-term? Lucian can play with the twins. And, of course, you guys also have to come to Keithy's fiftieth in November.'

Fiftieths are a massive thing. We did Florence for Si's fiftieth, and we all stayed in the Savoy, and even the stationery in the room was monogrammed, not with the initials of the birthday boy but – a lovely touch this – of the guests, so Gideon and I had watermarked Florentine notepaper headed G & C. And the liveried Fiat Cinquecentos that buzzed us from the hotel to the palaces and parties had personalized number plates saying SI 50 3–4–2014.

I think, the last one we went on, everyone was flown on PJs to Venice, and the entire livery of the jets, from napkins to the little white antimacassars on the seat-backs, said www.robins50th.com – a detail which everyone pretended was naff in a fun way, or fun in a naff way, I wasn't quite sure.

Yes, there's a huge competition around fiftieths and sixtieths, which – even more than weddings – have become haute couture events on which many hands toil for months on tiny, sparkling details to make a showstopper, one very special night only, so lavish and unforgettable that the celebrants can say afterwards that their budget was unlimited and yet still they exceeded it.

'We insist,' says Oksana.

'Yeah, you must. I've got a little place there, too,' says Julien, coming back to sit down, glancing over at Mirabel, chipping in. 'You guys should definitely all come.'

I wonder why Julien doesn't ever mention Farouche. Maybe they are really living apart-apart, rather than together-apart, like the rest of us?

I'm sure this is what everyone round the table is wondering, Marguerite, especially – Julien is a catch – but then Mimi (you can rely on her for the full-frontal approach) goes in.

'Will Farouche be there?' says Mimi, staring at Julien with a challenging look, high colour on her cheeks.

Julien smirks. 'Who knows?' he says. 'Does anyone ever know where the hell Farouche is? I don't. She's a, you know, a movable feast. But I can promise I'll be there, and so will Fox.'

Then Ralph kicks Mimi under and across the table – I can sense it. He doesn't want to go. He never even says he goes on holiday, he says he's taking 'annual leave'. He doesn't really believe in holidays. But, still, I have to help make this happen.

Mustique is the perfect place for Stage 2 of my scheme. The soupy heat. The cicadas. The villa. The tropical lassitude that steals over everyone after four days 'on island'.

And I'll be mid-cycle.

Still, Oksana is not to know that the Flemings' USP is that they *don't* have a second home, let alone a Caribbean island paradise, a spread in Gloucestershire or Wiltshire, or a Cornish beach house, or an estate in Provence.

So Oksana is – like everyone else round here – grappling with the perennial amusing-guest deficit.

When everyone has so many houses, there's no shortage of staff, or things to do, or places to stay, or beds; there's only one thing missing: people like us. To fill them. And the funner and smarter and more unhoused they are, the further ahead you have to bid for them ('local author' Sebastian *Birdsong* Faulks and his wife, Veronica, get pre-booked up to five years in advance), as everyone's scrapping over the same pool of guests, who have to be solvent, good company, not themselves in possession of both a house in the country and one abroad, and also . . . completely available at peak times of year, like half-terms and holidays.

By that token alone, Ralph and Mimi are in high demand – almost as hot right now as that Latin tutor who works exclusively for the Abramovich kids.

But Ralph is looking stricken.

I can tell by his face. I can tell, anyway. There is no way Ralph is going long haul for half-term to stay with people he's barely met who possess the added disadvantage of being extremely rich.

Mimi is panting with excitement.

'Such a shame we can't come,' she says, but her eyes are glistening already at the prospect. 'Half-term's just around the corner . . . and, anyway . . .'

She's hinting she can't afford it. Good move.

Oksana powers up her BlackBerry.

'You fly BA to St Lucia, then you get the hopper,' she says.

Trish comments not on the fact that you have to rent a private plane to get to the Dunbars' but that it's so rare to see a BlackBerry nowadays, and Oksana smiles and holds it up as if owning one is proof of her charming authenticity.

'And BA has exactly six seats left,' she says, as if that clinches it, and lifts her arms in triumph so we can all see the outline of her famous breasts, those perfectly rounded, heavy globes with raspberry-pink nipples, through her cream, loose-weave silk top.

'It's a sign.'

'Gosh, it's lovely of you . . . Can we think about it?' says Mimi. 'But I'm really not sure if . . .'

The conversation disintegrates. I have to make my move. Mimi and Oksana have changed places so they can plot the Mustique mini-break. Keith is still banging on about the compelling economics of the basement dig.

I touch Ralph again, on the hand. I can't help it, I want to touch him, but I feel him stiffen at my touch. 'Hey . . . I'm so glad you and Mimi are back,' I say. I don't say why I'm so glad. Wouldn't want to put him off. After all, he's been here for three hours and he hasn't even mentioned Joe's name yet. I must be . . . realistic.

Ralph doesn't move his hand, though Mirabel is hovering, wondering whether to clear the cheese plates and bring the pudding.

'I was wondering – what I started saying . . . it's hard here. Are you free for lunch on Tuesday? I've got a table at Sweetings . . . Can you join me?'

I remove my hand from Ralph's, and he goes very still.

Sweetings is Ralph's favourite restaurant. Serving nursery food and comfort puddings since 1889. Well, it used to be his favourite restaurant, and Ralph's the sort of man who never changes his preferences.

'It's nothing scary,' I say.

There is a long pause. I can sense that Ralph is weighing up his desire for Bakewell pudding and proper, thick, eggy, yellow custard against his fear of everything else.

'OK,' he says.

I want to punch the air. It's as if my second baby, Joe's full sibling, is already well underway and I can start dreaming of layettes and converting Aida's room, next to Joe's, into a nursery, and moving her into a flat nearby.

I feel a reckless confidence.

'What sports is Joe keen on, by the way?' Ralph changes the subject. Speaks in a louder voice so others can hear our conversation. 'He's still at Ponsonby, isn't he? You know Lucian's started there?'

I admit that I do. I track and stalk the whole Fleming family's movements like a bloodhound.

'How's his cricket coming on?' He can talk about Joe to me, as only Mimi and I know. And nobody else is paying attention, anyway.

As far as the others are concerned – all except Mimi, of course, who is looking at us with puzzlement shading into suspicion – Ralph is doing his duty as a male at a social function and politely talking to another mother about her children and their schools.

As Ralph speaks, I have to drag my gaze away from his handsome profile. I don't want to give myself away, so I look at the women, at their anxious faces around my table, and I realize how dangerous all our projects are. And also how they are all . . . linked.

Fracking. Digging. Analysing. Drilling down.

When you go beneath the surface, as Ralph was just saying, you're in unknown territory.

When you dig deep, you never know what you'll find.

Ralph

I know Clare will already be seated at Sweetings when I get there, having walked in the drizzle from Cannon Street, so I drag my feet. I dawdle outside the cream-and-blue façade to admire the window display, which is a smorgasbord of plated fish – white platters of salmon, prawns and gravadlax arrayed around a wooden board containing a whole, glistening smoked salmon and fat red crabs – all of it garnished with wet, sea-green samphire and Cézanne-yellow lemons.

I'm already feeling advance guilt, as I fear that, whatever it is that Clare wants, I can't, or won't, be able to give her.

I pray it's about something I can handle. Something practical. Doable. Like she wants to send Joe to prep school and – even though I have no authority when it comes to the poor little chap – she still wants my blessing.

Lord, let it be something like that. 'No biggie,' as Cas would say.

I hand my raincoat to the girl at the desk and, before I go to the table, I wave at Clare and pop into the Gents.

As soon as I agreed to this lunch I knew it was a mistake. And, for once, I can't blame it on Mimi. I know she longs for me to say yes to things, i.e. ghastly, three-line-whipped Notting Hill dinners, weekends away, half-terms in the Caribbean – even though, on the whole, I prefer to say no to almost everything, and the first rule of life is: Don't say anything to anyone.

But I don't think even Mimi meant I should agree to lunch *à deux* with Clare, even though I love Sweetings – it's like a

Victorian urinal, in a good way. Plus, the menu – called 'the bill of fare' – hasn't changed for over a hundred years. Still: no escaping the fact that I'm now committed to an hour's singles with a married woman and neighbour who is – like so many women – basically unplayable.

An hour and a half if I'm unlucky.

I potter up from the Gents and join Clare at a small table for two. I sit opposite her, my left shoulder to the wood-panelled wall. She has a glass of wine and a bottle of water and is wearing some sort of brown frock with flashy green trimmings at the neck.

'Hi,' she says, and smiles warmly, her smile reaching her eyes so her cheeks crinkle. She gestures to her glass. 'Hock?'

She looks almost pretty, and I notice for the first time that she has Joe's hazel eyes. Or Joe has her eyes, as opposed to my blue ones, I should say.

'Hello,' I say, beginning to relax and deciding I'll join her. Just one glass. I have a meeting at the Environment Agency about fracking in the National Parks at 3 p.m. and I need to be on the buzzer. 'Why not?' I say. 'Well, here I am.' I smile back, non-controversially.

She starts firing questions. In answer, I tell her about the new place on Lonsdale Gardens, how it smells of damp and probably is damp, and the walls are thin, but how it's a temporary staging post. She nods eagerly, willing me on to say how horrible it is, her eyes sparkling. 'The main drawback – well, one of the many down sides – is you can't go out of the little back garden to the communal garden,' I say, not wanting to sound spoilt or self-pitying, but, in my book, one is allowed to whinge, but only on behalf of one's dog. 'We're basically fine – it's temporary – but as far as Calypso is concerned, it's a tragedy.'

It's all going well – so far.

'How's Mimi settling in? Home Farm was lovely and she was such pals with Rose,' Clare says. 'When I came to see you there –' she has the grace to blush. As well she might. She ambushed Mimi with Joe on my birthday, during a *fête cham- pêtre* in the garden, and Mimi fainted, either from an excess of prosecco, shock or the fact that the mercury was above 80 degrees for the first time since we'd moved to Dorset and, of course, she was just pregnant with Lucian, only hadn't dared to tell me.

'And how do the kids like it?' Clare was saying. 'Cas is at boarding school now, isn't he, so at least he's got plenty of room to run around and let off steam,' she adds, as if we unfortunate Flemings were living in cages like battery hens.

Clare does seem mustard-keen to dwell on the downsides of our new habitation.

'And have you decided what to do about Home Farm?' she asks next. I wait to answer, as we're ordering. I don't need to look at the menu.

Clare orders the gravadlax.

'I'll have the eel, please.'

'And for your mains?'

'The grilled Dover sole and steamed spinach,' says Clare. 'No supper for me tonight!'

'I'll have the fishcakes and buttered carrots, please,' I say. 'And chips. I know you'll end up eating at least one, Clare.'

'Any wine at all with your meals?' the waitress asks, and Clare and I grin.

I say, 'A glass of hock, please, a large one.' It'll help me get through this. 'At the moment we're holding on to it,' I say to Clare, reverting to the safe topic of Home Farm.

My wine arrives shortly, thank God, cold and wheaty, in a tall-stemmed glass.

'As I see it, having a house in the country is like having

savings, or a pension. It's for peace of mind. As I get older, I realize that having things, owning things, is not so that you use them, or spend them. They act as mood regulators. So the money sits in the account, the house on the hill, and both assets serve as a sort of security blanket, as a middle-class version of worry-beads. It's one of my insurance policies against lying sleepless in the small hours and thinking that I have done nothing with my life, I have nothing to show for it.'

Clare is gazing at me with shining eyes, and I regret having said so much, but I sip my wine, feeling expansive, and conclude, 'So I think you can enjoy a property even if you're lying in bed 200 miles away, trying to get to sleep by imagining that you've arrived at the bottom of the unmade farm track and making yourself remember every turn in the track, every tree . . .'

'I know just what you mean,' Clare says. She slides her hand across the table and touches mine.

My eyes swivel around the restaurant, just checking there's nobody I know who will spot me having lunch with a married woman who is trying to hold my hand. But mainly it's men in suits reading the 'Lex' column on the back page of the *FT*, on stools, with their backs to us.

'Ralph . . .' She trails off, suggestively, as if to signal we have reached the main item on the agenda. And then she starts talking about Joe. Which is fine. How keen he is on cricket. Also fine. There comes a point where she asks whether we're going to Mustique at half-term, which is still under discussion, and I just grunt.

I ask politely after Gideon, who's always been a useless arse, as far as I can see, but is undeniably successful, and she tells me he's been so busy with his new skyscraper that he's missing out on so many 'key milestones' in Joe's little life.

I can only bear a certain amount of this. The deal, and Clare knows it, was that Gideon was, and is, to all extents and purposes, and for the record, Joe's father. Not I.

'So how would you feel if . . . Joe had a sibling?' Clare hasn't taken a single chip, I note, and her Dover sole, flecked with parsley, on the bone, is congealing on the plate. It's not clear to me why she's taken the trouble to take me out to lunch at Sweetings to ask me this.

After all, the woman must be in her mid-forties. Gideon shoots blanks, and so the chances of her having another baby by anyone are vanishingly small, and the idea that she is asking me to provide another one is testing the outer limits of absurdity.

The waitress comes over, with her pad, and I'm trying to decide whether to have the steamed suet pudding or the spotted dick, but then I have a wild thought and change my mind.

I look at her with total sincerity, the waitress still standing with her pen poised, and say with conviction, 'I'd be absolutely fine about it, Clare. I can't think of anything nicer,' then turn to the waitress: 'The baked jam roll, please, with extra custard.'

Clare lets out a breath so hard I can hear it, across the table, as the waitress clears our plates.

'No pudding for me, thanks,' says Clare, and then I notice that her eyes have filled with tears.

I don't ask her why she's crying.

I have an awful feeling that, if I did ask, she would tell me. There's a limit to how much emotional honesty a chap can bear, especially over weekday lunch.

'And the bill, please,' I say.

Mirabel's blogpost 14/10/2014 9.45 a.m.
(in Caribbean; 14.45 p.m. in London)

Lying on four-poster-style bed with white muslin drapes and staring at view of toes at the end of the bed, admiring way pink nail polish – Secret Stash by Essie – pops against the darker-blue sea and light-blue sky.

Sipping a lime cooler. Made with fresh limes and fresh mint, pre-loaded with vodka.

In a minute we are all going off in golf buggies to Macaroni Beach for lunch and meeting Julien and 'everyone', like Clare and Joe and what Keith calls the local colour, i.e. international celebrities.

Am going to wear the New Look bikini and Top Shop micro Daisy Dukes that Dad said were probably illegal in several US states and, to be fair, do show my entire bum.

Still can't believe I'm writing this . . . Oh to the Eff to the Em to the Gee.

In Mustique!!

I still can't believe we've come. After that lame dinner. When Julien took my number 'for babysitting' – yeah, right – when Mum wasn't looking, because she was looking at Clare, who was kinda holding Dad's hand over what Clare called the 'artisanal cheese platter from La Fromagerie – not the one on Moxon Street, the one on the Portobello', as if it was somehow important.

I never get it when women think they're clever just because they've chosen something to buy, as if it's some sort of creative act.

Oh yes, and I heard Oksana saying, 'Take me home and fuck me,' to Keith as she passed him to go to the downstairs loo by the area steps, where Clare had lit a fig candle.

I'm sure some other people heard, even though Keith was shouting about basement digs, which, apart from money and the mansion tax, is all anyone talks about in London, apart from talking about sex, which old people do when they're drunk.

I helped Clare to clear, and she sent me home early with Mum and Dad (with a £50 note, thank you very much) and we walked round the corner, from our old house around the square back to Lonsdale Garden Court.

Dad: 'Darling, shall we take Calypso out to powder her nose? I hope you realize there's no way we are going to Mustique, not for half-term – not ever, in fact. Over my dead body, Hell will freeze over, etc. etc.' Dad never likes the same things as Mum, and one of his mantras is 'The pleasure I get from not going to a party is, I can assure you, far greater than the pleasure you get from going.'

I see where he's coming from but, to be fair to Mum, the most exciting it gets for Dad is a day's fly-fishing on the Test, with perhaps a cheese-and-pickle sandwich on his own in the rain in some fishing hut in Hampshire.

After a day like that he'll come back home and say he was even wetter than the trout, and he didn't even get a rise it was raining so hard, it was all hopeless, but as he talks and peels off his wet-weather gear he'll look so happy, lit up, and his eyes seem extra blue, like someone is shining a torch out from inside his head.

Anyway, Mum always gets her way in the end.

So here we are. I think Dad and Mum are trying to make an extra effort with each other or something. I mean, now we're in our new house/flat thing, it's true, nothing feels quite right yet. I'm sharing a room with Posy, Luc with Cas; the windows have got metal frames, not wooden ones; and, as Dad admits, 'There's not one single, decent, well-proportioned room.' But it's temporary, I know, so it feels like we're turning around in a new dog bed and haven't settled yet. Doesn't feel cosy, like it should. Not yet. And of course am spending most of my time with Sid.

Oh, yes – forgot to say – about the flight yesterday.

We didn't see anyone else until we were actually on the plane, as we were in World Traveller.

When we boarded the plane the Dunbar party were already

installed in their flat-bed seats, declining offers of further refreshment as if it was somehow common to eat or drink on planes.

So we had to file past them in their luxury in-flight casuals. Oksana was drinking fizzy water out of an actual glass made of glass, with a white napkin curled round it, which only happens on planes; and Keith was swigging champagne from a baby split, working on his iPad; and the twins were whining, 'Mama, Mama, what are all these *other* people doing on *our plane*,' which made me realize that the Dunbars usually travel by private jet.

When we'd taken off and Mum was dozing with her mouth open and dribbling, suddenly, Oksana plunges through the blue curtains screening off the poor people from the rich people and makes her way towards us at the back of the plane. We are in seats 47A–F – the Fleming family takes up a whole row, like refugees – and she has the white napkin in her hand.

Mum (wakes up): 'Oh, hi, Oksana! Gosh, isn't this fun!' she says, as we hadn't met properly at Heathrow, as they were in the exclusive Lounge and we were in Pret. Oksana and Mum tell each other how happy they are, how wonderful it all is, how exciting, and then Oksana puts the napkin on Mum's tray table and I can see there's some lines in blue Biro on it. She smoothes it down, so it's flat, and hands Mum the Biro.

Oksana: 'Mimi, I was wondering, to sign here, please.'

Luckily, Dad was asleep, head back, eyes closed, mouth open.

Mum: 'Sorry, I don't understand?'

Oksana: 'It's an NDA.'

Mum asks what that is and turns out it's a 'non-disclosure agreement'.

Apparently, you can't take pictures of the celebrities, or say anything either, and this has got worse since Prince William married, as the Middletons are always there.

Then she said that 'Keith hates personal publicity' and it was just to make sure that Mimi never writes anything.

Dad: 'I told you this was a terrible, terrible mistake,' as Oksana
tottered back on her heels like Posh to First. 'The bloody cheek,' etc.

Anyway. Here we are. This is the routine.

Get up around 8 a.m. and head past pool to open-air dining
area where breakfast has been laid by the house slaves: crispy
bacon, freshly squeezed orange juice, American cereals like Froot
Loops and Lucky Charms, eggs, platters of tropical fruits – mangos,
pineapples, melons, passion fruit – and there's a Nespresso
machine. Everyone arrives in shorts, T-shirts and flip-flops, the girl
twins in matching sun-dresses, and everyone's cheery. Even Dad
manages to be, even though he didn't want to come, is officially on
holiday and a guest in some billionaire's 'cottage', i.e. 12,000
square foot beach palace in the Caribbean with gym, pool,
atrium-style reception area the size of Westminster Abbey, yoga
terrace, sun terrace, yards from this beach.

So from 8 a.m. to 9.30 a.m. you drink about six Nespressos, as it
seems rude to leave the table until hosts Keith and Oksana have
completed their morning swim-plus-shag and joined us at the
Captain's Table looking all pleased with themselves, as if they have
already met all their key targets for that day.

Then the twins, Evgeniya and Blanka – Oksana calls them Ev and
B – go off to be nannied and tutored, and we talk about what we're
going to do today and which beach will we go to for lunch, who will
be on which beach and what does everyone want to do, from a
menu of options: play tennis/ waterski/ parasail/ boat/ fish/ shop/
paddleboard/ swim with turtles/ dolphins/ you name it – even
though you just want to chill.

It's honestly like paradise. Apart from the music. There is one of
these sound systems that pipes music everywhere, in the grounds as
well as the rooms, so when you walk from the guesthouse to the
pool or in the gardens the flowerbeds are playing Burt Bacharach.
This makes Dad groan very quietly under his breath and say he is
counting the days. Then Keith disappears to make calls, buy

companies, do massive deals and stuff, and when both he and Oksana are out of earshot Dad says, 'It's just like the Isle of Wight, if you think about it, only with better weather.'

After breakfast everyone goes back to base to 'get ready' for chosen activity – i.e. do a big poo – and the butler records each person's day and activity on a spreadsheet, with meal preferences, allergies and intolerances, and by the time breakfast is over he's slid each person's personal agenda under the door.

On our first night on the island we go to Mick Jagger's house and, of course, I wanted to Instagram everything and I was hoping Georgia May would be there – she's done two *Vogue* covers I really like – but Oksana had another go at Mum about how this is a private island and the whole deal is celebrities come here to relax, not to have to 'endure press intrusion'.

Dad, beforehand: 'Are you really saying we have to go to the house of someone called "Mick" for cocktails?'

Mum: 'Not someone called Mick. Mick Jagger. *Hello!*'

Dad: 'But I don't know him, nor want to, and I feel fairly sure he feels the same about us.'

Am itching to take out iPhone every five minutes. Oksana and now Mum are on the case, and even Mum has gone native and is behaving like taking smartphone pix of rock stars and putting them on social media is as bad as phone hacking.

Also, I am warming to Oksana.

Mum: 'I think she's on the spectrum.'

Dad: 'Yes, if you imagine she's managing some severe personality disorder, she actually comes across quite well.'

I don't think Mum and Dad are getting on that well. I tried to talk to Mum about it, after the sunset yoga session on the terrace, but she said it was just stressful, the move to London, and trying to pick up the threads of her career, and also the basement campaign was eating up her time and energy.

But I know Mum. There's something else. She's lost some weight and has a faraway look in her eye, as if she's thinking about something all the time.

I've been checking my sweet Sid on Facebook, and he's changed his relationship status to 'it's complicated'.

Wondering if that's cos I'm here, and he's cross? Should I be uploading pix of me romping in my bikini and flaunting my curves so he can see what he's missing?

And why hasn't he changed his Facebook status to 'in a relationship', like I have?

Just had this Buzzfeed link from Po!
20 Hilarious Camel-toe Fails You Must See

Mimi

Ralph, astonishingly, has made it on to the beach.

He's planted himself in a steamer chair dressed with white cushions, and is reading, in the shade, but still wearing a tobacco-coloured and crumpled panama hat. I am so happy he's here that I am being unbelievably nice; while feeling incredibly shitty, too.

I can't say the real reason why I insisted we came, which was that there was, or so it seemed at the time, a fifty-fifty chance that Farouche would be here, too.

'God, I'm baking,' I exclaim, cooking up to asking whether he wants to have a swim.

He doesn't answer, as he knows I know the answer to the question already, even before I've asked it. He doesn't do sun. Or sand.

After about five minutes of being 'away', he is pining for a small, grey, rainy island near his own dog and within driving distance of a chalk stream. But I didn't give him an option. The deal was, he said yes to things. And I wasn't going to miss this. And while wild horses wouldn't drag him on a freebie, I knew I'd lie on my deathbed and my one regret would be that I didn't spend half-term in October 2014 in Mustique when I had the chance, so here we are.

Still, I can't believe that, only two weeks ago, I was wondering whether we could afford to stay in London, as it's so expensive, and now we're here, now Home Farm is rented out to a telly company for Rose's latest foodie production, and now I am sort-of-working again.

What happened on that was Olivia called, again; I went into *Newsnight*, where I found that the editor, Josh Kurtz, is excited – 'aerated' – about the fact that every other person in Notting Hill is digging an iceberg house, so he wants to do 'a package' on it. Not so much the basements, but how 'London is the new Monaco,' he says, and the 'rage for subterranea' is a concrete symbol of the direction London is going, with property just an investment vehicle for the super-rich and not 'Bauhaus machines for living in at all'.

So then, feeling rather proud at having inside track, I filled him (Kurtz) in about the Ponsonby dig three floors underground and how it was going under the public highway at the front and the Ponsonby communal garden at the back, and he was very interested in this, and then he asked me to be his 'on the ground reporter' for the Monaco-stroke-basements package and could I hit it running hard.

So I said there was a mystery about the ownership and that Alpha Star was so far unplaceable and most likely offshore, and he went all quiet, intense and brooding.

'Well, I've got an idea about how to get around *that*,' he said, ruffling his dark hair and sticking a pen behind his ear, as if he were an extra in a *Washington Post*-in-the-seventies shoot.

His white shirt was unbuttoned almost to his navel, tucked loosely into belted jeans. 'We'll put eyes on the site.' A grin.

A producer who looks about Posy's age asks if that's 'within guidelines', and Kurtz says, 'Fuck the guidelines, we'll set up CCTV, I'm thinking time-lapse, the works.' He high-fives me and says, 'You and me, baby, we are gonna launch this baby down the *Newsnight* slipway!' So of course I say yes. I agree to everything.

I haven't told Ralph yet.

It's so comfy lying on the lounger, next to him. He's only said three or four times, 'Remind me never to come to the Caribbean again.'

Incredible to think that all the other people here have spent a day on a plane to get here and thousands of pounds, probably, and yet there is no place in the world Ralph would rather not be.

Salmon fishing in the Kola Peninsula, or Iceland, with only a mute ghillie for company, is what he calls a holiday. Even though we have our own house and butler, which is definitely a first for the Fleming family. 'Well, this century, at any rate,' as Ralph observed when he came into our bedroom and found Hennrick unpacking his things, taking out his Ede & Ravenscroft cornflower-blue shirts and chinos and putting them in drawers.

'Ah, thank you, Henry,' said Ralph, after Hennrick had introduced himself, even though Hennrick was wearing a name badge on his pale-pink polo shirt, but by that stage it was too late and, anyway, we are being very careful with each other at the moment and letting 'the little things' go.

Off to our right, under the palm trees, in the tiger-striped shade, even though we've only just had breakfast, they're setting out lunch (they being the lovely staff/crew). There's a boat, too.

Four young boys – well, men, really, but they look like boys to me – in matching pale-pink polo shirts embroidered with 'Villa Jacaranda' are setting it all out while chattering and laughing, and it all looks too pretty for words. I keep taking pictures and Instagramming them in secret, trying not to think about data-roaming charges: white tablecloth, tattered pink-and-orange-and-green bunting, flowers in livid pink and red shades in simple vases on the table, proper knives and forks – oh yes, this is a 'simple beach picnic' that has only taken six full-time members of staff a whole morning to set up on the strand in the shade.

'This is the life,' I say, prone on my teak lounger, sucking in my tummy and watching the beach scene. 'We could almost be on holiday!'

I am anxious, though, about my un-updated beachwear. The look is faded vintage kikoys and lots of bangles and tousled hair, and that's just the men – i.e. like Julien, who has instantly gone golden brown and sun-baked like Ryan O'Neal and is the only man I know who looks good in a sarong.

Julien is now flirting quite openly with Mirabel, which is on one level sad, as it rams home that I am too old for him, that he was never the slightest bit interested in me, despite having suggested coffee . . . whatever 'coffee' means . . . but, on another, I couldn't care less, as I didn't fancy him either and I am in lust, as it happens, with his wife, a woman who has turned my world inside out and upside down, like a clean new duvet cover before you stuff the old duvet in.

Anyway – I shade my eyes as I squint over the beach – to my far left, with their toes in the surf, standing and chatting, there is a . . . not sure what the collective noun is for a group of Young British Artists . . .

'What's the name for a group of YBAs?' I ask Ralph.

'A wank,' he says, without pausing, but looks up to see Marc Quinn and Damien Hirst and I think at least one Chapman brother twenty yards away in cargo shorts, ironic T-shirts and baseball caps, accessorized by various women-stroke-muses, who are brown and scrawny with sun-streaked hair and flat bellies. Some have those new bosoms that still stick up, like two half-coconuts, even when they are lying on their backs.

So, YBAs to the left of us, to the right of us the beach picnic, and dead ahead, on that strip of harder, damp sand close to the shore, Cas and Lucian are playing French cricket.

Mirabel has set up a roost a few loungers down, so she can be away from us, listening to her iPod and I hope not uploading pictures from last night's drinks with Mick on Tumblr.

'What about a swim?' I say at last, knowing the answer.

Ralph does at least look up from his book about the First World War, one of several he has lugged 5,000 miles, as he refuses to buy a Kindle.

He marks his page with a Heywood Hill bookmark, as if he is preparing to give me a quick toot of attention.

Ralph buys hardbacks, and only non-fiction, i.e. war histories, by Max Hastings, Antony Beevor, Michael Burleigh, and so on, but he draws the line at Niall Ferguson, who he says is too pleased with himself and 'not as clever as he thinks he is'.

He also says most movies are intolerable. He will point blank refuse to watch any in which the dog dies, or there are two stubbly men kissing (he always shudders: 'Velcro'), but Ralph's main objection to mainstream cinema at the moment is that all actors have beards – well, all the male ones do, anyway – and that they have to go on emotional journeys, and also that the director often expresses this emotional journey through slight but telling changes to the actor's facial hair.

That's movies. Fiction is also banned, as he has a theory that there is a secret law of publishing that requires all modern fiction either to be pornographic or to have a dark secret involving incest or paedophilia, or both.

This theory was formulated when he picked up what looked like a promising novel set in the Great War by an author called Pat Barker, only to suffer the double blow that it was 1. written by a Woman and 2. there was a dark secret and 3. the dark secret was brother–sister copulation.

Ralph glances at the shining sea, winces. I notice the lines around his eyes, and how they make him even more attractive, and how his face goes brown, even though he never goes in the sun.

'You go, Mimi. I'll watch.' He picks up his book again and opens it.

I don't stir.

'By the way, Meems,' he murmurs, as if it doesn't do to say this out loud, 'if we were paying full whack, what would the damage be? Week in Mustique, half-term?'

'Crumbs,' I say, applying a thick plastering of Boots Soltan Water-resistant Factor 50 to my face and chest, which I do on a continuous basis, like patrolling my unruly bikini line, ever since Oksana screamed when she saw me by the pool. (Later, I found that a vanity kit with a pair of industrial tweezers, a hand magnifying mirror X5, a razor and some nail clippers had been thoughtfully placed in our bathroom.) 'Impossible to tell. Dread to think. It's already the most expensive holiday we've ever had, and so far we've only paid for the children's flights, the Gatwick Express and putting our car in the long-term car park, and, presumably, we will have to lash out on lunches and drinks –'

'And then we'll have to leave tips for the scores of staff, too,' he points out gloomily.

I groan as I come off the lounger. 'Oh well, darling, look on the bright side. At least Home Farm's washing its face.'

I saunter past Cas and Lucian, and they throw the ball at me and I fail to catch it and it slips into the sea and bobs back and forth in the little frill of surf that breaks on the golden sand.

I toss the ball back; Cas catches it with a lazy flick of one hand and says, 'Good throw, Mum,' and I smile and slip into the blood-temperature water, lie on my tummy, and float face down.

When I begin to stagger out ten or so minutes later, hoicking up bikini bottoms and making sure my breasts, or most of my breasts, are cupped by the bikini top again – it is the ocean's mission, always, to separate me from my swimwear – this is the new line-up on the beach:

- Julien talking to Mirabel, both of them doodling in the golden sand with sticks, while Fox scampers about in bright-orange trunks with a kite
- Oksana and Keith talking to Mick Jagger and a mermaid with endless, coltish brown limbs and bee-stung pink lips and tumbling, beach-blonde ringlets who may or may not be a daughter or granddaughter, and Jesus Christ, there's Pippa Middleton, with some tall bloke wearing navy trunks and a white T-shirt
- Clare painting a thick white layer of Lancôme Factor 100 to the shoulders of Joe and chatting to Ralph, who is gazing out to sea with the look of the Ancient Mariner scanning distant horizons for a speck of smoke that could signal rescue
- Mal and Meredith Blacker?! Whaaaa?! Meredith's in a swoopy, black asymmetrical sundress and wide-brimmed sunhat, so silhouetted like a bat against the full moon against the white sand. Mal stands muscular and solid, in baseball cap. They must be staying with . . . Clare and Joe? Julien and Fox? In their own house?

In a sense, I shouldn't be so surprised that there's a Lonsdale Gardens . . . *cluster* here in the Grenadines . . . I'd just forgotten that the super-rich are tribal. They like to do the same things, at the same time.

Move in a pack from breeding grounds to wintering grounds, from London mansion to holiday residences, while picking up art on the way. So they go from Courchevel in the first week of April, to Miami to Basel to Maastricht to the East Coast; and then it's the English season – Ascot, Wimbledon, Chelsea Flower Show, Henley, etc. – followed by long summers in the Hamptons, The Vineyard, Nantucket, Mount Desert Island, Maine; and then it's to the Caribbean, or skiing again, for October and February half-terms.

The migratory habits of the super-rich are as reliable and predictable as those of the Arctic tern.

The breeze is drying the salt on my skin and I am longing for a towel and shade, in that order, so there is nothing for it. I have to emerge from the turquoise main all white and doughy, and say hi to everyone as if we are on Kensington Park Road at ten past nine on a weekday morning.

Still, there's a faint chance I can slip by and that no one will recognize me, as I am 'out of context' – I mean: the Flemings are very much not the Mustique demographic, as everyone has been at pains to point out.

So I aim for the Blackers, as there is no way I am going to approach Mick Jagger in a green bikini from Bravissimo's 'supportive swimwear' collection exclusively for DL cup women, and give a shy wave, as if polishing a waist-height window, and, to my amazement, they both appear delighted to see me, faces breaking into actual smiles, and then I remember: one is always more pleased to see people one knows abroad.

And the normal rules of Notting Hill engagement, when you see your own status reflected back at you in the gaze of the person you're with, are suspended until you are back in London, when normal rules reapply.

'Hey!' we all say, as if thrilled. We don't kiss, as I am dripping, so we wave and sort of air-kiss.

I long to get a towel to mop myself off. We all explain who we're staying with. They're at Villa Mimosa, they say, as if this is a slight coup, and I say, 'We're at Villa Jacaranda with Keith and Oksana,' and Meredith looks pensive and says, 'Oh yes,' she remembers: she was there when I 'scored my freebie' at Clare's dinner, but I let it go.

Then a peon from Villa Jacaranda comes up and hands me a thick, soft navy beach towel with a little bow and the Blackers look impressed, and then start talking about Clare again, who has been amazing, so welcoming, since they moved on to the garden.

Suddenly, I have a panic that more people than I think know about the Sturgis–Fleming ... *dynamic*. There's me and Clare, and Ralph and Gideon and Donna, and Rose: we all know.

But not even the children know, so why is Meredith looking at me in this weird way, as if I am suddenly more interesting than she gave me credit for at earlier meetings?

We agree that Clare is a really lovely person and her Nourish & Flourish business was wonderful, it was sad she didn't grow it, and also a wonderful mother. It is generous of Meredith to say this, as the only thing over Clare I have is that I have four children and she has one. I give a little shiver.

'Cold?' says Mal. He removes his cap, which says 'Rosehearty', runs a hand through his thick curly hair, then replaces it.

'Rosehearty?' I say in answer, gesturing to the word on the brim.

'Oh, it's Rupert's old yacht,' says Mal.

I'd forgotten that Mal was a non-exec at News Corp.

'So, how was the water?' says Meredith, giving me her full beam. Her pearly teeth and eyes flash whiter than ever in her face.

This is the longest I've ever seen her without her checking her phone.

'Oh, and I meant to ask,' Meredith goes on, 'did Josh or anyone from *Newsnight* ever get in touch, after the crisis meeting at the Tea & Coffee Plant?'

I squint at her. Now I'm out of the sea, the sand is roasting the soles of my feet. I start hopping from one to the other, making 'ow' noises. I can't help it, and out of the corner of my eye I see Mirabel lift from her lounger. I hear the whine of a Vespa, on the road behind the trees shading the beach.

I remove the towel from around my waist and arrange it on my head to fashion a sort of sunscreen for my face. I don't care how silly it looks.

'*Newsnight?*' I say, playing for time. What did this have to do with Meredith?

As far as I knew, I was waiting for the call from Kurtz to let me know when he wanted to start filming the double-basement package.

Meredith turns her perfect profile away from me and contemplates the villas on the hill, as if deciding which one she is going to grace next with her coveted presence.

'Oh. Didn't Josh say?' she says. 'You know it was me who suggested to the editor that you should come on board, don't you? I texted about it during the meeting, actually. And I'm the presenter. Aren't you – I mean, I think your title is . . . researcher?' she adds with a generous nod.

Josh had said 'reporter/ researcher' to me, but left me with the impression that, if all went well and I came up with the goods, I might be fronting the package. As presenter.

So all I say is, 'It's all good. Gosh. So we're working together! What a thrill! I'm . . . very honoured.'

I absorb the blow privately for a few seconds, then beam at her.

'Perfect. It's like blood. The water, I mean. But my feet are on fire.'

I smile at the Blackers, then pretend to wave to someone so I can get away, but I stop in my tracks when I see the boys.

Lucian, in his Boden trunks with yellow sharks on them, is now playing with Cas, in khaki board shorts and a white T-shirt, and Fox . . . and also with Joe, who is wearing a baggy sun-garment with an integral hat with a brim so only a small portion of his face is exposed, like a doctor treating victims of the Ebola virus.

Joe scampers towards Cas and Fox. Cas is batting. Joe marks out a wicket. Then he runs across the sand in his Ebola chic and launches himself skyward, his legs tucked up, and in mid-air he bowls overarm to Cas. He lets fly like an arrow, the ball hits the wicket and a stick comes out of the sand like an exclamation mark and arcs through the air.

The boy is a natural cricketer.

Ralph's mouth drops open, and suddenly he's on his feet, shouting, '*Owzat!!* Well *bowled*, my *son!*' as if we are at Lord's.

Ralph strides across the sand in his shoes and socks . . . and high-fives Joe, who then fist-bumps him.

I am stunned.

'I'll see if I can get you an upgrade to AP,' Meredith calls to me.

'What?' I say, still staring at Ralph and Joe.

'Assistant Producer,' she says. 'Oh, and see you tonight?' she asks, changing the subject.

Tonight is the Beach Blanket Babylon at Basil's Bar. Whatever that is. Ralph and I are dreading having to remortgage Home Farm to buy one round of drinks.

'It should be fun,' says Meredith. 'Oh, and have you heard?' she continues. I stop in my tracks and turn and look at her dark figure, standing by the sea. Mal has vanished, gone off, and it's as if she's revealing this only in his absence.

'Farouche's here. She texted me last night.'

'Farouche?' I ask, and I wonder if I'm going to faint again, like I did when Clare turned up with Joe. I feel dizzy, sick.

Why did she text Meredith first, not me?

'Yeah, Farouche is *on island*,' she repeats. 'She's been at Canouan, or Bequia, or both, but she got bored.'

I manage to get back to my lounger in one piece.

I collapse.

After lying with my eyes closed for several minutes, and when my heartbeat has returned to normal, I have recovered enough to ask, with an edge to my voice, 'What was Clare talking to you about?' I don't raise his reference to Joe as 'my *son*', as he somehow, in the heat of the moment, got away with it.

Ralph doesn't answer. I know there's something up there, but I'm too distracted to get to the bottom of it, and not sure I care right now.

'Actually, Clare was wondering if, next year, I could take Joe on one of my fishing trips, just for the day, on the Test, practise his casting, say,' says Ralph. 'Apparently, he's keen. I could . . . even . . . see if Keith might organize something here . . . take all of them . . .'

This is smart of Clare, I have to give her that. Cricket is very on-brand with Ralph. But it's not part of the deal. Ralph is *not* Joe's father. That honour, privilege and responsibility falls to Gideon.

'Oh. And where's Mirabel?' I ask, even though all I can think is – where the fuck is Farouche?

How can I get to see her? Without anyone else from our garden, or my family, preferably, present?

'Our daughter has gone off with that prick with the stubble – Julien, Fox's father. On the back of a motorbike, I'm afraid. They're meeting someone with a silly name at the jetty. Some artist. Apparently, she's his wife.' He sighs. I allow a silence to fall.

'Well, you must be in heaven,' Ralph says, before resuming battle with the latest Max Hastings.

'Isn't that the Blackers you were talking to? Well done, darling.' He smiles, as if happy for me, and stretches over and taps my calf. 'You've travelled 5,000 miles to spend time with exactly the same people you see every day back home.'

Clare

Mustique

It's 10 p.m., still sultry and warm, and we're alone. It's like a miracle.

I've popped Ralph on a sofa out on the terrace, and I've come into the open-plan sitting room and am fiddling with the remote of the wireless sound system, wondering whether to turn the Love Songs of Frank Sinatra up, or down.

Down.

I stand in the living room and watch him for a second, feeling like a stalker, as he sips his drink then places it on one of the boxy rattan side tables to his left. I hope he doesn't glance at his watch. Or check his phone – worse – which he dropped into the back pocket of his chinos earlier. Good. He does neither.

I take this as a green light and carry my own drink towards him on the sofa, and have to decide – his sofa, or the one at right angles to it?

The terrace looks out over the sea and has three low couches in an E shape – missing the middle bit – so that you can sprawl and watch the sun go down and lie there gawping at the Caribbean nights and feeling insignificant and also, somehow, deeply lucky to be there at the same time, which is the whole point of stargazing in the tropics.

In a snap decision, I plump down next to him, but I have to place my drink on the same side, which means I have to lean across him. My hair brushes his face as I clink it down on the glass top.

Then I sort of snuggle back beside him. Tuck my bare feet under myself. Sigh.

'So, Clare,' he says, and I get that feeling I always get with him, that when I'm with him, there's no one else.

'So, Ralph,' I say. 'I have to say I'm glad all the others have buggered off to the movie, as I didn't think I'd get a chance to . . .' I pause, with meaning '. . . see you properly this half-term.'

He looks nervous.

'Did you think about what I said during our lunch?' Light voice.

I am keeping my eye on the bright, blipping progress of a satellite traversing the horizon. The moonlight glimmers in concentric yellow streaks on the sea. I want Ralph to confirm he knows that it's time for Joe to have a sibling – provided by him – and there are two ways of approaching this.

One, we can have sex, as of tonight (my preferred option). Two, I can ask him to release the sperm held by Wigmore Clinic (presuming it's still viable, and presuming I need Ralph's signed permission to use it).

Suddenly, in the silence, it feels very quiet on the terrace. We can hear the cheeping of cicadas. The sweet clatter of steel drums on a distant beach. I wonder if he's going to answer. A new track comes on the system. A dog barks. Stops. Then barks again.

After all, I did mention the sibling for Joe, when he was ordering the baked jam roll at Sweetings. He said he couldn't think of anything nicer.

'Clare,' he sighs. And shifts on the sofa.

The next track starts playing, and I can't help myself.

"'I know I stand in line until you think you have the time/ To spend an evening with me,'" I sing in a soft voice, as if to myself.

I used to be in the choir at Wycombe Abbey.

And, suddenly, Ralph is singing along, too, chiming with me, and the atmosphere eases, and he even turns to look at me as we sing the last line, like Grace Kelly and Frank Sinatra, and it makes me think, when did a man last look at me, *really* look at me?

We are looking at each other, and he knows I am waiting for an answer.

So here we are. Sinatra on the SONOS. Cicadas cheeping. Starry tropical night. My three-stage plan is progressing.

Stage 1: Get Ralph to come to Mustique.
Stage 2: Get Ralph to reveal the secret of Joe's paternity on the island, this week, to his four kids, with Mimi, and blend Joe in.
Stage 3: Get Ralph to sign on the dotted line when it comes to delivering Joe's sibling.

I take Ralph's hand. I keep on doing this, I know, and he lets me this time, as if he's used to it now.

'What about it?' I ask. 'Hugh Grant's got three children by two different mothers . . .' I say, wanting to reassure him that what he did before isn't that unusual now, so why not again? 'And they all seem very happy.'

I get the sense that I have dropped exactly the wrong name.

'Hugh *Grant*?' he says with a start. 'You put me in the same category as Hugh Grant, then?'

The thing is, Ralph is exactly the sort of man one senses Hugh Grant would love to be.

He sort of moves away from me on the sofa, and I think: I've lost him.

'By the way, where is everyone?' He is trying, I think, not to sound too anxious. 'How long will they be at the screening?'

At his question – he knows where everyone is as well as I do; he is clearly panicking – I can feel my chance, the moment, slipping away.

'They're at Basil's. Meredith, Mal, your lot and I think the Dunbars are all at the screening at the Dunbars'.' I sip my drink and feel the raw cane rum scorch my throat. It helps. 'It's *Wolf of Wall Street*. They'll be gone for ages,' I conclude, hoping this doesn't sound too threatening, as if I am going to kidnap him and take him hostage in a well-equipped Fritzl-style cellar until he plays ball.

'So, what do we make of Farouche?' I say. It's time to bring her into the frame. I know that Ralph doesn't do gossip, but I can't think what else to say, and it's important that he knows about those two, as it could help him make up his mind, when it comes to us, to my scheme.

'You know she and Mimi are . . . really quite good friends?' I say this with meaning.

Ralph glances up, looking puzzled. I realize: he must be the last person in London to spot that all Mimi can talk and think about is Farouche. And also – he doesn't talk about other people, like the rest of us do. He doesn't regard it as proper conversation, which is a crunchy discussion about the life of an idea like liberalism, or which rivers in Scotland are finest for salmon in August, or whether the Tories should challenge the UKIP threat by being more, or less, like the Whigs of yore.

As a result, he has absolutely no clue as to what is really going on, poor lamb, in plain sight and under his nose.

Farouche. She'd tipped up at Basil's wearing a completely see-through white cheesecloth garment that wasn't so much a dress as two transparent triangles of sheer fabric stitched together.

Mimi was at the bar, with Mirabel and Julien, and Ralph, who was reading *The Times* on his iPad.

Farouche strolled in, barefoot, and the sun was behind her, so you could just see the outline of her body through the fabric, silhouetted.

She came right up to the bar, took off her hat and stood right in front of Mimi.

Mimi's gaze dropped and the guy behind the bar gave a low whistle. Then he put 'My Baby Shot Me Down', on the iPod and blasted it round the bar.

Farouche stood there, and her silver bracelets jangled on her lean brown arms. She had long, dark bed-hair, and tangled, bushy eyebrows but the clearest, brownest skin. Her finger- and toenails were perfectly manicured bright turquoise.

There were Jagger girls in there, and Delevingnes, taking selfies with their smartphones, and there was Mirabel in her denim hotpants, but all eyes were on Farouche.

'Of all the gin-joints in all the world,' said Mimi, pink in the face.

She didn't introduce Farouche to Ralph, to Mirabel, as if she wanted to keep her to herself.

'Julien didn't say you were coming to Basil's.'

'That's because I didn't tell him,' said Farouche.

She tilted her face to the sun and so she caught the last rays, bathing in it, and closed her eyes. Everyone in the bar, meanwhile, gazed at her, which was the desired effect.

'We have to catch the sunset,' she said. She clicked her fingers. The barman handed her a glass of punch, in Sky Ray lolly colours that matched the sky, and then she clicked her fingers again and the barman placed a lit Marlboro in her lips. She spun around and marched out of the bar.

Everyone watched as Mimi trotted after her like a pet lamb.

So Mimi and Farouche went one way, then Mirabel said she was 'going back', and then I said I had to put Joe to bed and wasn't going to make movie night at the Dunbars', after all, and I was praying that Ralph would feel he was at enough of a loose end to want to spend some time with me.

'I don't want to be around that houri,' he said. 'And I definitely don't want to watch a movie with the Barmy Burmese Beauty and her surrendered husband and Oksana talking in Russian on her mobile about some house she's buying and which needs decorating all the way through it.'

So he's here: he's mine for the duration.

'Clare. I know what you want but, in case you haven't noticed, darling, I am not, and never will be, Hugh Grant,' says Ralph, and he turns to me and gives me one of his blinding blue stares. 'I never will be a repulsive sperm-sprayer.'

I think we are both drunk.

That sounds like a no, but all I can think is: we are almost in each other's arms already. I am in a green dress and my skin is going brown, and my hair is streaked with gold. It has taken several weeks of female admin and many, many thousands of pounds (I am counting in air fares and the cost of renting the villa for the week) to bring me to this presentational peak.

And he called me 'darling'.

Plus, the 'fruit punch' back at Basil's was actually a lethal concoction of coconut, lime, mandarin and a rum so strong the barman called it 'moonshine' and winked as I handed Ralph his first tumbler, which he downed like a pint of Pimm's after three sets of tennis on a summer afternoon.

But I can feel it: he is relaxing into it. It's the heat. The drink . . . and the wealth. And I know what to do next. I've thought about it, and now I'm going to do it.

I scoot off the sofa, race to the sound system, turn it right down, then dog-leg back to the drinks table, clink ice into two tumblers and make us two more lethal cocktails. As I pour the rum into Ralph's, I suddenly think that now I see the point of Rohypnol – but I feel ashamed that I have come to this.

'You know what I want, Ralph, darling,' I say in what I hope is a husky voice. 'You and Mimi can have your old family house back, if you like, if that will swing it, I mean. For what I paid last time. Like for like. It's a fantastic deal, given how it's appreciated.'

'Don't be ridiculous, Clare,' says Ralph. 'I've never heard anything so ridiculous.' But he doesn't look insulted.

Then I think, What the hell, now or never. So I kiss him, sort of around the ear. Ralph doesn't respond, but nor does he push me away.

I am pulling him towards me, pretending to be drunker, looser, more out of control than I ever am.

I stand up, leaving my sandals on the deck, as if in erotic abandon. Ralph stands, too. I hear his mobile beep in his back pocket, as if someone has left a voicemail, but he doesn't appear to hear it.

'Do you want to see Joe asleep?' I ask. He can't say no to that.

'I suppose,' he says slowly. 'Quickly. But Clare. Then I really must go.'

I take Ralph's hand – I'm worried he will bolt if I don't – and lead him – well, drag him like a dog on his way to a hated bath – through the French windows and into the sitting room of the villa, which has low lighting, ceiling fans whirring, white painted floorboards, white sofas and splashy pictures of tropical blooms and a very relaxed, funky beach-house vibe.

As we go into the passage beyond the sitting room of the

spreading bungalow I push Joe's bedroom door closed, without checking to see if he's asleep. But I know he will be. Joe sleeps like a Labrador after a hearty walk, in a sort of collapsed heap, occasionally twitching.

Then I open the door to my bedroom instead, and pull Ralph in.

Mimi

London

'This is, I assure you, quite categorically, a terrible misunderstanding,' says Ralph. I glare at him. He stares back, and then we both turn to Mrs Hawtin. I know she wants us to call her Felicity, but we're finding it hard. We're finding everything hard.

Felicity Hawtin regards us neutrally, as if to say, Don't look at me, you two. I am not here to judge, but to listen.

Ralph twists in his chair, away from me.

'Sorry,' I say, though I'm not sure what I'm sorry for. 'But it's not, is it?'

I heard the whole conversation with Clare when he butt-called me in error in Mustique. All about giving Clare a bloody baby and her, in return, bribing us by giving – or should I say selling? – our old house back to us, as if I'll give up my life again and my pride and my husband, all to live in a proper house rather than a measly maisonette on a sodding Notting Hill communal garden.

My eyes travel over the top of Ralph's head to Mrs Hawtin's bookshelves, as if searching for answers.

Mrs Hawtin is a small woman in a battleship-grey dress, tan tights and clumpy shoes. When we entered the lobby after that sticky moment with Marguerite on the doorstep, she stood smiling at the top of the stairs. Waiting for us.

Seconds before, we'd been trying to work out where Harley Street 123a was. ('The numbering is complicated,' Mrs Hawtin had warned in her text.)

There was no one else around in the November damp and drizzle of medical London, apart from Polish builders and cabs cruising down a wet Harley Street, and then Marguerite Molton, of all people, emerged from number 125.

We'd greeted each other as if it was quite normal for all of us to be there together in Harley Street on a Wednesday morning, seeing various expensive private consultants about various confidential matters.

Then Marguerite had aimed one of those meaningful woman-to-woman glances at me, before hailing a cab.

So now the whole of Lonsdale Gardens, the Stop the Digs Collective and therefore the whole of West London already knows we are in therapy, en route to 'conscious uncoupling' or, in plain English, divorce.

And this is, in theory, mainly bad news for me.

This means, according to all my female friends, that Ralph will be in play, listed on the grey market of men who aren't MBA, who aren't even divorced yet but whom women speculators will come to view off-plan, like a property that hasn't even been built yet. He'll go to sealed bids without even being aware that he's being surveyed. As for me, I will join the ranks of Notting Hill divorcees (NHDs).

After this, we filed on in and up and, in a cosy, practised way, used to dealing with couples on the verge, Mrs Hawtin soon had us sitting in a tight equilateral configuration in her rented office on the first floor.

Our six knees are all pointing towards the low pine table that divides us from her, upon which sit three tumblers, a flask of cloudy tap water, a large bowl of pot pourri and a box of jumbo Kleenex impregnated with soothing aloe vera.

There are two pine bookcases on either side of the boarded-up fireplace and, above the mantelpiece, a framed oil of a single tree, painted in hopeful and spreading leaf.

On the mantelpiece stands a pair of two-foot-high wooden sculptures representing nurturing motherhood – female figures entwined with babies, both with round, chiselled wood balls representing their heads, and round chiselled wood balls in their mid-sections representing foetuses – against which Mrs Hawtin has propped a photograph of three children, presumably hers, at an appetizing age.

The blinds are down, scaffolding up. There are builders hanging off it, moving about the structure in their scuffed, tan work boots and paint-stained hoodies, talking cheerily, in Slavic.

'Well, shall we talk about the misunderstanding Ralph mentions now, or would you prefer to talk about your relationship?' says Mrs Hawtin.

Ralph and I glance at each other.

'But we don't have a relationship,' he protests. 'Not as such. We're *married*.'

He clears his throat. Mrs Hawtin looks expectant, as if what he has just said doesn't count, but he does have a point.

'We went to Mustique by mistake,' says Ralph. 'Where there was another misunderstanding. Mimi thinks I went to bed with the woman who I had a child with about eight years ago, at her request. I didn't.'

Now it's my turn to blink.

'Steady on,' I hiss. 'It was – or was supposed to be, in theory, an almost total freebie – that *you* agreed to, a *family* holiday, during which you shagged Clare, again,' I say. 'Did you shag Clare without meaning to on this accidental holiday that just happened to you on the island of Mistake?'

Ralph pauses before answering, as if waiting for his brief to leap to his feet and ask the judge to disallow the question.

'Mimi, I couldn't shag her *again*, as I never shagged her in the first place,' says Ralph, looking at me with his sorrowing default expression of infinite patience, the one he assumes when he thinks a woman is displaying excessive emotional lability.

'Mrs Hawtin. You know the ways of the world. You've seen it all.' Ralph is appealing to the therapist now. 'Do you think that Kingsley Amis did have a slight point when he said "All women are mad"?'

'But Ralph, I heard the conversation with Clare,' I say, raising my voice over Mrs Hawtin, who is telling Ralph that his last contribution wasn't helpful. 'I know you did. I heard what Clare said, and you went off to her villa. Did the dirty deed. So I've got the smoking gun.'

Ralph shakes his head, murmurs, 'As ever, you're wrong, darling,' and says the whole holiday was a mistake again, and that it was all my fault, and if he'd had 'his druthers' (one of his favourite phrases – Mrs Hawtin looks blank) we'd have never gone, and far from being 'free', it was the most expensive holiday we'd ever had.

'Please,' says Mrs Hawtin. 'We're going round in circles. Shall we go back to the beginning? Ralph, you say you went to Mustique by mistake. I see. Right. And something happened there. And now you are here, to determine if you are going to stay together or, perhaps, have a period of time apart. And separate.'

I study my nails. I must get them done, I think, at the same time as I absorb her words. So is this where we are? Facing a choice of splitting up or moving forward as co-parents – or however one puts it – or staying together?

All the options seem unremittingly grim. Bleak.

And I can't help thinking: if we split, where does Farouche fit in?

Farouche. Her name in my head makes me feel breathless, anxious, tight-chested and almost sick. It's as if I'm taking some mind-bending drug. I can't be expected to make life-or-death decisions.

Ralph and Mrs Hawtin are staring at me.

'Are you all right?' Mrs Hawtin asks.

I nod again. This is what I want to say out loud, but can't: *I'm either 1. late-onset lesbian, 2. having a massive mid-life crisis or 3. going through The Change.* This would make it all about me. After all, I am here to share at the cost of £170 an hour, which works out at almost three pounds a minute of my husband's money.

But I can't say any of that. I can hear Ralph's answer in my head:

There's no need to talk in bullet points, darling. I haven't noticed anything different. Can't you just leave lesbianism to the real lesbians? Are you sure you haven't just been listening to Woman's Hour *too long?*

'OK, before we go on, I just need to ask: have you done this before?' Mrs Hawtin asks. 'With another couples counsellor, marital, or sex therapist?'

'Certainly not,' says Ralph firmly, as if the mere suggestion was a slight on his manhood.

'Yes, we did!' I say. 'We went to see Sarah Pollen!'

We went to Sarah Pollen several times, in fact. Maybe three. I remember thinking that marital therapy most resembled my many attempts to go to Brent Cross Shopping Centre when the children were tiny. And, every time I tried, the same thing happened.

I would set off, with hope in my heart. I would manage to find the North Circular. I would see those grim signs on the Finchley Road, just saying 'The North', but I could never find the right turning off the A406 and would always end up circling East Finchley and looping back on the ring road, zooming over the flyover in the wrong direction, in tears on Hendon

Way, before giving up and turning the car back towards West London.

My marriage, it seemed to me, like most long marriages maybe, was trying to get to a shopping centre in North London but never finding IKEA, but never, ever, losing confidence that, one day, I might – even though, so far, despite many attempts, I'd never once returned to base with a flat-pack Fjälkinge shelving unit with drawers in the boot of the car.

My marriage was the Brent Cross I had to bear.

'Oh my God,' says Ralph. 'You're quite right.' He speaks normally, as if remembering that he did pay the newspaper bill after all. 'I take it back. I stand corrected. Yes, Sarah Pollen, we did.' I think both of us then remember the painful sessions at Relate in Godminster, in a room above the Quaker Meeting House, when I was bulging with Lucian, after I hadn't had the termination Ralph had asked for.

'OK, now, Mimi, Ralph,' Mrs Hawtin says, 'before we move on, before I ask what you'd like to unpack on this journey, and why you're here, and what you'd like to achieve from our sessions, I'd like to start by asking you both to sit still and to listen to your breath.'

Silence falls, and the Polish radio seems loud in the room.

'Be aware of your breath, and align yourselves with the here and now.'

We both sit still. Ralph loathes this sort of thing.

Even I recoil from anything that involves any journey, to find myself, somewhere on life's path.

'Draw air into your nostrils,' she says, 'and expel it through your mouth.' She pants, like a midwife showing Mum how to pant when she wants to push in the final stage of labour.

'I'd like you to think of it like this. In this room,' Felicity Hawtin explains, as we pant together, 'there is me, and there are you both. I would like you to think of the space between you both as a separate entity. I would like you to think of the space as a *sacred space*. And to think that your relationship is a living thing that exists in the space between you.'

Ralph and I glance at each other, and his lips twitch with amusement.

'So bring your full and authentic presence,' she commands us, 'to the world of the other. And now, please, I'd like you both to cross the bridge to each other.'

We don't know what this means.

'Pull your chairs closer together so we are facing each other,' she commands, so we shuffle our chairs so our knees are touching. 'Closer!' she orders.

'Take each other's hands,' she says.

We do so.

I feel his dear, familiar, warm hands in mine and my eyes start brimming. Something strange is happening.

The back of my neck is prickling, and our hands – well, it's as if mine are plugs, connected into the live socket of Ralph.

'Now look into each other's eyes,' she goes on.

I do so for a bit, but I can't help looking over Ralph's head again; it feels so intense, too intense, and I see titles like 'How to Move On after an Affair', and 'Should I Stay or Should I Go?' and 'The Relationship Rescue Workbook', which doesn't help.

How can I ever explain the shaming truth, which is that I mind far more about Farouche, right now, than I do about my husband of twenty years shagging Clare or not shagging Clare and there no longer being an 'us' and, as a result, him being predated by one – or many – of the raptor divorcees of Notting Hill?

And I've known her for all of six months. As for that supposed 'smoking gun' conversation with Clare I overheard that I've gone on about, I used it as a get-out-of-jail-free card. I decided it granted me licence to *betray him back*.

I needed him to be the guilty party, as it *gave me cover*.

And then, I can't help it. I can't help thinking of that first time, the first proper time, with Farouche, at the villa in Mustique, while everyone was at the *Wolf of Wall Street* screening, and when Ralph had disappeared with Clare.

The upstairs bedroom. Shutters open. We are lying on a big, white bed, there's mosquito netting, but Farouche has hoicked it over the top. She is brown and taut. She is naked, apart from sweat and a liberal spritz of the scent that makes my head spin and my stomach flip –

'I only ever wear Frisson in bed,' she says, her hands trailing over my doughy body as if shaping a pot of rough clay and trying to make something beautiful out of me to offer to a stranger in the night.

I just grab her in response, and I lick and kiss and caress her silky brown skin . . . as if she's been lightly sprayed with some glaze . . . her hard nipples are the colour of mulberries.

I am fearless – I surprise myself, even – as I dive into that extraordinary, mysterious bush and track my way through it to the pink, wet heart of her darkness with my fingers, lips and tongue, and OK, yes, I'd had too much tropical punch at Basil's and I was disinhibited, but also, I was more alive than I'd ever been . . . and so I did.

I did things that I could never, in a million years, imagine I would ever do to another woman . . . and brought Farouche off, and then held her hands back above her head, and did it again, and again, four times in a row, and so far from being ashamed, or guilty, I felt so proud and pleased I wanted to jog around the whole island doing a victory lap, perhaps holding a Team GB flag aloft.

Never have I been so grateful that, for once, a movie was at least an hour too long, and I remember I lay there and closed my eyes, inhaling the scent of dried sweat and Frisson on her sun-baked skin until it was my turn to moan and clutch the white sheets, and tug her hair, and when I opened them, feeling proud and floaty and ready to go again, Farouche touched me as if I was the only woman in the world and these were her last moments on earth.

Something swims into focus during my reverie.

For the first time, I remember.

When I opened my eyes, they'd focused on the little white camera in the corner of the room. Its lens was pointed at the bed.

'Oh,' I say.

I don't realize for a moment that I've said this out loud, and I am back in Harley Street, in mid-couples counselling, on a wet Wednesday morning.

'Mimi?' asks Mrs Hawtin. 'Come into presence, please. Or is there something you want to share?'

My mind is turning over this fact, and I decide it's fine.

Rich people always have CCTV cameras everywhere, they're paranoid – but no one ever watches the film. So it's pointless.

Both Ralph and Mrs Hawtin are staring at me.

'Please, Mimi, cross the bridge,' she repeats.

Then she starts saying that grown-ups are persons with a big body and a little child inside, as I begin to question if my attraction to Farouche is real, whether it's hormonal – something to do with testosterone kicking in in your forties? – and as I'm thinking should I get my bloods done, Mrs Hawtin is saying that marriage is the space in which two grown-ups can help each other become adult. She is saying that Ralph and I could make each other complete, if only we could connect.

It all sounds very familiar but, it has to be said, sensible. Of course, put like that, it *is* much more fruitful, and rewarding, to have a connected, intimate relationship than a strained and distant one.

Fair enough. But easier said than done.

'We have thirty minutes remaining,' she says. 'So let's establish what you both want to achieve.

'Ralph?' says Mrs Hawtin, cocking her head to one side like a sparrow. She fingers her pendant, a large silver ring on a leather thong.

By mistake she pronounces it 'Ralph' as opposed to 'Rafe'.

Ralph winces.

'Well. Since you ask. And I can't speak for Mimi,' he says. 'I did make a big mistake, once. With Clare. But I would never make that same mistake again. So this – is a misunderstanding. I'd never do anything to break up the family. Mimi, my wife, has picked up the wrong end of the stick. And so, I fear, did Clare. At one point, I remember saying yes to baked jam roll, but never to giving her . . .'

I gasp.

'Jesus, Ralph,' I say. 'Have you taken leave of your *senses*? What the fuck have nursery puddings got to do with this?' I hiss, followed by 'Sorry.' I subside.

'I find confrontational or accusatory language to be unhelpful in these sessions,' says Mrs Hawtin. 'Ralph, don't look and speak to me, speak to Mimi.'

Ralph looks at me.

'Do you really think I would go off behind your back and go to her villa, while my whole family are on the island, for a family holiday, and have sex with her, while Joe is in the house?' he says. His blue eyes bore into me. 'If so, you need help.'

'But he *did* – he did do it, before,' I say to Mrs Hawtin.

She says, 'To Ralph, please. Remember the sacred space.'

'You *did* – you did it before,' I say to Ralph. 'You had a baby without asking me. With Clare. Even if it didn't involve sex, which is the story you're sticking to. Plus, you sold the house, to her. Not acknowledging that the children – our children,' I say, hotting up, feeling choked, 'and our house were the sacred space, the sacred thing, the only thing, we shared that no one else had, that was unique to me and to you, that made us, that made the family, and yet' – I turn back to Mrs Hawtin, wanting her on my side – 'and yet he allowed this woman, Clare, to sabotage both, our family *and* our home.'

'Still to Ralph, please,' she says, without reaction.

'So you did once,' I say, with a break in my voice. 'Mirabel, Cas, Posy, then Lucian, and of course Calypso – were *ours*,' I say. 'The precious, private things we created equally, that we shared and loved equally, together, the four beings on this planet that meant the same to each of us, that bonded and yoked us together whatever our feelings for each other . . .'

Ralph is nodding.

I grind to a halt and swipe a Kleenex. The way I put it, it's surprising we're together at all. I thought I was over it. The betrayal. But I'm not. I am almost waiting for the shrink to give Ralph what for.

'Now, Ralph, tell Mimi what you have heard her say and repeat it back to her,' says Mrs Hawtin.

And he does. Word for word. Then he grasps my hands and gazes at me and, as the tears roll down both our cheeks, he says, 'You've never forgiven me for Joe. I accept that. I should never have done it. But you have to believe me that nothing happened with me and Clare. It never has, and it never will.'

Mrs Hawtin is looking at Ralph with what seems like admiration. 'Clare doesn't mean anything to me. I'm sorry about Joe, but we are where we are. And he's turning out all right, isn't he? The makings of a decent off-spin bowler. Do you really want to split up over spilt milk, over Joe?'

How can I explain that it's not Joe, or even Clare, but that I am about to run away with Farouche, that my heart is elsewhere and I'm not sure that I can do it any more. I know that any marriage, however happy or unhappy, is more interesting than any affair, however passionate, da da da, but it doesn't feel like that now.

I know Ralph is a tremendous sticker, and I'm no bolter either – love the one you're with, and so on, but what if it's as simple, or as complicated as this? What if the other person, the one you're with, suddenly and fatally doesn't smell right and *someone else does*?

But I can't say it. I shut my mouth. Sex. The subject that everyone – man, woman, married, unmarried, single, coupled, young, old, parent, child – always lies about. The single line no poet ever wrote is, 'Tell me the truth about sex.' As nobody ever does.

'Let me summarize, then,' says Mrs Hawtin.

She looks down at her notes. And then she repeats all our words back to us. I could do this, I think. Get couples in. Make notes of what they say, listen, then tell them what they've said. Charge £170 an hour – yes, cash is fine. Job done.

'Ralph' – correct this time – 'you want to work on your marriage, and salvage it, despite' – she looks down at the notes again – 'the fact that you have what amounts to a second family. And that family lives in your old house, the former marital home in Notting Hill.'

'Hold your horses,' says Ralph, without heat. This was classic Ralph. If one of his oldest friends suggests he'd chosen the wrong fly during a day's trout fishing on the Test, he wouldn't speak to anyone for days. But now a marital therapist has accused him of selling out his ancestral home for commercial gain and having what amounts to a secret second family on the side, he can only muster a tone of mild reproof. 'That is a complete misrepresentation of the facts. I told you the facts earlier. It wasn't an affair, with Clare. It wasn't emotional. It was clinical. Actually involving a clinic, as it happens. It was a sort of financial transaction.'

'Indeed, yes, you told me the facts as you see them, but I am telling *you* the facts as I hear them,' she says. 'This is the emotional *takeaway* so far, of today,' Mrs Hawtin summarizes. 'And neither are you, Mimi, admitting that you, too, are not entirely without fault.' I nod. Fair play. I'd had an affair. A year or so before Lucian was born.

I look at my husband of almost twenty years.

I don't know what to feel, or to think. Whoever said – maybe it was my mother, maybe I read it – that big decisions take themselves was a big fat liar.

It's so easy getting together. And yet so hard breaking up. Nobody tells you that splitting up can take years. And that getting divorced, or separated, is yet another thing you can never agree on, let alone meet each other halfway on, and when you do contemplate it, all you can see is loss, the loss of everything you've made and done and said together and, above all, you lose the jokes.

OK, agreed, Ralph never wants to *go out*. Or see people. If we ever do go out, he wants to know in advance, 1. who will be there and 2. whether the fayre will comprise canapés, 'substantial nibbles' or a sit-down dinner and 3. when will we be able to leave.

'So . . .?' presses Mrs Hawtin. 'I have to draw it to a close, as time's up. I think, and do correct me if I'm wrong, but you two have come to decide something. Whether to work on your marriage, or whether to part.'

Then she comes up with some good lines, which she trots out as if for the first time:

'The truth about love and marriage is that you have to live with the choices you make.'

Then she says, 'Marriage is a longitudinal study establishing how much a couple can tolerate for how long.'

'And how much therapy they can afford,' adds Ralph.

'Ah, but marital therapy is an exercise in working out how much each of you is prepared to put up with,' she replies, as if this exercise alone was a reason to carry on doing it.

We both give hollow laughs at this.

My mobile vibrates. It's at the bottom of the hessian sack. It vibrates, then stops. Then, a minute later, it vibrates, then stops.

I can't help nudging the bag with my foot so I can see the screen.

Snapchats (2) and a text.

'Mimi?' says Mrs Hawtin.

'I thought I asked you to switch off all mobile devices at the start of the session. I asked you to be present, in every sense.'

'Sorry,' I lie.

I pretend to be switching off my phone but in fact I am opening the Snapchat and pressing down the button to view the images.

I am leaning into my bag, peering at the screen.

Ralph clears his throat.

'I was wondering, darling, whether there's anything else you'd like to bring up, as we're here?' He says this in the neutral voice of someone saying, 'As you're up,' when you're all having supper, 'could you bring the mustard from the larder?'

My phone, set to vibrate, buzzes again. 'Like what?' I ask.

The first Snapchat is from Farouche. It must be a mistake. Why has she sent this to me?

The selfie is composed of Farouche and Meredith Blacker, both making that gurning selfie-grin to camera.

The Snapchat time is set to ten seconds, but I only have to look at it for a couple to go cold, and quiet.

What's she doing with Meredith?

I drop the phone into my bag as if it were a live grenade.

'I have to go, sorry,' I say. 'I've had a text . . . the children.'

I can't believe I am using the children as an excuse to rush off to The Cowshed, where Farouche is having a pedicure, but I am.

'Ralph – can you sort out Mrs Hawtin?'

I run downstairs and take out my phone again in front of some Polish builders eating bacon butties from the Italian café on the corner.

The first Snapchat isn't there.

The second Snapchat has been set to only five seconds but again it takes only two to work out, to my joy, that Farouche has sent me a selfie of her bush.

Then I look at the text:

'You guys OK? Just checking. I'm here. So. xx'

It is from Marguerite Molton. She sounds concerned, but I know her game. She's checking to see whether she can officially list Ralph as a male who's not actually divorced but who could be liberated from his wife and repurposed elsewhere.

I know it's officially impossible for women of my age to find another man – you are more likely to be killed by lightning – but I don't want another man. I want Farouche, and it makes me scared.

If behind every fear is a wish, then I'm pretty sure that behind every wish there's a fear, too.

And mine is that I'm going to lose them both.

Ralph, and Farouche.

Clare

Lonsdale Gardens

I leave Aida with Joe, having made sure he's practised his instruments. The child is sitting in front of a fly-fishing DVD in the playroom, with a naughty treat – some unsalted popcorn from the boutique in Blenheim. When the popcorn shop first appeared on the other side of the Travel Bookshop, we all hoped that POP would be a pop-up popcorn shop, but it's stayed up. Unlike books, popcorn is a thing.

As I walk down Hornton Street, I realize how big this is. The Stop the Digs Rally.

As expected, the whole of Ponsonby Prep is here, and there are also several market traders, angry about the council's planned sell-off of the mews where they keep their barrows. I can see Mirabel's tall boyfriend, Sid, in a denim jacket, a head taller than most of the blonde blow-dries.

Trish is waving a sign saying 'We don't dig the DIGS,' and has even donned a student-protesty navy pea-coat for the occasion. Sally Avery is in a short red trench that could be Isabel Marant but could also be a Boden knock-off. It's so hard to tell high street from high fashion.

But, best of all, Sally has mounted the Solidarity Quilt – three yards wide, two high, with the letters 'S T D' picked out large in appliqué over the myriad squares sewn with beads, feathers and crystals – on to two poles. Marguerite is holding it aloft, along with two of her sons.

'What do we want?' shrieks Trish.

'To *stop the digs!*' the crowd squeals raggedly, a medley of soprano children and women's voices, and deeper Cockney tones from the costermongers.

The Ponsonby contingent hold their sippy cups from Ottolenghi and Starbucks or their electric cigarettes in one hand and their signs in another, the laminated ones the school got all the kids to make up in the art room.

As well as the film crew, who look bored, as if they'd far prefer to be in the Ukraine or Gaza, there's a smattering of the photographers who daily pap the celebrity parents and the supermodel mummies.

Filming the scene is a tall man with hipster facial hair and high-top red basketball boots and a zipped hoodie, a skinny girl in Uggs holding a boom mike, and oh. Here we go.

Here comes Meredith Blacker, in House of Cards tight grey body con.

The crowd parts like the Red Sea and she takes up a position in the middle of the waving signs to record her piece to camera.

Nervelessly, she delivers her link into the shiny, dark circle of a film camera, the red light as unblinking as her deep, dark eyes.

'Tonight, the stage is set for an almighty clash as local takes on international. Residential takes on offshore. Rate-payers challenge planning experts,' says Meredith in a special newsmaker voice, looking tough but toothsome at the same time.

The crowd quietens, eager to hear her expert analysis on the monster spat that has engulfed Notting Hill.

'In just a few minutes, these people are going to attend a meeting to hear arguments in what is seen as a test case on many levels: will the Tory council follow big money again and grant permission for yet another iceberg house in a crowded, built-up, conservation area? Or will it hearken to local pleas that such a massive private development should never be allowed to disrupt two public amenities, a school and a community centre, not to mention cause the closure of a public highway?

'Everyone here's up in arms. But are the residents of Notting Hill protesting too much?'

She pauses. The director in the hoodie gives a thumbs-up, and then makes a keep-camera-rolling sign. With a swish to her right, Meredith wheels about and, suddenly, Trish is at her side, as if by pre-arrangement.

'With me now is Trish Dodd Noble, who, together with Sally Avery' – and there's Sally, alongside Trish – 'founded the Stop the Digs coalition. So –' She turns to Trish first, with professional crispness. 'Trish Dodd Noble. Not to put too fine a point on it, you're married to a banker. What right do you have to complain?'

Everyone knows this is a low blow, and I hear the sucking sound of breath intaken around me. Where is Meredith Blacker going with this? She lives here. She's a neighbour. Is she one of us – I mean, at least a quarter of the borough works in finance – or is she here as a journalist? But we are also thinking, Good for old Meredith. Killer question.

Trish takes a deep breath and looks into the lens.

'Look. He's a hedge funder, as it happens. And we all accept that development has brought wealth and prosperity to the property owners of the borough. We all support building works, within reason,' she says.

This is good. She sounds reasonable, not like a whingeing NIMBY.

'But the planning regulations were never framed to cope with huge subterranean bunkers plunging three storeys down into the subsoil towards the earth's crust underneath a capital city!' she cries, as people start whistling, and shouting, 'Yeah!' as if we are at a happy-clappy evangelical service.

We all start chanting. I take out my phone and send an email as I join in the chant.

'*Stop the digs!*'

'*Stop the digs!*'

'We are now excavating on a scale not seen since Victorian times,' Trish continues. 'But these are not sewers or train tunnels created by industry for the public good. No!' She gathers steam. The scruffy director in red basketball boots says within earshot, 'Keep this running. This banker wife's cooking with gas now.'

'These are private, underground *palaces* for the super-rich! It's a land-grab by the billionaires at the expense of ordinary folks –'

She continues, and then, suddenly, I feel it, we all feel it: a surge, a rush of feeling, and a sense of being – yes – a part of something bigger than ourselves, our own lives, something *important*. In the face of such utter selfishness, the mutinous crowd is united in spirit, if only for a few seconds.

Market traders, yummy mummies, tired children in navy corduroy pinafores or shorts waving balloons in the colours of Ponsonby, silver and scarlet; elderly widows with tiny ankles wearing those Ferragamo pumps with square heels, their hair like marmalade candyfloss; even passing Japanese tourists recording, pointlessly, the event and camera crew on their smartphones – we all, for once, feel the same.

'And so it is *past time*,' Trish continues, and I sense a peroration building, 'that local government put a stop to this racket, and finally, finally, step up to the plate. The council represents our shared common interests, and not just vested ones.'

The crowd cheers.

Meredith has a final question.

'So who is, or are, the applicants?' she asks. It is a rhetorical question, as nobody knows. Trish and Sally shrug.

'Let's see if the anonymous Dirty Digger of Notting Hill is going to face the music!' Meredith broadcasts.

The camera follows Meredith Blacker as she stalks, like Morticia Addams on Hallowe'en night, across Hornton Street. The crowd follows like trick or treaters in her wake, me shuffling along with them.

We can't all go upstairs to the town-hall meeting room, we've been warned in advance: so the mummies with small children go home, job done, and we make a bonfire of placards in a corner.

Most of the upstairs committee room is taken up by a horse-shoe table. The planning officers sit on one side, the councillors on the other, paperwork before each, and at the head of the table sits the chairman, flanked by advisers. There's a projector on the table, near the planning officers, ready to relay plans and photographs of the site to a white screen against one wall.

The chairman – a man, clearly retired, with papery skin, white hair and spectacles – calls the meeting to order. 'We have ten applications to get through tonight . . .' he says in weary tones, as if he's done this many times before and will do it many times again.

The planning officer in charge of the application has already flashed up an image on the screen.

There is another audible intake of breath in the room as we attempt to take in the cross-section of the planned underground edifice. It is so huge that the 9,000 square foot, double-fronted villa above ground looks like a Victorian doll's house perched atop a submerged aircraft carrier. The drawing makes it crystal clear that the iceberg is not just underneath the house. It extends out under most of the street, too.

I check my phone. No reply yet to the email I sent ten minutes ago to the clinic.

'Quiet, please,' says the chairman, in a raised voice. 'Mr Blundell. You know the drill. If you would. We have a lot to get through.'

I gaze at the design for the rear elevation, but I can't see the architect's usual stamp or initials on the drawing. What's obvious to me is that the architect is a copycat.

That's Gideon's design for the garden room: the glass wall, the sliding doors that disappear so it looks as if the room doesn't have a fourth wall – he calls it the stage-set effect. It's a signature feature of his work.

The chairman then opens proceedings to the other officers, who ask all the right questions: what if the digging hits power lines, springs, sewers, causes flooding, causes other houses to disappear into sinkholes, causes damage to properties that were not covered by party-wall agreements, and so on?

Mr Blundell, who looks like an efficient vole in a suit, seems to relish taking each of the questions in turn. He talks of bore-holes and tests and refers frequently to the multiple, highly technical engineering and structural reports specially commissioned by the owners and conducted by the top experts in the field in the bundles of papers put before us.

The nub of the Q&A is this. The removal of a cubic mile of earth from a hill in a conservation area already known for its geological instability and propensity for flooding will be a breeze.

It is then the turn of three pre-selected objectors to outline their opposition in their allotted three minutes, and no more.

Trish Dodd Noble explains that the dig will disrupt the opening of the Giving Back Centre, put schoolchildren at imminent risk of death and possibly also cause structural damage to the school and the centre, as both are on a slight slope. Then the Ladbroke Association speaks, and then someone else I don't know.

'At this point, would applicants like to say anything in support of their application?' says the chairman.

Meredith leaps to her feet. Just in case. The *Newsnight* camera pans the room.

No one rises to their feet, raises their hand, comes to the table.

'Any applicants?' says the chairman. 'Does anyone from' – he glances down – 'er, Alpha Star, the registered applicants, want to speak?'

Silence. We still don't know who Alpha Star are.

'Ah. Well, in that case . . .' He seems relieved that we are not going to have to sit through any more.

The PAC chairman clears his throat. A hush falls.

'I understand the Ladbroke Association's concerns about the possible precedent set by digging a private property under a public highway and a communal garden,' he says.

The room rustles in apprehension.

The chairman appears to be wrestling with his thoughts. He gathers himself.

'But, according to common law, the owners are presumed to own the land underneath up until, anyway, the midpoint of the street, or *ad medium filum viae.*'

Gloom descends instantly. Those of us who have attended many planning-application meetings know to our cost that when the chairman starts quoting Latin, it's all over.

'There is nothing in common law, I would add, about the ownership of communal gardens which are presumed to be collectively owned by the properties that surround it.' The chairman surveys the room again. Clears his throat. 'And now we have much to get through, and it is time to put this to the vote.'

One cameraman zooms in for the money shot on the councillors; the other has raced behind the chairman so he can film the room at the moment of truth.

'Councillors opposed to the triple-basement dig in Ponsonby Terrace, please raise your hands.'

One elderly man in a bow tie raises his hand.

'In favour?'

The chairman and four councillors stick their arms up.

'Shame on you!' comes a brave voice from the back.

'*Quiet, please!*' shouts the chairman. I'm sure I heard a shout of '*Bung!*' from the back.

The chairman shushes the room. A reporter dashes out, phone clamped to his ear, already talking.

Behind me, the head of the Ladbroke Association, Sir Crispin Borwick, is saying audibly, 'It's very simple. The rich always win in the end. If the planning application is rejected, the applicant simply submits appeal after appeal until they get the right verdict, and then the council ends up paying all the costs. The last man standing wins.'

The chairman is wrapping up. 'Subject to the proviso about the alteration to the rear extension, of which I would like to see a resubmitted drawing, then' – he shuffles one stack of papers aside and moves another to under his nose – 'application approved.'

Uproar.

Even though he has just explained why this was a predictable outcome, I hear Trish gasp. Then I hear Donna's voice. She must have sneaked in, as she is right behind me. When I peek over my shoulder, I see her cradling Trish, who has almost collapsed into her lap, and both have assumed a stricken pietà pose for the photographers from the *Evening Standard* and *Kensington News*, not to mention the unblinking lens of the *Newsnight* camera.

'Make sure you get that, won't you?' says Meredith, pointing to the pair, before stalking the room for reactions. 'We can't report anything about bungs, obviously, as it's actionable, and this application has simply been assessed on compliance, not on any other criteria. OK, that's the story. And the owner's no-show.'

I hear Donna say, 'Don't worry, darling. The Feel Your Forefathers' Pain workshop will happen, whatever. I promise. The GBC will go on.'

Donna is stroking Trish's hair.

'But what about the children? What about the *children?*' one sobbing Ponsonby parent is shrieking.

The white-haired chairman strikes the table with a gavel. Case closed.

'Well, thanks, old chum, for fucking the whole street!' shouts someone from the back.

'And now, committee, can we move to the next sub-basement application – this one, I believe, in Lansdowne Walk. Mr Blundell?'

As I leave, I pull out my phone again. Wigmore Fertility has emailed back.

'We confirm we do have the samples and written permission from the named donor is not required for you to retrieve it, as we have a signed release form dated 2006. Please call reception to make an appointment.'

Result.

If Mum's in Paris, why is her passport in the drawer?

Dunno. She's on a 'work trip', which is jokes. Since when has *Mum* made dolla from actual work?

Where is Mum, really? It's Monday.

Where are you? At Sid's?

I'm at Keith and Oksana's, like I said, for the second time in a weekend £££. I'm in their weird 'media suite' in their double basement, which has a gym and a cinema and a spa. Oh yes, and a fucking *waterfall*. Am watching *Frozen* with the owl babies (why emoji for rat but no emoji for baby owls??).

Mimi

Oh God, I love her flat so much.

It's always hot and it's got a huge period drawing room painted the colour of bleached bones adrift on the clean white sand of a desert island. The high ceilings are adorned with a frilly cornice with bunches of grapes and leaves, a vast gilt mirror over the fireplace, and there are always fresh lilies everywhere.

And it's got other rooms – study, kitchen, Fox's bedroom, bathroom, Fox's bathroom – but we're in bed. Have been all weekend.

When she comes back from the bathroom she smells delicious, as usual, and I go, 'Mmm, you smell so good. Why do you smell so good?' and she says, '*C'est toujours Frisson,*' so I ask Farouche to sum up her creation and to tell me its component parts. She likes this question, her wild eyebrows knitting together.

'Lilies. The top of Fox's head. Sex. The neck of the woman I love.' I blush with pleasure, hoping she means me. '. . . the fumes of the chocolate factory just by the Gare du Midi in Brussels when I was a little girl,' she says. 'When you got off the train you would try to drink the air. Simple. Frisson.' Private smile. 'And I'm going to tell you another secret, now, Mimi. I'm working on a new scent.'

'Are you?' I say. 'Golly. Tell me about this one.'

'The smell of Ambre Solaire on the beach, in the south of France . . .'

I imagine oiled, brown flesh. Topless women.

'All my favourite smells, plus a secret ingredient.'

'What are you going to call it?' I ask, my fingers dabbling in the declivity between her throat and her shoulder.

'Maybe . . . *Frivolité*,' she says, and I close in on her, fill my nostrils with her perfume, overlaid with the heavy, fleshy, rotting sweetness of the lilies. 'Brilliant,' I say, 'I always say frivolity is far too important not to be taken seriously.'

Farouche's is what I imagine an apartment in the Left Bank would be like, but in Kensington Park Gardens, on the largest private garden in London, so every window opens out on to green vistas, weeping willows, Filipinas letting out Labradors and NHMs kickboxing with their personal trainers.

I've spent the whole weekend here, not in Paris, which is the baddest thing I've done since I went to a country-house hotel and spa with another man, but that was so long ago, in another lifetime, and this – this is bad in a different way. Some people say being in love makes them feel safe. It doesn't make me feel safe at all.

There are thick, arty French photographic magazines and coffee-table books on every surface. I've spent ages looking through them so I can understand Farouche's 'vision' and 'commitment to her art'. Also, Farouche made me look at the Annie Leibovitz photos of her lover, Susan Sontag, in life and in death, in sickness and in health, which were very, very . . . real, shall we say? I now feel I know the late, distinguished, badgery-haired essayist's bush and body like the back of my hand.

I love being here, coffee brewing in the silver pot on her stove, which we drink from bowls, dunking whole, thick, chunky fingers of Côte d'Or chocolate into it and then sucking the fat ends in front of each other so our lips have a balm of chocolate.

There is no actual food in the sense of 'potential meals' at all in the flat. There's only Dom Perignon in the fridge. A small round tin of pâté de foie gras in a cupboard. And some Nesquik and some Cheerios next to the Côte d'Or stash, for Fox, when he comes.

We spend most of the time in bed, in the bedroom. There's a storage drawer underneath her side. It has compartments.

Sometimes she takes something out for us to play with. I never object, even though sometimes I feel as if I am floating above the bed, watching us, and I have a sense of total unreality. Is this really me?

If we're not in the bedroom I flip through the magazines, impatient, and the Vanity Fair books, while Farouche works on her installation.

The last show – she says 'expo' – she had was somewhere in Switzerland. The theme was lost art, and it almost landed her with a lawsuit: from the StClair family, her own in-laws.

The StClairs failed, apparently, to appreciate whatever it is she had revealed of the private, unlisted dynasty. Farouche regarded this as very bourgeois, unimaginative and dreary of them. Hence the split.

'I've detached from them all,' she says. 'Including Julien. He doesn't get me any more. I'm sure all their art was stolen. I know it was. I had a moral obligation to tell the world.'

We are lying on the bed as she relates this.

'The family didn't like the fact that I made a video, of inside one of their houses, in Zurich.'

This is ringing a distant bell. Of course, now I remember. She had done a video tour of one of the StClair properties, and this one happened to be full of Old Masters of dubious provenance. The installation was a sensation. Farouche made the cover of *Newsweek*.

'So what's the new, erm, installation about?' I ask.

She's being very secretive about it. She clicks out of it when I stand in the study and stare at her, like a dog loyally monitoring its master's every move.

Farouche says, 'I don't want to talk too much about it, *chérie*. These things are all about *éclat*.'

'Oh, go on,' I beg, kissing her shoulder. 'Please. I won't even understand it.'

'No, honestly, Mimi. This is my work. It's important.'

I roll on top of her and pin her arms behind her head, allowing my hair to brush over her breasts. She shuts her eyes and starts moving slowly underneath me. As Ralph could spot at first glance, back in Mustique, when she appeared in that white cheesecloth dress, she is, without a shadow of a doubt, what he calls a 'dark wriggler'.

'The piece is an exploration of two contemporary themes,' she says, muffled by my chest. 'Surveillance, and the sex tape. I explore how in one medium subjects are exposed without their permission and, in the other, they expose themselves.' She turns sideways for air. After a little recovery time, she says, 'But who is violating whom? The person or persons who are filming? Those who witness the film?'

I've never been particularly bothered by the thought that someone is reading all my emails, despite the best efforts of the *Guardian*, but at the words 'surveillance' and 'sex tape' my eyes patrol the room. No security cameras, so far as I can see. Unless they're concealed in the directional light fitting by Tom Dixon above us that looks like an origami explosion.

'That sounds interesting,' I say. Then I mention something I keep forgetting to bring up.

'Oh yes, I did notice you had one in the bedroom in Mustique,' I say in a light voice. 'A security camera.'

'Is there?' she says, her fingers stroking my breasts. 'How

funny. Maybe it was there when I bought the house. I must switch it on – that would be fun, huh, one day?'

I roll over and kiss her – I love it when she talks about the future – and grab her, twining myself around her like a vine, inhaling the intoxicating scent, thinking, How can I get enough of this? Can one fall in love with another person's smell? And how can one persuade oneself to fall out of love again before the whole teetering edifice of one's life – husband and children and dog and work – crashes on top of one's head and crushes you for ever?

Then, as her lips part and she nibbles my lips and her hand slips down between my legs, I think: Who the fuck cares?

'What do I taste like?' I ask, hands playing with her dark, rope-like hair.

I push myself up on one elbow and gaze at her, I hope winningly, as she stares at the ceiling.

She turns her head to one side and contemplates me.

'You taste like you,' she says.

I think this is quite the most romantic thing anyone has ever said to me. I pull her up, bury my face in her neck.

'I'm scared that I'm not myself when I'm with you, but I'm more scared that I am,' I say.

She goes quiet. After this – I'm not sure Farouche does *feelings* – I tell her all about the *Newsnight* cameras that are rolling 24/7 at the Alpha Star dig (mounted on a lamp post) and how we're trying to catch the owners, and she seems very interested in that, which is nice, and she murmurs, 'Excavation, installation . . .' and then I try to show off by telling her that a TV company is making a series in our house in Dorset, and that it is likely to be a big hit, and why. I namecheck *Kirstie's Homemade Home*, the *Bake Off* and *Allotment Challenge*, even though we don't share cultural references and she doesn't read the English papers, or ever watch TV.

I tell her that the cover of the *Telegraph* magazine on Saturday had my farm on it, and many pages inside showing Home Farm. I had kept the mag specially to show my lover. I hop out of bed and fetch it from my case, and snuggle back in.

'Look.' I dump it on Farouche, open on the right page. 'My house, in the country.'

In the epic shoot that clearly took many hours and changes of clothes to achieve, Rose is doing something with preserves at the Aga, standing in an apron in front of tall, jewel-toned jars of jam, or smiling as she places a large ham on the cold shelf in the larder (I see she has taken down my home-made gingham curtains and replaced them with some cream ones), or stirring curds in her own dairy at Court Place, where she is also pictured, amidst wheels of cheese, and, lastly, there's another series of pictures taken in her own farm shop amid country plenty.

After a brief glance Farouche rolls off the bed and starts making her way out of the bedroom. It's as if something I've said has given her what Mirabel calls 'inspo', but I can't think what it is.

'What do you think of my house in the country?' I shout at her brown back and jutting buttocks.

'Is it on the sea?' Farouche asks over her shoulder. The magazine is spread-eagled on the floor by her side, like a crashed pigeon.

'No,' I admit. 'Not far, though . . . driveable.'

'*C'est mignon*,' she says.

I feel a flicker of annoyance. As I do when Americans come to Dorset and call the River Lar a 'stream' or Home Farm a 'cottage' and the briefest post-prandial ramble across a field becomes a full-blown 'hike'.

'*Félicitations!*' Farouche says, and blows me a kiss, grabs a wrap from the back of the door, ties it around her hips and leaves the room, as if carrying a bow and arrow in search of fresh prey.

I follow her, as if attached to her by toddler reins, to her study, where she is already working away at her over-sized Mac, the size of a billboard.

Everything in the room is monochrome. Black-and-white photos. Her cameras and film stuff are stacked neatly: rolls of film, in black leather cases, with stickers on them saying the name of the project, the year and a file number. There are also photo albums for each year of Fox's life, filled with photos she's taken and annotated herself; she's even already stuck in Mustique at half-term – I know because I checked, hoping there might be one of me. (There wasn't – only the back of my head.)

She's busy, so I back out of the office and find my handbag dumped in the hall. It crosses my mind that I should pack and go. I dig in and find my phone, and switch it on.

Ooh. There's an email from Olivia Featherstonehaugh of *Newsnight*, but first I read the text from Mirabel:

'Mum! When are you coming back?'

'Soon,' I tap back, going into the bedroom so as not to disturb Farouche's flow. 'I'm on the Eurostar,' I lie. 'Everything OK?'

I am amazed how guiltless I feel. I begin to wonder whether having an affair with a woman is as disloyal as having one with a man. If it is, why don't I feel more awful?

'Yes! Have something *amaze* to tell you,' Mirabel texts. 'About Keithy. Not about Scary.'

I can't call her. What if it goes to voicemail? The children have their mobiles on only silent, and what if she calls back, and I'm in England, not Paris, pretending to write a piece about the decline of the long lunch for *ES* magazine? Would she recognize the dial tone? In Europe, it goes long ring, long ring, not ring-ring, ring-ring. I can't risk it. I'll have to wait until I get home for Mirabel's shock news.

Email from Olivia.Featherstonehaugh@bbc.co.uk:
Hi Mimi
I tried to call but your phone is switched off, or are you away?
Anyway! Just to say the Monaco Notting Hill package is pretty much done, exciting – Josh is pleased with it and wants to roll Fri.
Meredith is all set. We'll need you in the studio after. We've bids in, but we want you in the discussion. Thanks. O xx

This Friday? This *Friday*? But Friday's the night of Keith's fiftieth. And, as we took their hospitality in Mustique, we really should go. Oksana and Keith have decided not to fly their two hundred closest friends to Venice, or St Petersburg; they have not hired the whole River Café for the night and booked Elton John. They have not, as Keith's hedge-fund partner Chris did for his fiftieth, built a whole edifice next to Blenheim Palace, including a round swimming pool, and seated five hundred people for dinner, including the Russian synchronized-swimming team, with Bryan Adams as after-dinner entertainment, for a revel that the Duke of Marlborough himself (who was also hired for the occasion, when he was alive) said made 'Wafic Saïd's sixtieth look like a vicarage tea party'.

They've decided they want something lower-key.

So they have only taken over Tate Modern for the night.

I sent Ralph the Save the Date email a few weeks ago. But I haven't dared tell him the full extent of the horror.

I pack my things, and before I leave the bedroom I go to the bed and fling myself down on it, on her side, and bury my face in the pillow and inhale until I'm dizzy.

The musky scent of the sheets, of her, makes me reel and

catches my throat. I crave her presence even though she's one of those people that you miss when they're around, when you're not with them . . . but you also miss them when you're with them, too, because they're never *actually there* with you.

I go and stand in the doorway of Farouche's study.

'I'm off,' I say.

'*Ciao, bella,*' she says, and remembers to look up and smile.

Ralph

Am sitting on the sweltering Tube. Everyone is reading *Metro* or the *Standard*. Or playing Candy Crush. God, I hate going out. Especially in London.

St Paul's already. The Central Line has its drawbacks – it is hot and full of people eating, and if you get on at Holland Park you have to say hello to at least three bankers – but at least it's fast.

Oh God, usual fiddle at the barrier, removing my Oyster card from my wallet just as a tannoyed announcement tells me to keep it separate to avoid card clash.

Then usual scrum debouching from the station, as it's post-rush-hour, plus a school trip to the cathedral of quite large kids in high-visibility vests in a crocodile, Health and Safety gone mad. I can see why they need these high-vis vests, though. None of them is looking where they are going. Glued to their smartphones.

And then my own phone beeps. I pluck it out of my jacket pocket. I never keep it in my back pocket any more, not after that unfortunate episode in Mustique, when I pocket-dialled Mimi while I was at Clare's. I don't want to look at it, but I do.

Then I wish with all my heart and soul that I hadn't.

It's another picture message. From Clare.

I don't open it. Instead, I press on, up the stairs, past the dump of *Evening Standards* from the pile at the mouth of the Tube. I don't pick up a paper, as I've already flipped through it on the Central Line. Keith's party is the lead in the 'Londoner's Diary', complete with a picture of Oksana.

Le tout Notting Hell is heading south of the river to the fiftieth birthday party of Dunbar Asset Management founder Keith Dunbar, hosted by his third wife, Oksana, the Soviet-born model and designer, 34, at Tate Modern. The glam fashionista-ski Oksana – whose body-con designs are worn by the likes of the Duchess of Cambridge, Tracey Emin, and film critic Camilla Long – insists that the revel is, by current Gatsby-esque standards of entertainment by financiers hitting the Big Five Oh, or Six Oh, anyway, a modest affair.

'The couple are looking forward to celebrating this happy milestone together, among family and friends from all walks of life, many of whom have travelled a long way to make it tonight, from many countries,' a spokeswoman said. 'It's not a formal party, there's no dress code, and Mr Dunbar will be wearing jeans from Oksana's new range.'

The Londoner learns that the occasion will see the launch of a new piece by the performance artist known as Farouche.

Ah, but the artist is seen in public only in white. Will La Farouche be in stone-washed double denim tonight?

Hard for heart not to sink reading this. I could live with the poor grammar – 'the couple are' – it was that dread warning about that awful fraud Farouche who has bewitched Mimi and her 'new piece'.

I cross the wobbly bridge across the river, and instead of thinking that earth has nothing to show more fair, I have to admit that, these days, I always think the mayor – well, one has to blame someone – has made an absolute Horlicks of the riparian built environment.

All these hideous residential glass-and-steel developments, the towers spearing the grey clouds, even that hideous one called The Phallus that I think Gideon has a hand in.

As I approach the South Bank I notice the Tate doesn't have the usual message to JOIN THE TATE TODAY AND SEE MALEVICH – or whatever – FOR FREE.

My pace slows on the wooden slats of the bridge, through which I can glimpse the oily, black flash of the river flowing beneath me as I absorb the full horror.

'Happy Birthday Keith HEART Oksana,' it says instead.

It reminds me somehow of one of those little planes that fly over beaches in the north, dragging banners saying 'Happy Golden Wedding Anniversary Marjorie love Geoffrey'.

I am making good time – it's just gone 8 p.m. – and as I zigzag down the wobbly bridge stairs to the entrance of Tate Modern I see a sign pointing to the back entrance, to the concrete ramp that pours visitors down the slipway to the Turbine Hall.

As I come round the corner, a light rain begins to fall, and I can see the tiny beads in the lock of hair that always flops over my eyes.

Then I grind to a halt. There is a queue, corralled by a naff red velvet rope and stretching from the entrance, which backs up to where I am standing.

I canter down to the front to check I haven't come to the wrong place at the wrong time and then realize to my horror that I have, and the entire Notting Hill has witnessed my shameless queue-jumping. And at the head of the queue is Meredith Blacker. In tight black jeans.

Then I remember. Not only the bit in the *Standard* diary. It also said on the invitation, which Mimi finally allowed me to inspect, 'The birthday boy will be in jeans.'

'But you have to let me in,' she is saying, in a loud voice, looking paler than ever.

'There are two policemen, and two clipboard Nazis, ranked in her way and barring everyone's passage.

'Everyone has to wait, ma'am,' says the policeman. He has an earpiece. 'There's a delay. We have to hold the line.'

'But don't you know who I am?' Meredith goes on to say, to general delight that someone has actually said those words out loud. She has an iPad in one hand, her press pass in another. Then, to her credit, she blushes.

Margy, the deputy head of Ponsonby Prep, is immediately behind me. We mouth, 'VVPP,' at each other. This is the school's official acronym for Very, Very Pushy Parent, which actually doesn't apply to the Blackers, who are without issue as yet. Or as far as I know.

'Doesn't matter who you are, ma'am,' says the same policeman, who looks about twelve and is a head shorter than Meredith. 'We have a VIP arriving and we can't let anyone in, whoever they are, till after said VIP arrives.'

'But my name is Meredith Blacker, and I have to come in soon because I'm doing *Newsnight*.'

She barrels forward.

At her lunge towards the velvet rope, the policemen lock arms 'Auld Lang Syne'-style and form a barrier as if a poll-tax riot were breaking out.

At that moment, a fleet of three Range Rovers with blacked-out windows crest the top of the concrete rise and proceed, in silence, to descend the long concrete slipway into the museum.

The Range Rovers proceed in a convoy towards us and park at preordained angles on the sloping apron. Simultaneously, doors open in the front passenger seats of both. A man with a headset jumps out of each passenger side, and then one opens the doors of the two back seats simultaneously while speaking into the mics in their necks, much as waiters whisk silver domes off dishes at the same time in pretentious French restaurants, in that way that says, I have a simple job, but I take it seriously as a vocation, and I like to do it well, and with a certain, sombre style.

A pair of cropped green trousers, an orange blouse and some teetering heels come out first, followed by the slim trunk of Samantha Cameron, who is not in jeans.

'She's wearing Oksana,' I hear someone say with confidence in the crowd. 'Autumn/Winter 2014. Very tactful.'

Samantha gives a gummy smile and tosses her head as she emerges, so the overall impact is of a thoroughbred chestnut mare in green-and-orange livery.

Then David Cameron emerges from the other side, taller than I thought, with the ruddy glow of a yeoman farmer and backswept brown hair, and he gestures towards his wife like a successful estate agent showing off his prime property.

They come together by the side of the car, smile at each other and hook arms. They are about to make a triumphant entrance two-by-two into the concrete Ark when, suddenly, there's a high cry from the crowd.

'Dave! Sam!' Meredith calls in her fluty voice. She is only feet away.

There are three or four photographers off to the side, taking pictures. To my surprise, they are not being allowed into the event. Not yet, anyway.

Dave's head snaps to the left. As Meredith propels herself forward again, his eyes do a reptilian flicker from side to side, but he takes a split-second decision and puts a restraining arm on his security detail. As if to say, 'I can handle this.'

But Samantha Cameron gets there first. 'Meredith!' she calls out, with a beneficent wave.

Meredith Blacker knows she's won. She beams at the policemen on the door, slides her press card into the back pocket of her jeans, as if she has no need to prove her credentials now, and then, in slow-motion relish, breasts the velvet rope somehow and greets the prime minister and his wife. Without even a backward glance to the waiting queue, she puts a cosy arm around Sam and does the walk of triumph, three abreast, into the party, and I can hear the words, 'Actually, I can't stay long, so nice to catch you both *now* as I've *got* to do *Newsnight*, so annoying . . .' floating on the damp air, as if she had far more on her crowded plate than the prime minister and they were lucky to have face-time with her.

It is only then that she pivots and gives a bountiful backwards wave to those penned behind the velvet rope.

It is not until the VIP party has descended into the bowels of the Turbine Hall, where Keith can be glimpsed, with a score of waiters in long white aprons waiting motionless on the plain of polished concrete, bearing aloft round trays adorned with pale-yellow chilled champagne flutes in one arm, that they start processing the rest of us. Behind me, I spot Clare and Gideon, Virginie and Mathieu, all the Averys wearing jeans, but the security somehow find it within themselves to expedite three further couples – Dasha Zhukova and Roman Abramovich, Jemima Khan and her plus one – I don't know who it is, not Russell Brand, anyway – and David and Victoria Beckham.

Still, I am one of the first to enter the Turbine Hall, and I meander slowly towards the waiters holding drinks. I don't see anyone I particularly want to talk to, so I bite the bullet.

I look at the picture Clare has sent me.

What I see makes me grab a cocktail from a tray.

I march on, towards the sound of gunfire, i.e. other people at the party, who are streaming down the Turbine Hall towards the end, where a white, ghostly structure towers at the end of the space.

As I approach, I realize it's a bouncy castle. Two female

figures have taken off their shoes and are already bouncing wildly inside the white rubber playpen.

I watch two women do star jumps, scream and hurtle themselves against the walls.

'Wonderful party, old boy,' I say, as Keith has wandered up to say hello.

We continue to watch the women jump up and down. One is in a black satin playsuit, I think it is called, with spaghetti straps, embroidered with gold stars; the other is in a red boiler suit, but open almost to her waist. I begin to say, 'Well turned up,' which is what I say when a man makes a social effort, before I realize it's his party, so he had to. Turn up, that is.

'What I love about English women,' sighs Keith, as the women bounce joyfully, as if solely for our viewing pleasure, 'is how their, you know, still . . . actually, move? Go to LA, it's extraordinary, and rather unsexy, actually. It's as if they're cemented on.'

I stare at the women in the bouncy castle. It does appear that Keith makes a fair point.

I suppose it is something to be proud of, these days, that women in this country, by and large, have their own breasts. To celebrate. We should have National Breast Day. After all, we have National everything else day, and so little left to be proud of, which was why Casimir tweeted, after watching a Channel Four documentary, that it was a matter of personal pride to him that the fattest man in the world was English.

I finish my drink – the same very cold, lemony cocktail that Keith is necking back and which is no doubt lethal – and wonder where to leave my glass.

I gaze around – the hall is filling up. There are stands for food. Good. I am just making my way towards the lobster-roll area, to mop up the alcohol, when I spot Clare and immediately determine to take evasive action.

Only she has spotted me, too.

Without wanting to, I wave back. Might as well . . . get it over now.

Or I could turn on a sixpence and make off in another direction, have a few more drinks, but that would put myself at risk of being mugged by several women who suspect I'm second-husband material for one of their many single, divorced girlfriends.

No. Grip it now.

I'm going to pretend to Clare how thrilled I am, for her.

Or else I'm going to say that I never got the image of the scan she just sent.

I need to grip this. Whatever Mimi is up to, I need to convey my position on my own status, which is this.

I am a married man.

I don't want to meet any dynamic, fit forty-five-year-olds who used to work in the City and have their own houses in Fulham and the bodies of teenagers thanks to Bikram yoga, even if some of them do have nice dogs.

Even if I can't be in Dorset, which is my fault, at least I could be back at Lonsdale, reading Lucian a bedtime story about pirates, before having something eggy on a plate, the Sotheby's catalogue on my lap, and sitting in front of part two of that BBC2 series about the Georgians, with that rather attractive presenter with a blonde bob, can't remember her name. The one with a slight speech impediment who at least speaks audibly, even in paragraphs.

I don't want another wife. I have a wife – I refuse to use the word 'partner' – and that is Mimi.

She may be a nightmare, but she's my nightmare. And that's all there is to it.

Good grief! I can't leave now.

Here's Clare, holding two soggy lobster rolls in napkins:

one for me, one for her. Her hair has been sort of ironed and made shiny and she's wearing a strange outfit, like a batsuit on top and a skirt that sticks out. She looks expensive. And determined. She talks about the bouncy castle for a bit and then she pins me like a butterfly.

'Did you get the picture?' she asks.

Sheezus! Dad keeps saying, 'My life is like a Channel Four documentary,' and now I get it.

Mum. **Mum**. Doesn't she know, and doesn't Dad know, that if they save a picture from Snapchat or wherever on to an iPhone, then charge their iPhone to their MacBook and sync, which is what they do, it saves pictures, images, songs, videos – *everything* – to iCloud? And the whole point of iCloud is that it is on a remote server and anyone with a login can view it, and we all – every single one of us – have a login, except maybe not Lucian?

So not only can I see their pictures in iCloud but so can Posy and so can Cas, and, in theory, so could Dad, even though he did ask, 'What is iCloudius?' the other day. 'Is it by Robert Graves, or am I behind the times?' – Dad's idea of a joke – and thought that was very funny indeed.

Only Mum laughed.

So our family life could finally fall apart, if, for any reason, Cas or Posy decided to look at iPhotos, which they often do, even though Posy has terrible Instarrhea, but, say the others wanted to find pictures of Calypso when she was a puppy, or of us in Dorset – or let's say Lucian has some project for Ponsonby, for PHSE: teachers are always asking pupils to write about their families; they pretend it helps them to understand the inner child, but in fact they do it to get the dirt on all the fucked-up parents from the horse's mouth. It's an old trick.

And, meanwhile, I'm the one who gave Mum her scoop on the basement dig that's being revealed tonight.

I have to do something – change the password – on iCloud, so the others don't find out.

Don't find out that Mum's cheating on Dad.

With another woman. Which is such a cliché.

Yawn.

She's not a display celeb lipstick faux lezzer, nor is she older-woman

hot, like Jen Aniston, say, or Halle Berry, or the entire frickin gay-for-the-stay cast of ***Orange is the New Black***.

Mum. Wears. Boden.

Plus, she and Dad are too old to split up. What would be the point?

Oh shit, it's Pose – she's come in and didn't even knock, showing me a tweet from Jo Elvin of @glamour saying, 'What do we think about printed yoga pants?'

We share the biggest bedroom, with a window that looks out over the communal garden, so she can just barge in.

What the actual ***fuck***? I'm staring at the screen, and something else has just uploaded.

Maybe Dad was suddenly connected to wi-fi rather than 4G. (Don't ask me to explain, but sometimes apps and downloads are kept in some sort of holding pattern?)

This one really is wack.

And I know what it is. I think I do, anyway. I've seen them on Mailonline. What I don't know is why Dad's got this on his iPhone.

I'm calling Mum.

Clare

I regret my Prada wedges as I clop past a grid of motionless waiters who are standing still in a diamond formation in the middle of the floor, like the Terracotta Army, holding round trays laden with cocktails and champagne.

My feet must have already gone up a size.

I've spotted Ralph's tall figure by the bouncy castle. His back's to me, and I think, that's Keith – in Dad jeans and a white shirt – with him.

Perfect time to make my move. I'll join them, which gives Keith cover to slip away and mingle with his many guests 'from all walks of life', as I read in tonight's *Standard*.

I pass the Maine lobster-roll stand, where a hungry mob is forming, push my way through and grab a couple, wrapped in napkins, that a waiter is placing on a tray, at the same time keeping an eye on the two men, and see Keith clap Ralph on the back. They nod and laugh and then Keith moves off.

I dart forward. 'Going in,' I say out loud. After all, the die is now cast.

I approach Ralph with resolved purpose, as if he is a rare and fragile library book that needs careful reshelving. He is wearing a dark wool jacket and one of his soft cornflower-blue, very fine cotton shirts that makes his eyes pop blue.

'Hi,' I say in a quiet voice. I make no attempt to kiss him. I am worried that if I did, he might recoil, as if I were hitting him.

'Oh. Hi, Clare,' he says, without expression.

I don't talk about it straightaway.

'You know this' – I gesture towards the Taj Mahal white-rubber edifice – 'this isn't a bouncy castle, you know.'

He looks at it again, as if not quite sure how to take this. 'Well, it looks like a bouncy castle, and sounds like a bouncy castle and it's even beginning to smell like one,' he says.

'It is, in fact, a Jeff Koons installation,' I say, handing him a lobster roll wrapped in a napkin, as if we're on a private picnic on a riverbank together.

I take an encouraging bite of mine. Men love being fed. You can't go wrong with food. 'It's not any old bouncy castle,' I say, chewing. 'This is a *Jeff Koons* bouncy castle.'

I say it in the same voice as the M&S ads for hot chocolate soufflé with a melting middle, but both the phrasing and tone are, I sense, lost on Ralph.

Maybe it was a bit full on, sending him the blurry 3D image of our child that I am carrying in my womb.

I say the only thing I can think of saying.

Even though I am standing in front of a bouncy castle in which Meredith Blacker and the prime minister's wife are now star-jumping, thus providing a useful talking point in anyone's book.

'Did you get the picture?' I ask. Light voice. As if I'd emailed a picture of something that I'd spotted at auction, a ratty tapestry, say, that I thought might appeal to Ralph and only to Ralph.

Given I've sent Ralph an image every few months or so of Joe, I didn't think he would find it that unsettling that I continue the tradition as we expand our blended family together.

I think he pretends not to hear. There's a distraction – oh yes, I see now. The PM's wife is gambolling about in her tailored trousers and Oksana top. And some woman's holding up an iPad and filming, and it's Oksana. Tricky. For Sam Cam.

We were told that we had to bring photo ID, to arrive at 8 p.m. sharp and that photography within Tate Modern and during the art installation was strictly forbidden.

But, on the other hand, it's Oksana's party, and she can film if she wants to.

So Oksana's holding her iPad up, smiling with satisfaction as she films the prime minister's wife doing a chest-bump with a well-known media personality, i.e. Meredith Blacker, and then of course everyone gets out their phones and starts filming the jumpers.

At which point Sam Cam notices, and freezes, as if the music's stopped in Musical Statues. And then everyone else stops jumping, too, as if they suddenly realize how silly they are, how silly they will look when the pictures start appearing all over social media within minutes, and in the papers tomorrow.

Sam Cam laughs, bumps-a-daisies out of the castle and, flicking her hair, goes up to Oksana, and they air kiss. Meredith follows close behind, pretends she doesn't know I'm watching. Oksana and Samantha embrace – it's a goodbye embrace – and Sam Cam comes in for a hug, and goes to put on her shoes, together with Meredith, who is checking her phone.

Ralph and I watch them as if all this is normal operating procedure at parties we both go to. And I wonder how soon the video will end up on YouTube, or whether people are too scared of Oksana to do that.

I can't eat my roll. My heart is too full. I am waiting for Ralph to speak, holding my soggy offering of bread, napkin, mayo and lobster, probably in that order of ingredients.

'Picture? The one you sent an hour ago?' replies Ralph, waving to a waiter and making drinking gestures. 'I didn't get it, actually.'

He is not making this easy.

The waiter glides over, carrying a tray, and Ralph swipes a tumbler of cool green liquid in a glass, with mint, lime, ice and a plastic swizzle stick with a flag saying 'Keith 50 not out' on it.

He is playing for time. I sent it as an email and a text. There is no way he didn't get it. He's received all the other pictures, and he sometimes even sends a response, like he did when I sent him a picture of Joe in the nets at Lord's in cricket whites.

It's as if Ralph doesn't want to admit he's seen it.

I understand.

Having a baby with someone is not like going through an economic shitstorm as a country.

You are not in it together.

Ralph and I are in this on our own.

'But I know you did,' I say, 'because my phone tells me if texts, and so on, have been opened and read.'

'I didn't say I didn't receive it,' Ralph says, enunciating in a words-of-one-syllable voice.

'I said: "I didn't *get* it."'

Oh my God, I can't believe this: Meredith is coming to talk to us, stooping sideways and hopping on one leg as she fastens her sandal.

With her heels back on, she's easily as tall as Ralph.

She leans down to peck my cheek. Her black hair, cut in a trademark long bob, or lob, brushes me, soft and shiny as a raven's wing.

Then Meredith turns her full attention to Ralph. Barely an acknowledgement for me, which I accept.

I do not count in this setting. Maybe back on the garden, because I take care of the allotment, and I notice who's cutting the flowers and the sweet peas for their own use, and from which bed, but I don't count, not here. It's all about context.

'Well, neighbours,' Meredith says, her dark eyes shining, 'I hope you're all going to be *glued* tonight. *Newsnight*, BBC2,

10.30 p.m.' She says this as if we are both too clueless and unsighted to have heard of, let alone seen, the BBC's flagship evening analysis programme before.

'For Mimi's triumph!' she adds.

'Mimi's on, after my package, so I'm off to NBH now – the Camerons are kindly giving me a lift back into town. So. Off I go! Ta-da!'

Meredith moves off at speed, as if she has a fire to put out, or, knowing Meredith and her taste for being in the thick of it, a fire to start.

I turn back to Ralph as Meredith goes off in search of the Camerons. I smile. Men like it when women smile.

Ralph senses my gaze.

'Ralph,' I say. 'Please. Please don't make this so hard.'

His blue eyes snap back to mine.

'Hard, Clare? Hard? For you? Well, try being me. Not only am I in charge of the government's most unpopular proposal to date, which is saying something, of forcing through legislation to make fracking under private property a human right – a human right in this country, like Sky Sports on widescreen TVs for those on benefits, or free school meals for the under-eights – but that stunt you tried to pull in Mustique? Are you *nuts*? Why are you *doing* this?'

I drop the lobster roll into the pocket of my trapeze skirt in my panic.

'You realize, don't you, that my children don't even know about *Joe* yet,' Ralph goes on, his face close to mine. 'They don't know about Joe. Now, I don't have anything against Joe. He's done nothing wrong. None of this is his fault. It's mine, Clare. But this has got to stop. It's never going to happen. OK?'

I feel my stomach twist. I worry I'm going to be sick on his brogues.

There is no way I can tell him what I've done now.

214

But how can I not? It reminds me of the T-shirt I bought from the GOOP website, for only £75, with the slogan 'To reveal is to heal.'

After all, I know, but he doesn't, not yet. But it's got to come out.

If you don't tell your story, your story will tell you.

Mimi

Am walking briskly across BBC forecourt as if I do this every day.

As everyone else has their nose in their phone, I've taken mine out of my pocket, too, to look as if I'm checking it for important missed calls and emails from heads of departments or star presenters that might have flooded in since I had to go on the Tube.

Oh.

I do actually have a couple of missed calls. But both of them – are from Mirabel.

Doesn't the blessed girl realize? I'm at *work*! Children these days don't know they're *born*.

I hesitate by the revolving doors, as staffers in low-slung jeans carrying lattes, lanyards round their necks, enter them gingerly as if risking certain decapitation.

I stop to send a quick email to Rose Musgrove, as the mobile signal in Dorset is too dodgy to rely on:

Watch *Newsnight* TONIGHT – am making BBC2 debut with
hard-hitting revelations about local planning scandal love
'Jere-Mimi' Paxman! xxx

As I press send, I realize that Rose is most likely going to be at Tate Modern, as of course Rose introduced me to Farouche, and it's Farouche's big night. I text Ralph to much the same effect, reminding him where I am and to look out for Rose at Keith's fiftieth.

I also email my brother, Con, by copying the one I've just sent Rose and pasting it to him.

I wonder whether to switch off my phone, in case Mirabel keeps calling. I haver, thinking that there's never any signal in TV studios anyway.

You wonder how channels manage to broadcast at all. I know this, as I did some breakfast TV show the other day. I said yes because I am supposed to be building my brand. Some researcher had turned up a piece I'd written for the *Telegraph* about a million years ago, about birth order. Or so I thought.

They sent a car to fetch me to the studio, I had half an hour in the chair, i.e. full make-up, and then they put a 'hot brush' through my hair and I went back to the Green Room to get stuck into the fruit plate and mini croissants. I was just thinking that I could get used to this, when the producer comes back in, looking sheepish, and it turns out the researcher got in a muddle and they wanted the Mimi Fleming who was the pelvic-floor expert.

They explained, as if it made it better, that if you put my name into Twitter, hers is the only one that comes up, apparently – or comes up first, at least – she even has a verification blue tick, whereas I have an underscore in mine, i.e. am @Mimi_Fleming, and have 507 followers. And if you put Mimi Fleming into Google, the first 45,000 results are about her, not me.

It was *awful*. I sat there munching an apricot Danish and, in front of the other guests, i.e. Vince Cable and Keith Vaz (there's a law that they have to be on every programme, I think), and Ben Fogle (ditto), this producer came up and said, 'There's been a slight change in the running order.' He was flannelling.

Then he said, 'Er, listen . . . we can find a way through this, if, um, might you be comfortable with talking about what is the optimum position for giving birth? The good news is, we don't have the right Mimi Fleming, ha ha, but we do have *the* Miriam Stoppard, and a woman who gave birth squatting, so it would be great if *you* could offer a different perspective.' He looked hopeful, as if it would make his day if I revealed I'd given birth in a tree, preferably during the Boxing Day tsunami, and that if I agreed he'd worship me *with his body*.

'We can come up with a fee if that swings it.'

I tried to call Ralph, as I wasn't sure – I thought they were paying me, anyway – and, unlike me, my husband is a private person and, strangely enough, doesn't like having intimate, messy details of our lives broadcast to strangers. But it said 'No service'. Hopeless.

I tried going up a floor in the lift – to the floor above *Daybreak* or *Good Morning Britain* or *Sunrise* or whatever it was – I now forget – but I still got 'No service'.

So I came down, back to the Green Room, and said, 'Sure' – after all, I'd had my make-up and faux dry done, and my hair regime is usually 'no-dry' and my facial regime no make-up.

I went on, and even managed to have a 'row' – i.e. a cooked-up cod TV spat for the cameras – with Miriam Stoppard. I said the only satisfactory position was flat on your back with every drug possible administered into every orifice and by mouth and needle and, if needs must, suppository, a statement I didn't even believe myself. (I actually had Posy and Lucian naturally and still feel smug about it many years later.)

I was tempted to follow this up with the story of how Ralph offered the consultant who was stitching me up after Cas a £50 note, to do a super job on me, like you do at Simpson's on the Strand when they bring the beef on a trolley and you incentivize the carver to give you the choicest cuts, but by this stage Miriam Stoppard was in full spate, so I never got another word in. And I don't think Ralph would have been that pleased.

I put this latest TV appearance out of my mind, whirl through the revolving doors and approach the desk.

I tell them my name and they write it down and invite me to take a seat.

So I'm on a modular plastic sofa gazing out over the shiny grey floor, phallic grey pillars and red plastic fascias. The decor is horrible.

On one entire wall there is a huge photograph of Annie Lennox in a sparkling white gown with huge angel wings, in full-throated voice. The receptionists have to stare at this uplifting image of a powerful woman artist in her creative prime all day. Behind them there is a selection of photographs that convey the broadcaster's close embrace of diversity, public service, older women on screen, the Scots, science and all its other charter commitments.

I'm on my own in NBH, and I'm beginning to wonder if *Newsnight* has forgotten me.

It's now almost ten o'clock, and there's no one else waiting apart from a man who is sitting facing the other way.

I suspect he's a tramp, only the BBC is too wet to stop him living here.

At the transport desk, drivers in black suits and white shirts are waiting for their next pick-up or drop-off, and the two black female receptionists are slowly processing other guests and sending them up with waiting runners.

Meanwhile, crews are surging in and out of the revolving doors, carrying tripods, trailing scarves and bits of digital equipment and looking harassed; and then skinny, middle-aged men in Lycra wearing bike helmets and carrying fold-up bikes are scurrying in and out, too, even though it's Friday evening, like drones coming in and out of the hive.

Oh, here we go. Someone is making their way towards me with a clipboard. How does he know, I wonder, who I am, and also which Mimi Fleming I am?

I brace myself for another case of mistaken identity.

He's in uniform of low-slung jeans, T-shirt, V-neck sweater and Converse. Hand outstretched. He looks about Cas's age. I can pinpoint the age of a woman down to the last month – but only with those over forty. Anyone younger of either sex, it's impossible. They all look like my own children.

'Hi, you must be Mimi, right?' he says. 'I'm Chris-from-*Newsnight*. Though I do *WATO* – *The World at One* – too, haha. Got your pass OK?'

I say yes, then I follow him like a tracker dog as he shades through a series of revolving doors, lifts, fire doors and down into the basement, where he installs me in a small, Stygian, low-lit room with purple sofas and beige walls fashioned of plastic squares. There is a fridge with Cokes and white wine in it, and a coffee table on which there's a bowl of fruit and about a dozen copies of the in-house magazine, *Ariel*, on it, with Jeremy Vine on the cover.

I sit down and am about to pick up *Ariel* to find out what Jeremy Vine's been up to, but then another runner comes in, a skinny girl in specs this time, called Abby, and she takes me out again, along a corridor to a cupboard. I pass Kirsty Wark, having her make-up done while reading a script and texting on her phone, and wearing a mustard-yellow top made out of a blanket and a hooped skirt from which her spike heels poke, but she doesn't see me.

I sit in the next-door booth, and the nice make-up lady asks what I want and I have to think. I have no idea.

I say, 'Do what you like,' and she squints at me and she says, 'We need to bring your eyes out, maybe zhzh the hair a little,' and so she gives me 'big, smoky eyes', and then she backcombs my chestnut frizz and sprays it with Elnett, and it is then that I begin to have serious second thoughts. Doubts. Like when Justin Welby goes jogging and he worries that God doesn't exist, these doubts are perfectly legitimate and understandable.

I mean, what if I'm wrong? What if, between us, Mirabel and I have completely cocked up?

I leave Make-up, go back to the Green Room, open the fridge. Take a Diet Coke.

As I crack it open and take the first slug, the best one (in fact, the only really good one), I allow myself to mind that I'm missing Keith's party, too, where everyone else is. Where Farouche is screening her new film . . .

I check my phone, but now we are in the sub-basement. I can't call Ralph to say I've changed my mind, I'm on my way to Tate Modern, don't leave, I'm not doing *Newsnight*, it was a bad idea. A very bad idea. I knew if I spoke to Ralph – told him what I was going to say – he would forbid me to step on to the set. After all, his operating principle is 'Don't say anything to anyone,' and here I am about to tell everyone everything. On live TV.

Chris, the teenage producer, bursts in.

'Er,' he says. 'You OK? Need a drink? Water?'

I gesture to the Diet Coke on the side table next to the Jeremy Vine magazine.

'We have a situation with the package,' he goes on.

'What do you mean?'

'Meredith will be here at 10.15 or so, she's on her way, she just called from David Cameron's car, actually,' he says, as if this makes him more important, by association.

'Nothing major. Nothing you need to know.' He runs a finger down the running order on his clipboard.

'So, Meredith cues up the package, package goes out, you'll

go on set, Eleanor will introduce you and the other guests, then there's the disco, discussion, which is you, the Tory leader' – he glances at his pad – 'Giles Goodenough. You'll challenge him about the decision to say yes to three hundred or so basements.'

'Four hundred, actually,' I say.

'And then, specifically, the Alpha Star dig in Ponsonby Terrace. See what he says. Then you go in for the kill. You dob the owners in. OK? All set?'

The sheer horror of what I have agreed to do sinks in for the first time.

When Mirabel was babysitting the Dunbar twins, she wandered into Keith's study, looking for a DVD. And she found everything. A folder marked 'Alpha Star'. And, inside the folder, she found that the two directors of the company were –

Well, that's what I'm about to reveal on screen.

Mirabel screen-shotted the documents and emailed them to me.

It is my debut scoop. And not a bad one, though I say so myself. Even Josh Kurtz, who must be super-busy, found time to text me:

'Proper investigative journalism, so great for the prog. Well done, Kurtz xxx.'

The teenage producer is continuing to brief me.

'You drop the two names – *boom boom*,' he says, as if the names were hitting the floor, 'and we'll flash up on the screens behind those documents your daughter screen-shotted via the ImagetoText app and emailed. The names will be highlighted, for effect. OK?'

'I think so,' I say. I pick up my Coke.

I wish I could call Ralph. Just to warn him of the extent to which I am about to dump on our own doorstep. I always turn to Ralph in times of trouble.

'So I just need to know. Are. You. Sure?' the teenager is say-ing. 'The last thing *Newsnight* needs is another, you know, libellous misidentification catastrophe, like that time we said Lord McAlpine was a paedophile, and he wasn't, which was unfortunate.'

'But he's dead,' I remind him.

'Exactly our point,' says the producer. 'That's what people blame us for. So we have to be super-careful, or' – he does a slicing motion across his throat – 'it's curtains for the pro-gramme.' Then he glances at his watch. 'You OK? The other guests are on their way. Help yourself to anything. More Coke. Wine. Water. Whatever you like, help yourself.' Glances at his watch. 'OK, I'll be back shortly.' He turns to leave.

If I don't do it now . . .

'Chris,' I say. 'I can't do this. Sorry. I've changed my mind. I don't think it works, I'm not sure . . .' I gabble.

Of course I can't. I am committing public hara-kiri. I am, officially, mad. I have to leave.

Chris turns back. Runs his hand over his chin, which has the mandatory light beard worn by every man in his twenties and thirties who works in the creative industries. He stands at the door and smiles at me, as if humouring me.

'I've had second thoughts. I don't think this is a good idea. Why do you need *me*? You've got all the information. You've got the screen-shots. Kirsty can do it,' I gabble. 'She can be the one to challenge the council, talk to the chairman, and what-not. You don't actually need me . . .'

A steely look comes across Chris's face, and I realize he's older than I thought. At least thirty-five. And he probably has an enormous mortgage on a two-bedroom flat in Hackney to pay for.

His mouth sets into a line, a farm track across a wintry, stubbly field.

'Too late, your name's on the tea towel, as Kirsty's already trailed the discussion,' he says. He makes it sound as if the die is cast. And there's no going back.

'Don't worry, you'll be great, I know you will,' he says, and darts out. 'You'll be great,' he sings, 'I know you will,' and locks me in the Green Room as he leaves.

Ralph

I'm swept along in the riptide to the east wall of the Turbine Hall, where a lively crowd, tanked on cocktails, is gathering for speeches, followed by the various, much unanticipated entertainments.

Marguerite, who is surprisingly forceful for someone so slight, has got me in a sort of armlock on one side.

It must be all that Pilates.

'Hurry,' she's saying. 'Can't miss speeches!'

Virginie, in a white, sporty dress, as if she is about to play some lawn tennis at the Hurlingham, is escorting me on my other side, so I feel like a battleship being guided into harbour by two determined tugs.

Virginie leans forward and whispers in my ear.

'You can always come and talk to me,' she says, laying a brown arm on mine, and I watch her slim brown legs scissoring alongside my soberly trousered ones. 'About your trobble . . . Ze wan important sing,' she continues, 'is to remembair. Nobody's marriage' – she actually says 'ma-ri-age', i.e. three syllables – 'is purr-fect.'

'Well, yes, Virginie,' I say. 'Into each life some rain must fall,' and she asks, '*Quoi?*' so I then say: 'Man is born to trouble, as the sparks fly upward,' but neither Virginie, nor, I might add, Marguerite, who read English at Bristol, appears to know what I am talking about.

Marguerite, at least, seems perky, or perkier, tonight.

Her plus one is Edward, a barrister whom she went bunny-boiler on – I seem to remember some grisly anecdote about a photo album after a dirty weekend in the south of France – but he seems to have returned for more. Or at least he has *pro tem*.

A waiter comes up as we surge forth and walks in lockstep alongside us, proffering mini-hamburgers and then crab sandwiches, as if we will need sustenance for what lies ahead.

The women decline, but I cram food in my mouth while Virginie and Mathieu, who is somehow managing to eat a hamburger on the go, with ketchup, without getting any sauce on his chin, chat away to Patrick and Tiggy, and the topic is whether the One and Only or the Aman chain of hotels is more comfortable, and Tiggy is saying that she prefers the latter but also how, when one is on the sub-continent, it's more enjoyable and profound and more real to live quite simply, and have one or two nights in a five-star hotel perhaps, but also to spend a lot of the time close to nature, living 'as the native tribespeople do'.

Then Sally and Bob Avery join us, which is a relief, as I'm not sure I can cope with two of Patrick's women at once, and they start telling the group all about a five-week holiday they did *en famille* in Chile last year, with white-water rafting, hiking and paragliding, during the summer vacation, and how they climbed a peak that 'no family has ever climbed before', and everyone says they feel exhausted just hearing about it, and indeed it makes me want to go home and lie down all the more.

When I think that, as a child, a holiday meant midges in Scotland or a pasty on a Cornish beach, I feel a wave of nostalgia, for my own family, for the West Country, and then Gideon forms up and I'm almost relieved at the sight of him.

The Sturgises don't do social events as a couple. Perhaps Clare's bailed and . . . I'm safe.

'What's the difference between a bonus and a penis?' he asks me.

'I don't know,' I say.

'Your wife will blow the bonus,' he roars, and hits me on the back.

Gideon may be a château-bottled berk, but at least he knows his onions, and he starts giving a TED-style talk about how the Swiss architects converted the power station into the Tate without detracting one iota from its form and allowing the space to remain an experiential piece in itself, and how the Turbine Hall provides a linear grain to a central spine in a public realm, but then, as he warbles on – Gideon wears his learning heavily – there is a palpable sense that something is about to happen.

The young, tall, dark waiters are corralling guests and herding us back.

So we surge from whence we came back towards the bouncy castle, and I follow the herd: the Averys, and the Lacostes, Patrick and Tiggy, Marguerite, her new chap Edward, and Gideon, but no Clare.

It is clear that, now the PM and Sam have gone, the strictures about photography have been relaxed. As if in tribute to the greatness that is Keith, guests hold up their lit screens to record the deathless image of their host standing in the portcullis of a Jeff Koons bouncy castle in his red party socks.

He is holding a mic.

This is always a sight to sink the heart. Someone isn't just going to say a 'few words' impromptu. They have planned an entire speech.

Oksana is standing beside him, in a red, strappy dress, with cut-away areas at her waist, and she is gripping one side of the castle – a rampart – so she doesn't slip on to her bottom like a child coming down a slide in front of us.

Sitting at their feet, in a splayed pose, is Farouche.

She's in a white frock, which is slipping off her shoulder, and has bare feet.

She almost disappears against the white rubber of the castle; only her brown limbs have a spectral phosphorescence.

I remember Farouche saying in Mustique, to no one in particular, at the beach bar: 'White is my colour. I own white.'

'Oh my God, it's Farouche-time,' groans Gideon in my ear, which is my feeling entirely.

Then he says, his breath tickling my neck, his peppery after-shave filling my nostrils, 'The ghost at the feast.'

I wonder how much Gideon knows. Of course he knows about Joe. But we've never discussed it. As for Clare's latest manoeuvres . . . the least said.

Someone tings a glass. The chatter continues. The glass is tinged again. Chatter subsides.

Speeches. Even though I haven't exactly been looking forward to them, at least they're happening, which means that soon – Lord, I hope soon – the end will be in sight and I can leave, with full battle honours.

'Lords, ladies, gentlemen, editors of the Murdoch press and bankers, ha ha,' booms Keith, to polite laughter and a smattering of claps. 'Thank you very much indeed for coming so far tonight – some of you from as far as Kensington Park Gardens and your offices in Mayfair.'

Oh my God, Keith is trying to do funny.

'Thank you all for coming tonight, because I know how busy you all are, and how far Battersea helipad is, but one's not fifty every day and, as someone said, you're only old once.' Keith pauses for a laugh that never comes. 'But seriously' – he speeds up – 'you're all here.' He shades his eyes and looks across the sea of guests, stretching across the acres of concrete floor, past the food stands with little, sweet baby burgers, the bars with ranks of filled glasses waiting to go, past the lobster-roll stand . . . The monumental scale of the building makes dwarves of us all, even the masters of the universe and the

colossi of the financial world. 'You're all here for my Hawaii
– my Hawaii FIVE OH – because you are all in some way special to my lady wife, Oksana, and I.'

Everyone knows the exact opposite of this is true, but
drinks it in anyway. The truth is, everyone is here tonight
either because he has to have them, or because he has given
them money or done them some favour or other, or vice versa;
or their children are at Ponsonby (his children by Oksana), or
the Harrodian (his children by his previous wife but one)
together. And a number of the guests are here as a down payment on future calls on Keith's good credit. They are paying it
forward.

'Special to *me*,' says Gideon. 'To *me*!' In my ear. 'Not to *I*.
Didn't he go to school?'

Then Keith namechecks some especially special people
whom he wants to thank particularly for making such an effort
– the prime minister, of course, and Samantha, who might have
left to go to attend to important matters of state –

'You mean date night,' someone shouts.

And he thanks all his team from the New York office and
the Beijing office, who subsidize the losses of the New York
office, ho ho; he wants to thank someone called Patrick, his
dear friend, for all his good advice over the years, especially his
tip to get out of newspaper publishing five years ago, and book
publishing getting on for ten, and then he pauses.

Everyone presumes he is going to get maudlin about
Oksana.

'But, lastly, I would like to make a special mention of Gala,'
he says. 'Mother of my beautiful wife, Oksana, who has flown
in from Donetsk to be here tonight, as have Oksana's twin sisters, Tasha and Masha. Where are you, Gala, Tasha and
Masha?'

Tasha and Masha reveal themselves in the front row, and I

am amazed I haven't spotted them before: they are sulky, stringy blondes from the same stable as Oksana, but their dam, Gala, is a revelation: a stumpy woman with her hair in a headscarf, clutching a large leather handbag. It is completely beyond comprehension that she produced these three Amazons, but, as Giddy whispers, 'Russian genes – total hotties in their twenties. Then, *blam*, they go baboushka. Keith: be warned.'

'Gideon,' I say. 'For once. Shut up.'

'So I would like everyone to raise their glasses, as this really is a Gala – ha ha – occasion,' says Keith. 'Everyone I love and care about is here, even my first and second wives, and both mothers-in-law.' Laughter. 'So happy birthday to *me*. I really am one lucky bastard! Now, come here, Scary, and give your old man a kiss.'

Someone shouts, 'To Keith!' and everyone echoes, 'Keith!' and raises glasses, empty or full. Gala scowls, drinks and dashes hers to the ground, as do Masha and Tasha, and the three women stand there as if hoping to start a fight, but instead, everyone cheers and claps, and Oksana starts bouncing up and down with excitement in the castle.

Mimi

I follow Chris-from-*Newsnight* from the Green Room, past various dressing rooms, down a wide, neon-lit corridor.

There are large double doors at the end. Studio 2. There is a warning red light on outside over a sign that says 'ON AIR'.

'Watch the cables,' he says, as we penetrate the darkness. I now feel that I have been held hostage so long by Chris that I will do anything he asks.

We part a dark curtain and stand in the wings, together with a score of preternaturally young people in uniform of trainers, jeans, stubble and hoodies, wearing headphones and clutching clipboards. Only the blue-backgrounded set is brightly lit, and three cameramen are filming as the presenter – a ferret-like blonde who shows her lower teeth while she talks – is finishing up her interview with Vince Cable and Keith Vaz and the package is being cued up to roll. That will last, I am told, five minutes, and then I'm up.

The studio manager is a middle-aged woman in glasses who says she's called Jenni/Jenny – I think there is a rule that says all women over a certain age who work at the BBC are called Jenni/Jenny – and gives me a tired wave.

Chris has already warned me that I will need to be in place on set before the end of the Meredith dig package, and to 'scram' before the credits, as Josh has some 'jiggery-pokery' planned. As he says this, Chris does jazz hands and makes a funny face.

I've already been miked up, which involved untucking my

Zara shirt and then messily retucking it, and removing the necklace Ralph gave me for my fortieth.

As I stand waiting to go on, I think: in less than two minutes –

A tap on my shoulder.

'Please can you go and sit next to Eleanor,' says Chris, and gives me a little shove towards the blue sofas, where the other guests for the basement-dig discussion have already been seated.

I pick my way across the dusty concrete floor, the spaghetti of cables, smile at the presenter, who doesn't smile back. Meredith glances up briefly and gives me a curt nod, as she leafs through her brief for the interview.

I take a seat next to the presenter, at right angles to Meredith, and also next to the leader of the Royal Borough of Kensington and Chelsea, a Tory banker called Giles Goodenough in a pin-stripe suit. We all watch the package on the screens.

We see a panoramic view of one street in Notting Hill. It's Elgin Crescent, where every other house is digging a base-ment, so the street scene shows stucco villas obscured by hoardings, scarred with diggers, lorries, skips, Portaloos and crews of builders in hard hats and rigger boots. The theme of the package is not that Notting Hill 'is the new Monaco' and, as people can't build up, they are building down while they can.

Then an architectural therapist – no, me neither – is wheeled on to explain that 'the attic is the site of rationality' and the basement represents 'irrationality and the darkest manifest-ations of the unconscious', basically implying that anyone who digs down is a Fritzl-style psychopath, and then someone from some right-wing think tank explains how good the devel-opment is in every way, and then the package ends, and Eleanor is cueing up our discussion.

'In London, the vogue for iceberg houses is reaching fever pitch as some councils are threatening to pull the plug on works . . . gyms . . . underground swimming pools . . . months, if not years, of disruption . . . roads closed . . . structural damage . . . flooding . . .' Eleanor wraps up the cue.

'Now, with me, the leader of the Royal Borough of Kensington, Giles Goodenough, and local Mimi Fleming, who is active on the neighbourhood campaign to oppose a triple basement in the heart of Notting Hill, which has a primary school on one side and a new community centre on the other. Mimi will be giving us some fresh news on that in just a minute.'

We all nod and give curt smiles.

'Mimi, thank you for coming on. I know you have some information about the owners of the mansion in Ponsonby Terrace, which we will come to shortly, but turning to you first, Giles Goodenough, you're the Tory leader of the council' – she says 'Tory leader' with the same intonation as you might say 'people trafficker' or 'child rapist'.

'Perhaps you are able to explain why you've granted permission to the owners, whoever they are, to carry out works that are so obviously antisocial, when, as local resident, film director and Comic Relief co-founder Richard Curtis says: the council represents all its ratepayers, not just developers.'

Giles Goodenough looks pleased at the question. And disposes of it in a few practised soundbites. He sounds sorrowful when he explains that, as the planning law stands, the council can't turn down applications and actually can't afford to, as they often go to appeal and then the council has to pay costs, too. Then he looks into the camera and says that the 'direction of travel' is very much in the opposite direction of double and triple digs but, until the new guidance is formally adopted, the PAC –

233

'That's the planning application committee,' Eleanor says crisply.

Giles Goodenough then launches into a spiel that could have been written by the Treasury about how the bankers, the developers and the basement digs in the capital are the main engine revving this country out of recession, like it or not. 'We are where we are,' he concludes.

'And now, Mimi Fleming of the STD coalition.' Eleanor is turning to me, with a light laugh. 'I should explain that STD stands for Stop the Digs, not Save the Date,' she says.

'Or Sexually . . .' I say, then stop.

Eleanor raises one eyebrow. 'One of the main complaints – and there are many – is that the owners have gone through the planning process anonymously. But you have, as part of our *Newsnight* investigation, managed to uncover the identities of the applicants.'

'Yes, indeed,' I say. I've never said 'Yes, indeed' in my life, but it now comes out of my mouth.

I clear my throat.

At this point some documents were supposed to flash on the screen, so I wait.

But the screen behind me still shows the broken street scene of Notting Hill, while the camera to my left shows me sitting in a green skirt and a beige shirt with a white placket from Zara with my mouth open and, in front of me, in the unlit gloaming of the technical area off-screen, I can see the seconds hand ticking away on a clock, and the studio manager is talking to Josh Kurtz and they are both looking at me as if the white coats are about to charge the set, so there is nothing for it. I plough on.

'Yes, thank you, Eleanor,' I say, again. 'And it does appear that the people behind Alpha Star are – how to put this? – well-known Notting Hill residents, so this is going to come as a bit

of a shock and surprise, to say the least, to the STD campaign.'
I pause. 'According to documents seen by *Newsnight*,' I say
with care (this is the form of words Chris has told me to use:
thank God I remember) and phew! – the documents are now
up on the screen – 'the owner of the house with the triple dig
is –' I falter.

'So can you tell our viewers who it is,' says Eleanor, with
her pencil pointing at the screen.

I see Josh Kurtz glaring at me – he has left the gallery and
come down to the set. He makes a whirring movement with
his hand. Wind it up.

'Yes. The architect of the triple dig is the former eco-
architect Gideon Sturgis, who is now more famous for being
the architect of the Phallus in Southwark.' I am getting into
my stride now, even if I malaprop Phallus and Southwark.
'Gideon Sturgis, the architect of the Phallus' – comes out OK
this time – 'London's highest skyscraper. Apart from the
Shard, of course.'

I can't believe I've done it. Outed Gideon. Who is married
to Clare. Who lives in my old house. It couldn't get closer to
home.

'And the owner of the AXA PPP Healthcare tower?' says
Eleanor, making me think I should never have said 'The
Phallus' on air.

'Yes,' I say, and I realize my face has gone bright red. It's
hard to bite the hand. But I have to. It is my public duty to
report it.

'It's not Alpha Star, as it says on the Land Register, I mean
Registry. That's a front. It's the financier Keith Dunbar.'

'If I may interrupt . . . um . . . Miss Fleming?' Giles Goodenough emits a discreet cough.

Eleanor cocks her head in his direction with an enquiring,
beady look, like a woodland creature on *Autumn Watch*.

'If you check the Land Registry website' – and then Goodenough spells it out, as if he really wants us to go online right
then – 'yes, if you go to www.landregistrysupport.co.uk, I
think you'll find the registered owner is, indeed, the educational charity Alpha Star, but that is owned by Keith Dunbar as
one of his many philanthropic interests, and, indeed, I am a
director.'

'Well, then, it's good that you're here to defend your actions,
isn't it?' says Eleanor, terrier-like. 'Can you begin to justify
your development? How can personal selfishness trump public amenity here?'

'That's very easy,' says Giles Goodenough smoothly in
response. 'As Mr Dunbar can't be here tonight to speak for
himself, I am happy to fill you in. Alpha Star has bought the
house and, as I understand it, the Dunbars intend to set up a
much-needed boutique free school in the borough, to cope
primarily with the socially excluded,' he carries on. 'So the
subterranean development, far from being antisocial –'

I can hear someone jabbering into Eleanor's earpiece. I try
to interrupt Giles Goodenough, but my mic has been muted,
or switched off.

Giles Goodenough is now telling Eleanor that Alpha Star is
not only using compassionate contractors when it comes to
the new free school in Kensington and Chelsea . . . 'It is not
only using the best possible practices in the construction
industry, and investing in our young people,' he drones on,
'but the council has established that works will only take place
between the hours of nine and five, and only till 12 noon, as
opposed to 1 p.m., on Saturdays, as a way of protecting family
life and quality time in the borough.'

Eleanor is nodding him encouragement, as if she can take
as much of this from Goodenough as he's got.

'Two, we have changed the plans so that the sub-basement

floor will be a gym and the sub-sub-basement floor will be a decent-sized swimming pool.'

Eleanor is beaming and nodding, urging him on, as if he is inviting her to stay.

'And Alpha Star has decided, whatever the designation of the property, whether educational or residential, to make the pool, the gym and all the amenities available to both Ponsonby Prep and also to the users of the Giving Back Centre next door,' concludes Giles with a flourish, as if he doesn't want to draw too much attention to Keith Dunbar's own generosity, as he is, despite his billionaire status, a humble man. 'It will be, if you like, a community resource rather than a personal and private luxury for any one individual or their family.'

As I stagger off the set, we all pile into the Green Room. As I knew she would be, Meredith is all over Goodenough, telling him that the Alpha Star offer is 'Big Society in action', and how he and Keith are a 'shining exemplar of inclusive capitalism'. She has her iPhone out and is already inputting his contact details.

I collapse on to a chair.

Nobody seems to notice I am there.

Vince Cable is quarting back white wine with an assistant producer, while inhaling Twiglets, and Meredith is telling him and Keith Vaz, and Giles Goodenough, too, that Mal has been offered a knighthood but turned it down, as he made so much money selling his company that he didn't need the recognition and, for her part, she thinks 'Lady Blacker' sounds like something out of Cluedo . . .

Finally, Josh Kurtz, the editor of the programme, bursts in and someone – a runner – goes to the fridge and takes out a chilled full-fat Coke.

'Great show,' he says, cracking it open and waiting for the fizz to settle. He takes a long pull then wipes his chin. 'Thanks, everyone. *Newsnight*'s trending on Twitter with the hashtag #localhero and #alphastar, so that's good, and, so far I haven't had any calls from Legal about Mimi's – um –' He suddenly spots me on the sofa on my own, so I get up in a hopeful way.

'Couple of minor legals, but we're on it, I'm sure we'll be fine' – he looks at me then looks away – 'in the end.'

Chris sidles up to me, and I suddenly get the feeling that the entire crew has decided the most sensible next step is to medevac me off the premises asap.

'Your car's here,' he says, slightly pushing me towards the door so I stumble into the floor manager, who steadies me in a kindly way.

I gather my things, and switch my iPhone back on, but, of course, there's 'No service' still. Meredith has moved from the most important politicians in the room to Josh Kurtz. Her pale skin gleams under the strip lighting in the Green Room.

I decide that I will beat a retreat, but I will go with dignity. So I go up to Meredith and Kurtz.

'Well done,' I manage to choke out, as I hear her saying to Josh, 'I hope you're coming to my annual Christmas party. Just a few locals, neighbours, friends and lots of champagne!' She is touching his arm, and gurgling, as if to say, if things were different . . . you never know, you and I . . .

'There'll be plenty of telly folk and other media creatives, what with Mal's new production-company venture. The invitations have already gone out, but I'll make sure Delilah, the PA who runs my office, sends you one tomorrow.'

She doesn't turn to me once. Say anything. Say 'Well done,' for finding out who Alpha Star are.

Meredith has, in fact, been frosty for weeks now. Since Mustique. And she's been off about this *Newsnight* programme, too. And I've just been . . . sucking it up, because, I suppose, she's richer and more important than I am and, above all, she's a neighbour. And neighbours must make nice.

Meredith is staring at me now, as I stand with Josh.

I'm off home. This has been a tough evening. I unmask Keith – who has been nothing but a kind and generous host to me and my whole family – as the Dirty Digger, and then it turns out I am blackening his name as the mansion is going to be, according to the Tory leader, the local public baths or something. It doesn't really add up, but I am too shaken to speak.

'Just saying goodbye,' I say, as I pass Meredith, and kiss her on the cheek, as if we're friends.

She jerks away so that, instead of hitting her cheek, I bang her jutting cheekbone. Then she gives me a penetrating look, as if silently asking me something. As I draw breath again I know why.

I inhale her scent and almost faint.

She is drenched – as if she has self-basted – in Frisson, and there's a note of something else on her skin that I've only smelt on one other person, ever. Who I thought belonged to me.

Farouche.

As I leave the building, dazed, trying not to break down, my phone picks up a signal, and starts beeping. And beeping.

I have five missed calls. And seven texts.

'Where are you going, ma'am?' asks the driver, who is standing by a Prius holding a placard saying 'Fleming'.

'Home, please,' I say, falling into the back seat, almost in tears.

'And where might that be?' the driver says, his hand clawed over the satnav on the dashboard, ready to input my address. Home? Nowhere feels like home any more.

'Notting Hill, please, driver,' I say.

Ralph

As waiters rush forward to pick up the broken glass from the Russian toasts from the concrete floor, Gideon takes the mic again. Someone has come up behind me, and grabbed my bottom.

Only one person in the world does this to me.

It's Rose. A real person. From Dorset. I can almost smell the grass and the air on her cheeks as I kiss her. 'Is Pierre here?' I ask. 'No, Miami,' she says.

'And now, as promised . . .' Keith thunders on. 'Pray silence. In just a few moments, on the East Wall, you can feast your eyes on something truly special. For one night only.' Keith scans the room, over our heads, shading his eyes. 'I trust no minors are present?'

We all laugh politely, as it has been decades since any of us have been minors, but Tasha and Masha, I now see, have a selection of Keith's children and are escorting them up the ramp and out of the Turbine Hall, where limos and Ubers are lined up, the drivers puffing on cigarettes, waiting to take them home.

'What you are about to see may contain scenes of a violent or sexual nature and profanity – or, I hope, all three – and right from the start. On the occasion of my fiftieth birthday, I am proud to announce' – everyone quietens, to listen, obedient – 'the world premier of the new piece by internationally acclaimed performance artist Farouche. Let the wild rumpus start!'

Waiters circulate with trays again. I take what looks like a gin and tonic, drink a deep draught, and the waiter says, 'That's not fizzy water, by the way – it's a special cocktail made with fair-trade quinoa vodka,' but I am past caring. I'll take anything, drink anything, at this point.

Farouche's film has started.

On the screen, there is just an eye. It's like that awfully boring Salvador Dalí film I watched at boarding school once on a Sunday night in the Michaelmas term. Music plays. I'm not sure what, but it's loud and unpleasant.

'This is great,' says Rose. 'The Prodigy, isn't it? Remember? I like it.'

After a few minutes, we are all beginning to feel uncomfortable, bored, and also . . . as if someone is watching us. Then the eye turns into a camera lens.

Even I have watched *Big Brother*, so I am wondering where Farouche is going with this.

And then the camera fills the screen and you can see an image inside the fish-eye of the lens. It is two naked bodies on a bed. One pale, one darker. Both female, though hard to tell at this range.

'She's subverting the surveillance theme,' whispers Rose in my ear.

'Thanks, Rose,' I answer.

Then there is a montage, one that seems never to end. I can recognize some, but not all, of the jumbled collage of references, images and allusions: Edward Snowden, Julian Assange, men in Guantanamo, hooded in orange jumpsuits, drones, more men in orange jumpsuits, kneeling in the desert, ISIS jihadis wielding knives, children in kurta pajama being killed by drones, Bradley Manning in uniform, Bradley Manning in drag, blood in the dust, heads on spikes, the CIA HQ in Langley . . . it's like a dull double episode of *Homeland*.

The images are superimposed with screens dripping with

computer code, or the stock market indices going red and green, and intercut with screengrabs of Google searches, emails and images of the global HQs of Google, Yahoo, Apple, Microsoft, News Corp, the BBC . . .

People are starting to whisper and shuffle, but then the fisheye of the camera comes back.

And the image comes into focus and expands so that the screen is now filled by the two naked bodies lying on a white bed, entwined in a white sheet.

One is white, and plump, and face down under the sheet.

The other is a whippet-like dark woman, with Medusa-like corkscrew hair.

It is the artist currently known as Farouche.

I want to leave. Something about the scene is infinitely disturbing.

Farouche removes the sheet. You see her lips move, but you can't hear what she's saying. Then she pulls the sheet off the woman, who is crouching on her knees, so her bottom is in the air. I would know that bottom anywhere. As it has two moles or slightly raised brown freckles on the right buttock that exactly recall the constellation Canis Major in the night sky.

Farouche then proceeds to perform a sex act on the other woman, and I have to look away.

It all goes on so long that people begin to talk amongst themselves, as they do at the back of a room during a speech that over-extends itself.

'This is so cool,' says Rose.

'This is pornography,' I say, praying I'm the only one who has noticed who the other woman is.

'I can't believe everyone came south of the river to see this.'

'And now she's referencing the trope of the sex tape,' whispers Rose. 'So clever, no? And very brave.'

Gideon is now behind us.

'I say, Farouche, bravo!' he says in a leering voice. 'Doesn't muck about, does she!'

Farouche's head is bobbing up and down, and the other woman is clutching at the sheet, and the soundtrack has become a rap of Theresa May making a speech about civil liberties, and Obama talking about Iraq, and Syria and al Qaeda, intercut with the sounds of gunfire and screaming and YouTube beheading videos.

'Nom nom, hurry up, fatty,' says Gideon. 'We're all waiting for the money shot.'

Rose grabs my arm. Farouche has flipped over the woman on the bed as if she's a chop on a griddle and the other side needs browning.

Her face is pixellated, but I can see, and Rose can see, and anyone who has ever seen my wife even for a brief time would recognize that wild chestnut hair anywhere.

'Jesus,' says Rose. 'Isn't –' she blurts. Then claps her hand over her mouth.

Gideon looks at me with what I am afraid to say seems like fresh respect.

'Well, old chum,' he says, in a stage whisper. I wish he would stop talking.

Talking always makes everything so much worse. 'Was this all in the name of art? Or is it still called agitprop?' He looks at me narrowly, as if to say, 'You poor sod. Husbands and wives. Always the last to know.'

I admit that I am, for the first time in my life, completely stunned, at the sight of my wife engaged in *actual rumpy* with another woman.

Like a halal sheep.

I thought that whatever was going on – well, when it comes to Mimi's eruptions, my *modus operandi* is to keep my head down and hope, like a general in the Great War, that it will be over by Christmas.

'Terribly clever,' Rose says, as we stand frozen in front of the screen. 'I think it's about exploitation: who is exploiting whom – are the surveillance authorities exploiting us, or vice versa? And, in a sex tape, who is the victim – those who make the tape, or those who participate in the making of the sex tape?'

'Or those who view the sex tape,' says Gideon, with another awful snigger. Then he clears his throat. He has gone rather red in the face. 'Anyway. I can't see Clare carpet munching the business end like that. The *back* of the business end, at that. Impressive.'

I would punch Gideon in the mouth, but people are going 'Shhh!' as, believe it or not, the piece has not yet ended. What happens next is hard to determine: the filming speeds up, Farouche is no longer on a bed with Mimi, she's with several other women – but fortunately, or unfortunately, they are naked and also pixellated, and I don't recognize them with their clothes off but Gideon is whistling and saying, 'Pretty sure that's Virginie' and 'I'm guessing the tall dark one with the pretty tits is Meredith?' And then he says, 'Oh God,' and moans, then says, 'Well, if Farouche can, I see no reason why I can't have a crack at her, too.'

Farouche proceeds to have sex with a black man and several women and, even though the pictures are black and white and grainy and moving, they're so cluttered up with the political messaging about surveillance and personal identity that it really is hard to see who is doing what to whom, so there are small mercies.

She doesn't have sex with any animals, for example. Luckily, no dogs were harmed in the making of the piece. And the only person who hasn't been visibly harmed or abused in some way is the artist herself.

After twenty-five excruciatingly long minutes that I will never be able to forget for as long as I live, the piece seems to finish, and everyone feels the need to pronounce.

Virginie gives her verdict.

'What we 'ave just watched – *je te jure* – *Farouche, elle n'est pas stupide* – eez a long commercial for Frisson.'

But there's one more scene to come. The finale shows Farouche apparently inserting a CCTV camera up her front bottom, after which the screen goes mercifully dark.

Everyone claps and Gideon shouts 'Bravo!', which makes me want to hit him again.

Instead, I go home.

Front door slams at 11.30 p.m. It's Dad. He says, 'Hello, darling, hello, my puppy,' to Calypso, who always barks when someone she knows and loves comes in and never when a total stranger breaks a window and steals two MacBook Airs from the bedrooms of sleeping children (that really happened).

He stomps upstairs to use the toilet then goes down again. I can tell just by the leaden tread as he walks back into the kitchen below my bedroom that he's in a bad mood. I don't blame him. Mum was so embarrassing on *Newsnight*, when it turned out that Keith had bought the house to be a new school, but it can't be that – Mum's 'journalism' is always hideous; that's always been the cost of doing business with Mum, when I think of all the articles she's written about us, and the terrible photo shoots we've had to do.

Silence from down below, till I hear Mum come in just before midnight. She throws her keys down on the side by the front door and then they slide off and fall on to the lino by the mat, like they always do. Then she kicks off her shoes so they thud against the skirting. Then she goes into the kitchen. Dad is in there. I can imagine him sitting at the table with a tumbler of Famous Grouse. You can hear everything – and I mean, everything; I wear earplugs at night – as this is an old council block and the walls are like paper.

Mum: 'Hello, you're still up! Did you see me on *Newsnight*? What did you think of the fact that Keith Dunbar owned Ponsonby behind all our backs, cooked up the plans, got them approved, and now they're saying it's some charter, or free school and . . .'

Short silence.

Turns into long silence.

Mum: 'So . . . how was Keith's party?'

Dad: 'No, I did not see you on *Newsnight*, Mimi. I don't give a monkey's who owns Ponsonby Terrace, though it's a pity it turns out to be Keith Dunbar. To be honest, I always assumed it was him. You seem to have missed the fact that all Oksana did in Mustique was chunter on about the school run and how she'd told Keithy to buy a house nearer Ponsonby. It was plain as day. God knows how I'm going to look him in the eye but, anyway, what does it matter? To Dunbar, to that arse Gideon, too, it's just another property. It's just another asset to those people, and has the status of any other asset. It means nothing. It is only kept till it can be sold on to the next sucker for more money. It's not a *home*.'

Dad believes that new money has no sentimental attachment to its estates, unlike our wider Fleming family, like Grandpa Perry, who has clung on to a crumbling castle in the Borders for centuries.

Dad: 'No, I was, frankly, somewhat distracted this evening. I was disturbed by the main event at Tate Modern, which happened to be you making your debut on the big screen in that Belgian tinker's sex tape that was the *pièce de résistance* at Keith Dunbar's party. Jesus Christ, Mimi. I couldn't believe my eyes. Everything Clare and everyone else says is true. I've been an utter fool to tell them you'd never, in a million years, be such a pathetic, deluded trollop, but I'd forgotten' – in a hiss – 'what a total tart you are.'

Silence from Mum.

Dad: 'You've done it before, you're doing it now, and you'll do it again, I expect. But I have to ask. Did you even *know* you were being set up? Did you know that, for Farouche, this wasn't love, this wasn't sex, this wasn't even art, this is – I don't know what to call it – a command performance of *Royal Variety Show* NARCISSIST EXHIBITIONISM?'

Mum, small voice: 'I still don't know what you're talking about. Please, Ralph. What are you talking about? You're frightening me.'

Dad: 'What do you mean, what do I mean? What. On. Earth do you think you've done *now*? Did you know you were being filmed? Did you participate in this pathetic, filthy rubbish, this pornography parading as art? I think you owe me an explanation. You owe this whole family an explanation. You *disgust* me.'

Sound of Calypso's tail thumping on lino. Trying to cheer them up.

Sound of Mum opening cupboard, looking for chocolate. Sound of wrapper tearing. Bin lid going up and down.

Mum: 'Darling!' Light voice, almost amused. 'Don't be nuts. Of course I haven't been in a *sex tape*. Darling, if you haven't noticed, I'm forty-four years old. I don't have a bikini body to flaunt, exactly, do I? Who would want to see *me* without any clothes on, let alone . . . getting jiggy . . . with anyone? Please. I don't know what you're talking about.'

Dad: 'Yes, you do.'

Mum: 'No, I honestly don't.'

I honestly don't either tbh. What the fcuk is Dad talking abt? Mum in a sex tape? That was shown at *Tate Modern*? In front of the prime minister and his wife. (There were pictures of her on a bouncy castle all over Twitter, as well as people trolling Mum for being 'the worst female guest on *Newsnight* ever in a very competitive market for that distinction'.)

I can see why Dad's cross, but Mum . . . stars in arty sex tape at posh top people's party! Get in! Booooom! Respect!

I clatter down, making a noise to give them a few seconds' warning.

They are both sitting at the table, and Dad is showing Mum something on his phone and saying, 'By some fluke, I managed to turn it from photo to video, so here's the proof.' He jabs at the play button and their heads come together as they peer at the screen.

I hear some audio – sort of messy – and Mum is very still as he shows her.

Then she bursts into tears.

Dad, shouting: 'Oh, for *fuck's sake*, don't *cry*. Why do *women* always *cry* –'

Mum: 'Please don't shout, you'll wake the children.'

I clear my throat.

'Word up, Detroit,' I say, so they know I'm in the room.

They look up.

Me: 'Hi Mum, Dad, in case you were wondering, I've made the packed lunches for tomorrow. Lucian's gym kit is by the front door. Posy's got swimming, but I can't find her regulation swim hat, so I've given her three quid from the jar to buy another one at the pool.'

Mum: 'Thanks, darling . . .'

Me: 'And I know you two are very busy with all your bad shit, but I have some news for you. I hope this won't make things worse. Sid's asked me to live with him and Cathy downstairs, and guess what? I've said yes. We're going into business together. Well, it's more of a charity thing.'

Mum opens her mouth to say, 'That's wonderful, darling,' as the truth is, the Garden Court 'maisonette' is poky and none of us can stand it, and Lonsdale Garden Court conclusively disproves the *Location, Location, Location* fantasy that it's better to have the worst house in the best street rather than the best house in the worst street.

Me: 'One last thing, as I'm tired.'

I carry my MacBook, open, and place it on the table, where both are sitting like waxworks, not looking at each other, Dad staring down into his Scotch as if reading tea leaves, Mum breaking off squares of chocolate with salted caramel crackle bits she buys in bulk from Lidl.

Me: 'Don't you think you'd better explain, to Mum, why that freak Clare Sturgis has sent you all these pictures of Joe?'

I click out of the link Posy had sent me, saying, 'Click on this if you've never seen a baby bunny in a bathtub before,' and get to the page.

I have grouped the pictures of Joe so that it's like a time-lapse photograph of the boy, from a baby to in his uniform for Ponsonby Prep, and there are also quite a few of him in cricket whites and swimming shorts, on yachts, in the garden, playing instruments, on skis and stuff. As the images get more recent, and I've looked at them carefully, I can see a theme emerging, more and more strongly.

He looks like Dad.

And then I point on the screen to the most recent image Dad's been sent, which is automatically saved to iCloud and dated today, and taken in St John and St Elizabeth hospital yesterday.

It's of a blob that looks a bit like William Hague, i.e. a foetus, and the host of the blob is a patient called Clare Sturgis.

Mimi

From: MimiFleming@gmail.com
To: FarouchedeG@wanadoo.fr.org
Date: 20 December 2014
I know you won't read this now, as you are at Meredith's Christmas party, along with everyone else, and I can't help wondering
– have you slept with *all* of them – Virginie, Sally, the girl who
does your toes at Cowshed, that little assistant in Paris called
Charlotte, as well as Meredith?
I wish I'd known your playbook before I fell for you. Before I knew
that what you do is light the blue touchpaper and not so much
retire but fuck off, laughing and pointing at the smouldering mess
you've left behind.
But I'm over it now. I'm glad we've talked. I don't want to go over
the sex tape again. As Ralph says, 'It's all right for you, Mimi, you
haven't seen it. Whereas I will carry those images in my head as
long as I live.'

My fingers have been flying across the keyboard, but the
sound of the party is almost too loud now for me to do anything else but feel left out and cross.

I can hear the roar of the Blacker party across the garden, a
festive revel which is partly in celebration of their works being
over, and to show off their new, knocked-through, lateral
mega-mansion, which has just been completed, after only two
years' solid work.

I'm sitting at my tiny, kidney-shaped dressing table, one that belonged to Ralph's grandmother, tucked in the small bay window which overlooks the garden.

I can see the lights on, blazing, and there's a huge Christmas tree in the Blackers' double-width back garden, which they've had done in the minimal fashion, lawn bisected by pleached limes, concrete, gravel. I know everyone wants to go out and stand by the braziers and have a sing-song, as the Blackers all love singing, and Meredith could have been an opera singer, as well as a ballet dancer, according to Meredith, anyway.

Marguerite kept saying, 'Do come, I'm sure Meredith *meant* to invite you, you're a neighbour, it must be a *mistake*,' not knowing.

The waiters are all in black and white, and all the curtains are open, so I can see them moving around on the lower-ground floor, the champagne, boxes and boxes of Pol Roger, stacked to keep cool outside, and occasionally I see a face or a figure framed at the window and look out over the communal garden, and a small part of me hopes against hope that it's Farouche, looking for me.

I carry on with the email. 'I should have known that you would move on,' I write, trying not to let tears fall on the keyboard in case they fry my laptop. 'I blame myself for falling for you. I blame myself for allowing "us" to mean so much more to me than it did to you. Enough of that.'

I sit still for ages, listening to the shouts of laughter carrying over the communal garden. I think about what to say next.

'F, it was sweet of you to suggest that we come to Mustique at Christmas. Sorry I haven't replied on that,' I type.

I don't write that 1. we can't afford it and 2. we're going to Rose's for Christmas, and the Sturgises are coming. (Clare hasn't been at all well, but we're all back on track. Phew, it's been a longish haul, as Ralph would say, but I can't go into all of that.)

I stare at my screen. I can hear people drifting around outside. Someone starts up an a cappella version of 'The Holly and the Ivy' in a rich, public-school *basso profundo* – I think I recognize the deep, rich tones of local author Sebastian Faulks – and more voices join in.

I know this email is going on far too long. Farouche never showed the slightest interest in the mundane details of my domestic life, my finances, my Christmas, Home Farm, the fact that Mirabel and Sid have started up a food-box scheme, delivering fruit and veg from the market after it closes on Saturday to local households in Notting Hill, Queen's Park and North Ken in food poverty, let alone my feelings, about how she took my heart and broke it in two, in front of hundreds of people at Keith Dunbar's fucking 'Hawaii', just as I was naming him as the Dirty Digger on *Newsnight* . . . I don't finish the email, let alone press send. When I'm asked whether I want to save the screed to draft, I don't.

I cancel it.

I promised Ralph that I wouldn't contact Farouche, and I must keep my promise.

It is only when I hear Meredith's voice soaring over the garden ('I had to choose whether to be an opera singer or a ballerina in my twenties') as she sings a descant solo of *'Adeste Fideles'* in a warbling soprano that I put my wax earplugs in.

I go to my bedside table, where I keep my secret, private things, and I take out the tiny round flagon she sent me, afterwards, as my consolation prize.

I ease the top off, and inhale, and I have my hit of Frisson, of Farouche, and I try to tell myself that I don't want more.

The little round flagon is numbered. She only produces 365 bottles a year. She designs and numbers each bottle herself, all are collector's items, and this is – I note – number 69. She told me that she would send me the first bottle of *Frivolité* when the batch arrived from Grasse.

I realize that she probably does and says the same to all her conquests.

I allow myself to cry, just for a little, before I dry my eyes and blow my nose and potter down, out of our maisonette, and down to the basement, to help Mirabel and Sid with their spreadsheet for their pioneering 'FreshBox' scheme, to bring free fruit and vegetables to the indigent of Notting Dale.

PART THREE

CHRISTMAS

Clare

Court Place Farm,
Honeyborne

I have to say, Rose really does the most perfect Christmas.

Goose *and* turkey. Four sorts of stuffing. Sprouts with bacon and chestnuts.

Christmas really can be a healing occasion. Rose must have had an instinct that bringing us all to Dorset would be like balm in Gilead, and so it has proved.

Even Ralph keeps saying, 'Well, it all seems to be going very well . . . *so far.*'

And, best of all, Joan, her cleaner, agreed to come in daily throughout the festive period on a triple rate, as well as another woman in her sixties known only as 'Mrs Clissitt from the village'.

Joan's a widow now and she said she was grateful for the extra, and says work keeps her out of mischief, and she did a little twirl in her Christmas tabard, white with a brown figgy pudding on it, spiked with flaming holly.

Rose was more relaxed, gracious and hospitable than I can say, even welcoming our new puppy, Tracker (in the end, every single class fell in love with the Sprollie to such an extent that the bidding went even higher than expected. Julien dropped out of the bidding at £40,000, so in the end Gideon paid £42,000 for a puppy that, on the open market, would sell for no more than £500, which serves him right, considering everything).

Yes, it's all been lovely. Pierre's been padding about in his pointed kilim slippers doing drinks and fires, and going off in the mornings in their new Range Rover to get the papers from the Post Office and Stores, which has turned into a community shop. But when he tootled off on a Wednesday morning I said I thought it was closed Wednesdays, and he whispered to me that he actually goes to the all-night garage on the Godminster ring road, as he prefers going to the ESSO service station, as you don't 'have to chat to people' there, unlike in the village shop, which is like a cross between a care-home outing and a cocktail party.

And Court Place is such a jewel, the sort of place you drool over in *Country Life*: a late-Elizabethan manor house, one of those places where the garden and the landscape beyond merge seamlessly and inside is light and comfort, the accents on pale, fresh and sunny: just eight bedrooms, slate floors downstairs, double-height hall, wide fireplaces where the home fires always burn, so the whole house always smells of flowers, polish, woodsmoke. As for the interior, Rose doesn't need a decorator, she deploys touches of William Morris here, Nancy Lancaster there, Arts & Crafts with Milan, so the house is a wonderful, heady mix. There are old and new pictures, so Freud drawings of whippets and Ivon Hitchens landscapes and a marvellous Stanley Spencer of cherries in bloom in the sitting room, and the new paintings, Endellion Lycett Green still lifes, landscapes by Freya Wood . . . There are only a few flies in the ointment.

I'm afraid that Mimi is wearing Frisson, but no one has mentioned it. I know that she's still in pain, and I would never dream of telling her what Virginie told me Farouche has said. (That Merde-eeth was 'eeen-credeeble' in bed.)

Anyway, the children love it, as there are tall glass jars everywhere full of jelly beans and peanut M&Ms, and a fifty-two-inch flatscreen TV, there's Netflix, and mobile reception, and wi-fi.

So far, touch wood, it's been a very happy time, apart from the occasion when Lucian and Joe were playing on the twin sculptures that frame the vista from the house to the lake.

One is of a vulva and the other is Pierre's take on an aroused kouros. The vulva is a monumental piece of stone with a fissure down the middle, which Pierre says symbolizes the gateway to the universe. Lucian managed to insert himself so deep into the cleft that he got stuck and we thought we'd have to ring the fire brigade, but somehow Gideon, Ralph and Pierre managed to pull him out, 'without needing forceps', as Gideon joked. When he popped free, Ralph said, 'It's a boy.' Then I went into the house, my heart in about a million tiny pieces.

So yes, it's been nice. Considering.

Rose has put Gideon and me at the opposite end of the house from Ralph and Mimi, but Joe and Lucian are in the attic together, where there's an X-Box and bean bags and ping-pong table and a vintage set of Subbuteo – which the boys have fallen in love with.

Joe and Lucian are bonding.

We made a pact, all of us, not to do lavish presents for each other on the day, as we all have too much. As Farouche said in an interview with the *Sunday Times* after her Tate Modern showstopper (poor, poor Mimi): 'It's so important to go back to basics at this time – energy, not materiality.'

In the end I just got a season ticket for Chelsea for the Flemings, as the boys love their football; and for Mimi a spa bootcamp week at a clinic on the Wörthersee in Austria.

I told her she could fly to Klagenfurt on Ryanair, so all she needed to do was get herself there and it's all taken care of. I didn't tell Mimi how much it was for the week, as it sounds silly when you think that people pay four grand to have gruel at every meal and have colonic irrigation, especially when

Mirabel and Sid have established that many families in West London live on only three pounds a day and can't afford fresh fruit and vegetables at all.

I have to say Mirabel's FreshBox scheme is terribly impressive. She's got all the market traders on side. She's managed to secure funding from Tesco, in the Portobello, which has a collection point for the food bank, and she's working on Waitrose, too.

She and Sid seem very devoted. 'You'll end up in the Lords,' I told her on Christmas Eve when she arrived with one of the leaflets she'd just picked up from the printers. She's going to distribute them in the area so that people can apply for free FreshBox deliveries.

So I gave Mimi the week in the clinic, as she's always going on about how fat she is, and the boys the Chelsea season ticket. They were thrilled; luckily, they said they'd take Joe all the time if he wanted, but he said he preferred tennis and cricket; and then there was Ralph. That was tricky.

What do you give the man who wants nothing, especially from you?

What do you give the man from whom you took something, without asking?

On the grounds that we value life experiences more than consumer goods, I went off to Farlows, on Pall Mall, where they seemed to know him, and I bought him the most expensive fly-fishing rod they had, and a case, and some flies, even though I know he uses his grandfather's rod.

'My thinking was, you using such an old one is like a player at Wimbledon using one of the old wooden Dunlop tennis racquets rather than one of those new ones which connects to your smartphone via Bluetooth and counts your strokes and compares your stats to previous games,' I explain as he unzips it from its smart, dark-green canvas tube and fits it together with an expert hand.

I knew all about the new 'connected' Babolat, as I was planning to give it to Joe, but in the end we settled on just a normal racquet and junior membership of Campden Hill Tennis Club, and lessons with the pro, for him.

Just now, we were all slumped in the sitting room, watching *Downton* on TV, and Ralph suddenly says to me, 'Come on, let's give it a go.'

So we go on to the lawn, and he puts it all together and ties a fly, using special little scissors to snip, and takes up a position in the middle of the lawn and casts. I stand on his left; the kids are watching from the porch: Cas, Lucian, Posy and Joe; and Gideon's, Mimi's, Pierre's and Rose's heads appear in a cluster, briefly, at the mullioned windows of the sitting room. I know Gideon won't come out; he only likes the country if he's standing in a centrally heated room, looking out over a Poussin-like landscape with a large drink with clinking ice in his hand.

'No, it's not the same as using a very snazzy new racquet,' says Ralph in answer to my observation, as he swishes the rod, and it flexes and whips above our heads, making a fast swish in the air. 'But this is a brilliant rod. Thank you, Clare. It's very generous of you and, if only I still lived down the road, I'd be on the Lar with it the whole time.' He sounds wistful.

Then he says, in a different voice, 'You don't need to give us all these presents, you know. It's OK. We're OK.'

He is stiff with me. Understandably.

After all, I got his sperm out of the cold storage to get pregnant without asking his permission, and then, somehow, failed to tell him until the pregnancy was eight weeks underway. I wanted so much to tell him, but I couldn't.

So instead I sent him that image from my first scan, out of the clear blue sky, when I was so filled with joy and excitement that I couldn't help myself. Even though he'd made himself very plain in Mustique, that night, when it went so terribly wrong with him and he exploded – in so far as Ralph ever explodes; he does cold, hard, granular anger that's much more intimidating. He said he hadn't even told his children about Joe yet, and 'was I mad?' And then he left. Even though there was a golf buggy outside the villa, he walked, so it must have taken him hours to get back to the Dunbars', which would have been funny, if it hadn't been such an awful end to the evening.

And now, I think that maybe . . . yes. I was mad. I don't think men know that the yearning for a baby *is* like madness. It takes possession of you. You will do anything. It is like the most dementing sort of lust, and it consumes you, for years, and years.

And then, during those awful few days, after Mimi's disastrous appearances on that terrible sex tape and then *Newsnight*, so many awful things.

First, Ralph tumbled – with my help, I admit – to what Farouche and Mimi had been up to, and then Mimi realized Farouche was carrying on with Meredith, and God knows whom else, frankly – that woman really has no boundaries at all.

I really thought the Flemings were going to break up; I'd heard, from Marguerite, that they've been seeing a counsellor. Marguerite passed on the headlines, which were that what Mimi did was not about her redefining her sexuality or finding herself – she was merely externalizing her issues within the marriage.

It was at this point that I told Rose everything.

And Rose was a dear, and she agreed with me, that honesty was the best policy, and transparency, and we cooked up the Christmas plan.

And then, of course, I lost the baby. I like to think, I hope, that Ralph felt some faint flicker of loss, too. It's hard to be sure. He did have the grace to say he was sorry for me.

'Are we all set for the tea?' I ask, wandering back in.

Rose is in the kitchen with me, taking scones out of the oven. I am arranging cups and side plates, butter, clotted cream and a range of home-made jams on the square oak table.

It's all been prearranged. At teatime, Rose and Pierre are going to go off to see his mother in her nursing home in God-minster.

Ralph and I and Mimi are going to sit all the children down, in the kitchen, and Mimi will cut the cake – not the Christmas cake, but a triple-chocolate bûche de Noël that they all decorated on the twenty-third and have been begging to have ever since.

We will sit them down, all of them – even Mirabel, who is more grown up than all of us – and tell them the lovely news that they have an extra-special present this Christmas.

Yes, it's been the most perfect Christmas, and this is going to be the most perfect ending to the most perfect Christmas that I could ever imagine.

Rose kept going on about the special Boxing Day Tea with meaningful looks, so we knew something was up, and we all had to be there, rather than watching films on our laptops.

So we all go to the kitchen at Court Place, which is totally dope. It's got a huge fireplace, top of the range, as well as an Aga, a larder off one end, a pantry, a drinks chiller, and worktops where you slice stuff and there's a hole so you can just swipe the tops and tails and peelings straight into a bin. I love that. I am so getting that when me and Sid move into our house. Whenever that might be.

The chocolate cake's sitting on the worktop in the central island when we all come in, and scones, and the gallon teapot from the Bridgewater set, in the middle of a Stonehenge of cream mugs with black Labradors on them, is on a huge oaken table from olden days.

All the 'grown-ups' are already present.

Rose: 'How lovely, you're all here. Well, Pierre and I have to run into Godminster, as previously discussed, so we've got to scoot off. Enjoy the bûche de Noël – leave some for Pierre, he's very greedy – and see you all at suppertime!'

We all sit in chairs around the table and help ourselves to slices of cake, and Mum pours the tea. Shaking a little. Although it could be delirium tremens, as everyone's been putting it back big time this Christmas.

Dad/Clare, simultaneously: 'Well . . .'

OMG there really is going to be an Announcement.

Casimir: 'What's going on, guys?'

Clare: 'We have some news. I hope, eventually, you'll see it is good news.'

Posy: 'I knew it! We're getting a puppy!'

Mum: 'Not exactly, but close.'

Gids: 'Ha ha, Mimi.'

Then Mimi and Gids look at Ralph and Clare, as if this is all on them.

And my heart sinks.

Not Dad and Clare. Please. I don't want her being my new stepmum. Not now, not ever. She's OK, but – how to put this? – one day she really needs to grip her OCD. When Joe was helping himself to cake, she cuts his slice in half, and she's taken him off dairy, as 'the Sturgises have transitioned from soya to almond milk.'

Dad: 'There's no easy way of telling you this, children, and, of course, Joe . . .'

I am waiting for Posy to burst into tears, but she is ploughing through her second slice of cake.

Clare: 'I got this, Ralph.' Brave voice. 'Mirabel. Cas. Posy.' Looks at us each in turn. Makes eye contact. 'Lucian.' Soft voice. She loves Lucian, as he plays Subbuteo with Joe in the attic. 'I hope this doesn't come as too much of a shock, but Gideon is not Joe's actual, or as we say, biological, father . . .'

And then she says *Dad* is.

At this point, we do almost all fall off our chairs, and we just stare at her and then at Dad and back, like we're at the Wimbledon final, and wonder.

Did they, like, actually shag?

Clare informs us that we will all find this very traumatic and difficult to process. That she knows and understands our feelings of betrayal and anger.

Then, to our horror, she starts explaining that they didn't actually shag, it was all about Dad being a prize bull and she was the cow, and Posy just said, 'So Dada supplied the magic seed,' and then we all burst out into giggles and, luckily, Clare stopped.

We all look at Joe with fresh eyes. He's sitting there with his tufty hair, with chocolate cake smeared all over his mouth, like Just William at a birthday party, and Lucian points at him and then we all laugh.

And then Cas makes this little speech that breaks everyone's heart.

He says that he can't begin to understand why adults do the things they do, but he has learnt to accept them. He says that it's sad Joe is an only child, and he hopes that Joe feels that the four of us, i.e. him and me and Posy and Lucian, are his brothers and sisters, his proper brothers and sisters – he actually said 'bros and hos', and everyone clapped.

He said that he used to think we had the only boring family in Britain, but he is pleased to find out that we're just like everyone else (i.e. fucked up). I know he's been feeling left out because, at Canford, his boarding school, there're only two kids in his year whose parents are still together.

It was like something out of *Love, Actually*, only set in Dorset, on Boxing Day, which is usually the worst day of the year.

Then Lucian says, 'I really liked the Chelsea season ticket, but a new brother is better, the best Christmas present I've ever had.'

And all the grown-ups are wiping their eyes and smiling, and going phew, and the mood's so up, I thought, What the fuck. Time for *my* news.

Me: 'Guys, I have an announcement. Mum, Dad, Lucian, Posy, Casimir ' – I pause, and add – 'Oh yes, and new bro, Joe.'

They are all looking at me, for a change.

'I'm going to have a baby.'

Stunned silence. Mum drops cream mug with black Labrador on side on to Rose's slate floor.

Me: 'Sid wished he could be here to tell you himself,' I go on. 'But he's with Cathy, and her emphysema's terrible, and he's looking after her.'

I have the floor now, no doubt.

'You're going to be a *nan*, Mum.'

PART FOUR

2015

News item in the London Evening Standard

1 February 2015

A controversial property in Notting Hill has changed hands for the second time in six months, it has emerged.

The new owner of the property is the Malaysian government, according to the Land Registry. The Malaysians bought the property for £3.5 million more than the £12 million paid by billionaire Keith Dunbar, beating off a competing bid from a Russian oligarch looking for a pied-à-terre in the capital, the *Standard* understands.

At one point, the property was intended to be an Alpha Star free school but is now in the process of being converted into an eight-storey iceberg house with the council's blessing, as all planning permissions were in place.

The mansion is adjacent to the Giving Back Centre (GBC) community resource and also to a long-established private school, Ponsonby Preparatory. Prince George is expected to start at the nursery in 2017.

The news will come as a disappointment to neighbours, not just because works are expected to take two years and involve the closure of a public highway. Mr Dunbar, the City financier and Alpha Star chairman, had previously announced that the leisure complex in the sub-basement levels would be available as a shared community health resource to the pupils of Ponsonby and also to users of the GBC.

The Malaysian ambassador to the Court of St James would not confirm that the government had started investing in London property, mainly in

Knightsbridge, Mayfair, Hampstead and St John's Wood. Anecdotally, however, estate agents are reporting that the governments of Russia, China and India, as well as Malaysia, have been investing in the capital's super-prime housing stock instead of in government bonds or gold, despite the threat of higher property taxes, such as the mansion tax, and council tax rebanding.

In most cases, the properties are left empty after purchase and redevelopment.

This is the first recorded instance of a foreign-government investment in W11. Previously, it is thought that investors have been put off by the scarcity of parking in the neighbourhood, which boasts several bustling and sought-after private schools.

Mimi Fleming, part of the *Newsnight* team that last year tracked the ups – and ups – of this particular property, and long-term local resident, said, 'Nothing that happens in Notting Hill will ever surprise me.' It turns out that not even £15 million will buy you your own parking space here these days.

20 February 2015

Police have confirmed that the person who died at the site of the dig in Ponsonby Terrace, Notting Hill, on Valentine's Day, was Farouche de Gramont, of Kensington Park Gardens.

De Gramont, known as Farouche, was the internationally known performance artist and creator of the iconic fragrance Frisson by Farouche. She was the partner of businessman Julien StClair. She leaves a young son, Fox.

A coroner's inquest has been opened.

@GBC Everyone in the close-knit and compassionate Giving Back Centre family is mourning the death of our supporter the beautiful artist and incredible mother Farouche #RIP

News item in the London Evening Standard

26 February 2015

By a staff reporter

Farouche de Gramont, the Belgian multi-media artist and creator of the Frisson cult perfume, took her own life, a coroner has ruled.

The artist was discovered at the bottom of the 100-foot underground excavation at the triple dig in Ponsonby Terrace. The new verdict was recorded after CCTV tapes were submitted to the inquest.

Meredith Blacker, the *Newsnight* presenter, and the programme's editor, Josh Kurtz, provided the tapes. Tony Hall, the BBC chairman, has cleared the programme of any wrongdoing or breach of guidelines, according to a statement on the *Guardian* Media site.

Newsnight had installed the cameras as part of a covert operation during a previous investigation into the proliferation of double basements in the area.

'I viewed the tapes of the day in question, 14 February, and it is my belief that the artist intended to die and was aware that the CCTV camera was in place,' said the coroner. 'I do not wish to make any further comment and the tapes have been returned to the BBC.'

Newsnight said it was preparing a special package in tribute to the performance artist but would not confirm whether any footage from the CCTV tapes – possibly including the moment of the artist's death – would be broadcast or not.

De Gramont, who was born Marie-Claude Smets in Knokke-le-Zoute, was the daughter of

Manon Lippens and Kris Smets, who still live in Belgium.

She leaves a son, Fox, and a partner, the businessman Julien StClair.

The funeral is to be held next week, at Père Lachaise Cemetery, Paris, the resting place of Oscar Wilde, Chopin and Jim Morrison.

Mimi

Père Lachaise Cemetery, Paris

The taxis are nosing up, one after the other, to the entrance to the cemetery, and disgorging their solemn consignments of London mourners from the Gare du Nord.

Ralph and I follow the backs of those weaving up the cobbles to the wide mouth of the walled cemetery, flanked by two ornate pillars topped by funerary urns, wreaths and carved torches.

'Like Olympic flames,' I say.

'Almost, darling. They're to light the way to the underworld,' explains Ralph, who's benefited from a classical education and, unlike me, didn't go to a girls' school in Hampshire, where the only thing I've remembered after five years' private education is how to make a white sauce.

In front of us, white-robed mourners like winter druids are filing into the cemetery, being checked off by two women in white suits and high-heeled boots holding clipboards and keeping the press and paps at bay.

The women in white are bookended by two fridge-sized black men in black suits with earpieces and dark glasses who glower at each mourner as they give their name.

'Golly,' says Ralph. I didn't think he would come. But he knew this was important. He'd never use a word like 'closure', but when I told him, there was a bit of a silence, and then he said, 'Paris is always a good idea,' and I knew it would be fine. We would be fine. I probably won't make him come to the memorial service – well, one of them, anyway – which is to be held at the Giving Back Centre in May, in the atrium that has been renamed in Farouche's honour, and where the Solidarity Quilt, as well as several of her early video pieces, take pride of place.

He takes my hand. As our fingers touch, they begin to transmit messages to each other. He doesn't need to say what I want to hear, as his fingertips are imprinting the message on mine. You've been an absolute chump and a silly fool, but I still love you. It's OK. We're OK. We're still here.

I grip his hand tightly, in thanks and praise that, even though in the midst of life there is death, we seem to have made it.

'Thanks for coming, darling,' I say, sort of hoping that Ralph might go a bit *Brief Encounter* and say, 'You've been a long way away. Thank you for coming back to me.'

That's not his style.

It's been a long, hard fortnight and, at the beginning, I could hardly put one foot in front of the other, one word in front of another.

When we saw the *Evening Standard* story about the death, the lines buzzed all over the borough. I called the police station. I called the reporter who wrote the news story on the *Standard*. But nobody seemed to know, or nobody was prepared to divulge, the name of the deceased, and the manner of his or her death.

I wondered if it was Clare, depressed at losing the baby, but she picked up as soon as I called, and asked, 'Have you seen?'

She had. Things have been easier between us since 1. she lost the baby and 2. she told me, almost embarrassed, that the clinic in Wigmore Street had sent a letter saying that she hadn't been impregnated with Ralph's sperm after all; it had been a mix-up. Not sure I believe her, but it doesn't matter now.

I wondered if it was Gid, as he has been shagging the interns in his office again, and it did cross my mind whether Clare had pushed him over the lip of the dig for betraying her and for doing the designs for the Ponsonby iceberg behind her back, but I don't think Clare – though mad, of course, in the way that all women are a little bit mad – is a murderer.

I wondered if it was Virginie, as Mathieu has put up with so much from her over the years.

And I have to confess that a small part of me wondered with wild hope whether it was Meredith, as she's caused me such agony and jealousy. I am ashamed to say – I could never admit this to anyone, it's too pathetic – that I did hope, for a few seconds, that it was Meredith who had died.

I never in a million years wondered whether Farouche had died.

I've never met anyone less likely to kill themselves. More full of life. And so crazy for it. I still don't know if it was an accident or not. No one does. Whatever the coroner says.

So when I found out, I went into shock. Physical shock. I was sick, as in English 'sick', rather than American 'sick', as in ill, i.e. I actually vomited. The world went black.

I went to bed for two days but, after that, it was as if I was purged. I felt . . . relief. Lighter. After that, I found I could walk along the street and see – really see – the sky and the trees and the houses, rather than see and experience everything as if through a silkscreen of her.

That told me that life would be more boring without her in it, but it would be calmer, and easier, too. I wouldn't wonder and worry who she was seducing next. I wouldn't have to mark her at parties, like a Sunday dabbler running after a key Premier League striker. I wouldn't have to endure the pain I endured when I found out that she was sleeping with Meredith and heard the rumour that my rival was better in bed than I was, which had led me to lacerating reveries about whether I was adventurous enough, filthy enough, technically skilled enough, and to churning thoughts about what they did to each other that we didn't do and would never occur to me in a million years even to try.

That hurt so much more than sucking it up when Meredith was appointed *Newsnight* presenter. (There was some ungracious comment that she was thirty-eight, part Asian, and a woman, i.e. racially, age and gender appropriate, and so therefore Josh Kurtz could hardly *not* hire her.) In fact, it hurt so much that I realized that to love Farouche and to want her for only myself was a world of pain from which only her premature death would release me.

And then, as if to prove something, she did go and die.

'How much further do you think?' I say, as we plod past tombs, and I suddenly realize the turreted Gothic chapel on our left is the tomb of Abelard and Héloïse. A pale student in an overcoat, clearly starcrossed in love himself, is leaving a letter there. He looks startled as we file past.

Most mourners have observed the dress code – 'white' – a stipulation that has occasioned several full days of sartorial panic back in London, as all the key boutiques are in the tricky mid-season stage, heading for Spring/Summer 2015.

White in winter, in February – somehow, it works here, among the browns and greys and granites and marble monuments. It looks like life amid death, light shining in darkness.

Farouche must have known it would, and imagined all this in advance.

It is a wonderfully ectoplasmic procession that files into the cemetery, dark with ivy, lichen and rain-stained statuary.

Young, aesthetically pleasing members of the Haus of Farouche clad in boxy white jackets and tight white pencil skirts or tight white Levi's stand at key points, way markers along our journey, the stations of her cross, to the artist's final resting place.

After five minutes' fast but respectful walking, Ralph says, 'Over there,' pointing. There are about forty people clustered at a monument.

This is a private funeral, but there's a camera crew. Ralph and I approach. It's so good of him to come, considering.

I wonder where it's appropriate for me – the rejected ex-lover – to stand, but Ralph is gripping me, and we slide into the crowd next to Virginie, in a short, tight white dress over which she has flung a white mink for the full fur-coat-and-no-knickers impact.

There's the deep open grave, and I immediately think of Farouche hurling herself into the dig at Ponsonby Terrace, like Tosca off the battlements. And there's the coffin, on a bier, covered by a white velvet shroud.

I'm wearing white Converses, and the ground feels cold through the thin soles. Others have made more effort, presumably with an eye to the cameras recording the event, and posterity.

I wonder how many women present have bought a white fur coat simply for the occasion.

I nod to Clare, who's in pale shearling, with Michael Alexis, the minimalist architect, and minus Gideon, as usual. Poor Clare. The idea that we would move back into our old house. That we would want to.

No, we're moving to the house in Queen's Park that Ralph showed me the gatefold particulars of back in Dorset, which is miraculously still on the market now prices are dropping, and we can even afford to buy the pink beach hut, too.

Meredith may have her PJ, but we are very pleased with Bubblegum. (And thinking about the hut makes me realize. That's what Farouche did. She treated me like bubblegum: she chewed me and spat me out when there was no juice left.)

Meredith, who couldn't believe we were 'moving North of

the Westway' (it was as if we'd announced we were moving to Hull), is standing at the open mouth of the grave in a white cloak, as if she is chief mourner, alongside Julien and Fox. It's the first time I've seen her not wearing black, but white becomes her ebony-ivory colouring just as well.

'Eez ridicule, am going to complain to the *mairie*,' stage whispers Virginie. '*Farouche, elle n'était pas Parisienne. Elle était Belge!* Should be *enterrée* in Knokke-le-Zoute, *pas ici, à Père Lachaise.*'

As Virginie whinnies on, I whisper to Ralph, 'So annoying that I never managed to interview Farouche when I was doing my column on people planning their own funerals for the *Telegraph*, because this' – I can't help but gulp – 'would have made the best one ever.'

I clutch the little bottle of Frisson in my hand, my good-luck charm. And although I'm cold and my nose is red with a drip on the end, I feel warm inside.

It's not all about me now. It's about Mirabel. She's having a baby! After my initial gulp – Mirabel is nineteen now – I can see only advantages. I will be a young grandmother. Being grandparents is – unlike fishing – something that Ralph and I can enjoy together.

'Now your eldest child is having a baby I see a lucrative new future for you, darling,' said Ralph. 'Just as you were the first woman in the world to have had a baby, you can be the first woman in the world to have ever had a grandchild, and when Mirabel gives birth . . . you can do a blow-by-blow from the perspective of the mother of the mother. You don't need to compete with Meredith any more,' he teased. 'She doesn't even have children, does she? You can be the First Grandma of Fleet Street.'

It is ten past twelve now and yet still the druids are arriving: the Dodd Nobles, teachers from Ponsonby Prep, glossy people from the art world, and there's Alan Yentob, of course, who has to be everywhere anything is happening, anywhere in the world, in white Prada sneakers with little red tabs, white Levi's and a white sweater, looking like a teddy bear, Lady Helen Taylor in ivory Armani, with handsome hubby Tim Taylor of the Tim Taylor Gallery in designer specs . . . and there's actual Tracey Emin, in a satin negligee and white rug – which gives me a piercing pang.

I think, Please no, not Tracey, not her, too? Will jealousy torment me even after her death . . . I still mind what she did before she met me, what she did during the time we were together, and after it ended – even though she's dead, in that coffin, and I will never touch her, and she will never touch another, ever again.

Tears fill my eyes and, when I compose myself, I find I'm staring at Oksana, in white fox fur over a white shark-skin dress and high, wedged, white moon-boots, and Keith, who's in cream Ralph Lauren, looking like a fancy-dress Wimbledon umpire. They are being so sweet and forgiving; they really didn't mind the *Newsnight* debacle. They *had* bought the house in Ponsonby Terrace to be nearer the school, as Ralph had guessed, as Oksana was fed up with the school run, but then Oksana decided that she wanted to send the twins to Notting Hill Prep instead, and lo, they didn't need the house bang next door to Ponsonby any more, so Keith flipped it to the Malaysians, for a multimillion-pound profit. Ralph and I smile at the Dunbars in a funereal way, and then I notice.

I wonder if everyone else has already realized.

Fox and Julien StClair are standing like apparitions by the coffin, holding hands.

As the last mourners cluster by the graveside, there is a gathering silence, as if we are in collective shock.

The coffin is *open*. How could I not notice this before?

The funeral was supposed to start at noon. It is now half past twelve.

And still, nothing happens.

Nobody says anything. Everyone is looking towards the coffin, as if drawn to it. But we are too shy actually to crane in and look down.

Fox and Julien StClair don't say anything.

I have an awful, awful thought. What if she's not dead and this is some sort of prank? She's waiting to see how we all react to her death, and then she'll resurrect herself? I almost have to resist the urge to check my phone, to see if she's sent me a text.

It is quiet in the graveyard, and the tourists and sightseers fall silent when they see us.

A few flakes of snow begin to fall, and I want to cover Farouche up. It seems wrong to have her snowed on.

The silence, and the nothingness, extends. And yet, the longer it lasts, the more powerful it is. The atmosphere thickens, intensifies, the more it goes on, like the two-minute silence at Remembrance Day at the Cenotaph. Thoughts flit across my brain. Farouche is lying there, dead, in a coffin. Farouche, who said to me, 'If a kid says to me, "I am going to be an artist," I tell them they can never make it, for you are born an artist. It's not a choice, it's a condition, it is destiny.'

I also remember Farouche saying that 'art is made out of energy, not out of stuff,' and then, of course, it dawns.

She is dead – but we are her live material.

And this is her last piece of conceptual art. She is allowing us to make it, so it is our creation. It is her final gift to us, and this is our final gift to her.

As the cameras film, people weep softly. Someone starts chanting, in Sanskrit, I think, an American woman in a sharply tailored Stella McCartney white trouser-suit. When she stops, there is a moment, and then someone else recites a passage from *The Prophet*.

Sally Avery steps forward. She shrugs. Then she sings, in a pure, clear voice.

'From this valley they say you are going . . .'

Everyone knows 'Red River Valley'. It is one of the songs that every parent at Ponsonby Prep has sung, at some point, during circle time at the pre-prep, along with 'Little Rabbit' and 'The Wheels on the Bus'. So a ragged chorus, in soft voices, we sing in unison, 'We shall miss your bright eyes and sweet smile . . . For a long time, my darling, I've waited . . .'

As the singing continues, I noiselessly creep to the front. I stand at the open grave. I look into the coffin.

Farouche is lying there as if asleep, her dark hair fanning out.

I realize I am swaying, and Julien reaches out to steady me, but I shake him off.

Ralph is shouldering himself through the crowd towards me, as if playing British Bulldog, but I can't stop myself.

I have to do this.

I reach into my pocket, and as I do so, my trainer slightly slips and Ralph calls to me softly, 'For Christ's sake, Mimi!' and the crowd is stirring in alarm, and of course they think I'm so deranged with ghoul-chasing grief that I'm going to get into the snug, white-satin-lined interior with her. The film crew has come in for this close-up, this Grand Guignol finale, hoping no doubt for me to be a distraught coffin-jumper – but I disappoint them.

I remove the tiny, numbered flagon of Frisson from my pocket and kiss it.

Then I place it next to Farouche's waxy cheek and close my eyes.

'Goodbye, my sweet poison,' I say.

I squeeze my eyes shut, hoping I'm not going to cry, but instead of the bolt of agony, I feel light, unexpected joy. As if I'm scampering over a beach in white trousers, barefoot, without a care in the world, as in a million ads for bio-active yoghurt . . . pads with wings . . . or cruise holidays in the Nordic fjords for springy retired couples.

I breathe, deeply, filling my lungs with cold February air – in and out, in and out – and look up at the trees silhouetted against the dirty, yellow-grey sky. It's as if – for the first time in months – I'm seeing the world as it is. Look, no filter. No Farouche filter. Then I see the crow sitting in a branch, and it seems to catch my eye.

The bird swoops down, towards the crowd, and for an awful second there is a murmur of alarm from mourners, and I think it is going to settle on the edge of Farouche's coffin, or dive-bomb the open grave. Instead it lands, yellow claws first, on the edge of the pit.

'Shoo!' says Fox. The boy moves towards the open grave. Julien grabs him back. The crow rises with a squawk, then flies close over the crowd, seemingly straight for Meredith, who screams and flaps her hands.

And then the crow is gone.

I re-take my place, to find Ralph staring at me with a familiar expression of befuddled irritation and heightened tolerance.

He takes my hand.

I don't say anything, because I don't need to. He knows I've come back. I know there's a Frenchman standing in the front row in a Loden coat and a charcoal suit who keeps catching my eye – it's so cheering, the way Frenchmen regard women *d'un certain âge*, i.e. old, worth flirting with – and holding it a fraction too long.

But I am not going to give him The Look – even though I would, he's terribly attractive – as I know, to my cost, and to my pain, that when you do that it always goes wrong in the end. You can press the refresh button on your life, but – in the end – when you're married, thank God, it always takes you back to the same page.

I'm never going to do that again.

'Well done, darling,' says Ralph, guiding me away from the graveside with a firm hand, as if leading a wayward Thelwell pony.

'It's rotten bad luck about Farouche, but I don't know how much more of this I can take.' We walk on a bit, in lockstep.

'I know you were fond of her.' He gives me a consoling pat, and I wind my arm around him as we wander back through the wintry cemetery. I know this is all he will ever say about her. The subject is now closed. Ralph has always been good like that. And then he says, 'How about steak-frites and a *petit quart* – actually, make that maybe a *demi* – of red in a little brasserie I know round the corner?'

News item in the London Evening Standard

5 March 2015

Moratorium on Iceberg Houses

The Royal Borough of Kensington and Chelsea today announced a go-slow on the proliferation of massive digs in the most expensive and sought-after areas of West London.

Following widespread consultation, the borough has said it will not be determining applications for development proposals which include subterranean development, and that such proposals will not be reported to the Planning Applications Committee unless there are site-specific material considerations which make this appropriate, or the proposals comply with the current core strategy and emerging policy.

This means that, from now, basements will be accepted only if they are limited to 50 per cent of the area of the garden, confined to one level and not dug under listed buildings, public roads or communal garden squares.

The moratorium does not apply to properties that have already received planning permission.

3 December 2015

The Turner Prize 2015 has been posthumously awarded to the performance and conceptual artist Farouche for her last piece of work, an immersive fifteen-minute video entitled *The Artist is Absent*.

The artist committed suicide, apparently by hurling herself into the 100-foot foundations of an iceberg house in Notting Hill, a coroner's inquest ruled.

Her last piece includes a scene of the artist lying in a coffin during her funeral at the Père Lachaise Cemetery in Paris in February (see picture).

Disciples from the Haus of Farouche filmed the scene and events according to a script and storyboard emailed to them via computer program on the day of her death. Footage from the artist's mobile phone taken by Farouche of her last moments, and video from the cameras on the dig, were included, on the late artist's instructions.

She left no other note.

The judges, who included Oksana Dunbar, the collector, and gallerists Ben Brown and Tim Taylor, as well as the artist Grayson Perry, were unanimous in awarding Farouche the prestigious award, which is given to an artist under the age of fifty who lives and works in Britain. It is the first time the Turner Prize has been awarded to a dead artist.

The BBC has announced that Alan Yentob will be presenting a two-hour 'Imagine' special devoted to Farouche's life and work, with the working title 'Frisson', the name of the costly, limited-edition scent which the artist created.

Comments (3)

This is a joke, right?
Snoddy

So her death was like some art thang? Or is this the first recorded instance of the hashtag 'Selfie Suicide' confused.com?!
DeckMyBalls

Some people will do anything for publicity even kill themselves
Little Englander

Comments have been closed on this article.

Acknowledgements

Thank you, Juliet Annan, yet again, for your faith and humour, your impeccable taste and occasional brutality, and to all at Penguin and Fig Tree. Thank you, Sarah Day, for being the sharpest copy-editor on the block. Thank you, Peter Straus, my literary agent, at RCW.

After a whole second's reflection, I have decided not to identify the many people – friends, colleagues and neighbours, enemies and other NHMs – who have helped me with this, the third and final (many must hope) volume of the Notting Hell trilogy, as I don't want to incriminate them. No names, no pack drill, etc. They know who they are. I thank them all.

RACHEL JOHNSON

NOTTING HELL

'Our neighbours divide into the haves . . . and the have yachts.'

Meet Mimi and Clare, two married women making the most of their Notting Hill postcode. New best friends, and close neighbours, that doesn't stop them being rivals, in fact it compels it. Both are aspiring Notting Hill Mummies (Clare needs the baby, Mimi needs the six figure income) and, keeping up with all the area's fads, fashions and fabulousness is a full-time job. But the arrival of sexy billionaire Si in their exclusive communal garden strains loyalty to friends, family, spouse and feng-shui guru alike . . . and only one of them can win. But who will that be? Clare or Mimi? Are they friends, or just . . . neighbours?

'Shiveringly brilliant' Jilly Cooper

'Witty, sharp, outrageous and cringingly real. I was riveted!' Sophie Kinsella

'A wickedly funny comedy of modern manners' *OK!*

RACHEL JOHNSON

SHIRE HELL

Mimi and Ralph have left social climbing, pushy parenting and their marital problems behind them in London, and moved west to the bucolic green depths of the country. Or so they thought. Yes, there's mud and masses of fresh air, plenty of handsome hayseeds and there's Rose, Mimi's new best friend and Dorset's answer to Martha Stewart. But what should be Shire Heaven is, it turns out, just as tricky to navigate as Notting Hell.

There's low-level conflict between the racehorses in vintage/Diesel/Ralph Lauren and the brood mares in Barbour/Boden, there's guerrilla warfare between the landowners and eco-warriers and naked hostility between Old Money, New Money and No Money. Yes, in honeybourne, if you don't have:

• A landscaped garden within 1000 acres (minimum) of prime land
• A helipad for your trophy guests
• An organic farm shop selling 16 sorts of home-made sausages
• Four pony-mad polo-playing children
• A literary festival in your mini-stately
• A bottom that looks smackable in jodhpurs

Then, well . . . you're Mimi basically. And that's just the start of her problems. Mimi also has a secret. But can she keep it?

'An irreverent romp through the wilds of the English countryside . . . hilarious. Johnson's humour is wickedly delicious' *She*

RACHEL JOHNSON

THE MUMMY DIARIES
Or How to Lose Your Husband, Children and Dog in Twelve Months

Rachel Johnson's hilarious take on life as a yummy mummy in West London and on Exmoor has been making her newspaper readers chortle for the last couple of years: now they are seamlessly turned into a diary of her year, from the dog's birthday party in January (games of Paws-the-Parcel) to the June sports days (where the mummies turn up at the school sports day in sports bras and running shorts with little back packs containing high energy drinks - and that's just for them) to summer on Exmoor hosting demanding visiting ponies.

'Wonderful! Such joy, such giggles - Rachel Johnson writes beautifully and I thank her for cheering me up' Jilly Cooper

'Very, very funny . . . [a] must-read for all you yummy mummies' *Heat*

'Strong on jokes and self-confidence . . . whether one falls within or outside its social pale, *The Mummy Diaries* is a sprightly footnote to the official history of our strange times.' *Telegraph*

RACHEL JOHNSON

A DIARY OF THE LADY

'The whole place seemed completely bonkers: dusty, tatty, disorganized and impossibly old-fashioned, set in an age of doilies and flag-waving patriotism and jam still for tea, some sunny day.'

Appointed editor of The Lady – the oldest women's weekly in the world – Rachel Johnson faced the challenge of a lifetime. For a start, how do you become an editor when you've never, well, edited? How do you turn around a venerable title, full of ads for walk-in baths, during the worst recession EVER? And forget doubling the circulation in a year – what on earth do you wear to work when you've spent the last fifteen years at home in sweatpants?

'A total romp . . . wonderfully readable' *Guardian*
'Hilarious' *Daily Mail*
'Action-packed, entertaining, marvellously indiscreet' *Sunday Times*

RACHEL JOHNSON

WINTER GAMES

Munich, 1936. She doesn't know it, but eighteen-year old Daphne Linden has a seat in the front row of history. Along with her best friend, Betsy Barton-Hill, and a whole bevy of other young English upper-class girls, Daphne is in Bavaria to improve her German, to go to the Opera, to be 'finished'. It may be the Third Reich, but another war is unthinkable, and the girls are having the time of their lives. Aren't they?

London, 2006. Seventy years later and Daphne's granddaughter, Francie Fitzsimon has all the boxes ticked: large flat, successful husband, cushy job writing up holistic spas . . . The hardest decision she has to make is where to go for brunch - until, that is, events conspire to send her on a quest to discover what really happened to her grandmother in Germany, all those years ago.

'The Jane Austen of W11' *Scotsman*

'A rip-roaring read' *Evening Standard*

'As addictively, fizzily invigorating as the Alpine air itself' *Daily Mail*

He just wanted a decent book to read ...

Not too much to ask, is it? It was in 1935 when Allen Lane, Managing Director of Bodley Head Publishers, stood on a platform at Exeter railway station looking for something good to read on his journey back to London. His choice was limited to popular magazines and poor-quality paperbacks – the same choice faced every day by the vast majority of readers, few of whom could afford hardbacks. Lane's disappointment and subsequent anger at the range of books generally available led him to found a company – and change the world.

'We believed in the existence in this country of a vast reading public for intelligent books at a low price, and staked everything on it'
Sir Allen Lane, 1902–1970, founder of Penguin Books

The quality paperback had arrived – and not just in bookshops. Lane was adamant that his Penguins should appear in chain stores and tobacconists, and should cost no more than a packet of cigarettes.

Reading habits (and cigarette prices) have changed since 1935, but Penguin still believes in publishing the best books for everybody to enjoy. We still believe that good design costs no more than bad design, and we still believe that quality books published passionately and responsibly make the world a better place.

So wherever you see the little bird – whether it's on a piece of prize-winning literary fiction or a celebrity autobiography, political tour de force or historical masterpiece, a serial-killer thriller, reference book, world classic or a piece of pure escapism – you can bet that it represents the very best that the genre has to offer.

Whatever you like to read – trust Penguin.

read more
www.penguin.co.uk